T0246301

SISTER
SNAKE

Also by Amanda Lee Koe

Delayed Rays of a Star

SISTER SNAKE

a novel

AMANDA LEE KOE

ecco

An Imprint of HarperCollinsPublishers

SISTER SNAKE. Copyright © 2024 by Amanda Lee Koe. All rights reserved. Printed in the United States of America. No part of this book may be used or reproduced in any manner whatsoever without written permission except in the case of brief quotations embodied in critical articles and reviews. For information, address HarperCollins Publishers, 195 Broadway, New York, NY 10007.

HarperCollins books may be purchased for educational, business, or sales promotional use. For information, please email the Special Markets Department at SPsales@harpercollins.com.

Ecco® and HarperCollins® are trademarks of
HarperCollins Publishers.

FIRST EDITION

Designed by Jennifer Chung
Snake silhouettes © AnyaCher/stock.adobe.com
Snake skin textures © PackagingMonster/stock.adobe.com

*Library of Congress Cataloging-in-Publication Data has been
applied for.*

ISBN 978-0-06-335506-4

24 25 26 27 28 LBC 5 4 3 2 1

For those who no longer hide.

Miraculous animals are commonplace around West Lake, made from moisture or magic. In one grotto lived a white snake who could take on the skin and shape of a beautiful woman with ease. A dedicated and fastidious practitioner of the art of self-cultivation, this snake spirit did not desire anything immoral. No one, but herself, could tell the difference between her and a human.

— **Chinese folktale,** *Legend of the White Snake*

. . .

Nothing I accept about myself can be used against me to diminish me.

— **Audre Lorde,** *Sister Outsider*

SISTER SNAKE

Before

Before they had legs, they had tails. This was way back when.

Before the buzzkill of data and doomscrolling. Before the inception of the steam engine and the stock exchange. This was more than a thousand years ago, under a majestic weeping willow whose hollowed trunk was home to an inseparable pair of snakes who had sworn to be sisters: one pure white, the other jewel green.

The willow tree afforded the two snakes an unparalleled view of the famed West Lake in their hometown of Hangzhou, a garden metropolis feted as the most beautiful city in all of China. But even a beguiling paradise grows drier than dust when you can't have what you want.

A hot kernel of desire was ripening under the cool scales of the white snake. She wanted so badly to be human. She had spent many a morning slithering under the viaducts of West Lake—Broken Bridge, which is not broken, Long Bridge, which is not long—where scholar poets liked to practice their speeches and amorous lovers stopped to cop a feel.

You may be disappointed, the green snake signed with her forked tongue, as her sister gazed wanly at passersby crossing the bridge. *At their core, humans and animals are not so different.*

Don't you want to see well enough to read a scroll? the white snake asked. *To have a wrist you can slip a jade bracelet onto? To have a name, and hear your lover sigh it in your ear?*

The green snake was satisfied with their way of life, as long as she had the white snake with her. Every skin had its pleasures. She loved the freedom of flexing her spine. The clarity of existing as one sinuous length, unencumbered by clumsy limbs. The thrill of the chase, how fierce she felt when they hunted side by side. The lush ripple of spring grass along her underside.

But she knew how much her sister desired to be human, and she would try anything once. And so that fateful mid-autumn night, when the moon was at its brightest, in the year 815 in the Tang dynasty, the green snake swam to an underwater cave and obtained a lilac lotus sown by the hand of a great goddess. The lotus seeds were capable of bestowing human form and ageless immortality.

Happy Mid-Autumn, the green snake signed jauntily as she presented the seeds. *May you rise up along life's ladder.*

The white snake stared in sheer disbelief. *It wasn't just a rumor?*

Only one way to find out. The green snake split the seeds.

Tails touching, they swallowed.

Before they slid into the lake to begin their transformation, the green snake looked into the white snake's eyes and signed to her:

This body itself is emptiness. Emptiness itself is this body.

1

Thotty Baesians Are in High Demand

Emerald tells him she won't be drinking, but clearly her sugar daddy thinks the decision is his to make because he's paying. "Single-malt scotch for me," he says, "and, for the lady, let's see." He narrows his eyes and cocks his head, making a show of sizing Emerald up. He prefers girls with long tresses, but Emerald carries her seafoam-green buzz cut with easy panache. Heads swiveled when they walked in. "You're the fun sort, aren't you?" He winks. "Let's get you a cute little cocktail!"

"I told you," Emerald repeats, "I'm allergic to alcohol."

She smiles at him. He doesn't know what alcohol does to her kind.

"C'mon." He waves what she's saying away. Holding the menu back for long-sightedness, he's still unable to read the fine print. Grudgingly, he reaches for the glasses perched on top of his bald head. "She'll have a Sencha Daiquiri," he tells the bartender. He takes the glasses off and places a hammy hand over Emerald's. She's been fiddling with the fringed cords on the velvet armchair.

He grins. "Don't these look like nipple tassels?"

"No." Emerald says. There is a finality to her tone that throws him off. For a moment, it even makes her seem much older than she looks. He shrugs that off and grabs her hand. "Don't worry," he says, slightly sulky, "you don't have to finish the drink."

"Ah." Emerald deepens her stare by just a fraction. "I wasn't worried about me." If she were to turn it up a few more notches, he might start to quiver. But it's still early, so she eases up and finishes playfully: "I'm worried about *you*, Giovanni."

Giovanni is the name he goes by on the app: he thinks the Don Juan reference is a nice touch. He'd asked Emerald to put on something form-fitting for their date, but he was still floored when she showed up at this cocktail and ceviche bar in knee-high boots and a tiny dress. All in bright-lime-and-black faux snakeskin leather. He traces a knuckle along her knee. "Is it a kink?"

Emerald is amused. "Wouldn't you like to find out?"

The bartender wields the muddler like a ceremonial mace, winking at Emerald as he stirs peach puree into rum, then tosses the shaker from one hand to another behind his back.

Everything in this bar is breezy in that dry-cleaned, coat-checked, doormanned Upper East Side way. Emerald still loves New York, but she can no longer be bothered to take part in its ritualistic repartee. Born-again cougars with tousled blowouts on a girls' night out comparing alimony packages, androgynous borderline bulimic models making out with each other in the corner booth, square-jawed banker bros spilling vodka shots as they whoosh like rockets to herald the week's gains on the stock market, out-of-towner families in overcoordinated Burberry feeling good about bringing country-club chic to the big city when really they look like plaid-gift-wrapped Christmas presents. On the walls are David LaChapelle celebrity portraits of Britney Spears and Paris Hilton, whose pop irony is derived at the expense of the subject. Mouths smiling, eyes dead.

When Emerald requested wealth verification, Giovanni didn't reveal his real name or job. He offered to show her the art he collected. He couldn't take her to the SoHo town house where his prenupped wife of many years roosted, so he drove her to a climate-controlled Long Island storage facility, unlocked his vault, and unveiled a Damien Hirst vitrine. A white lamb with black hooves, preserved in a formaldehyde-filled tank. Its mouth was open, which made it look caught off guard.

"So, what do we think?" Giovanni prompted. "Game on?"

Relatively well endowed, he'd said the same thing when he flashed his penis at Emerald in his Tesla. Size didn't matter to Emerald. It was qi that kept her fresh. She could draw that vitality out of a human's body once they were in close proximity. If she could hear them breathing, in general, that was near enough for her to get down to business. Sex was just an easy time to feed on qi because humans got so distracted, they would never notice the slightly translucent stream of breath and life force leaving their body through their nose or mouth and entering her own.

Everyone's qi tasted different. Giovanni's reminded her of burned ends and ranch dressing. By now, she knew her limits. As long as she didn't feed on any one partner for too long, the harm done to them was minimal. They might feel tired or look haggard for a couple of days, but the human body's qi naturally replenished itself if it wasn't continually and aggressively depleted.

Emerald stared at the dead lamb, wishing she could reach in to help it close its mouth. "Game on," she said, tiptoeing to kiss Giovanni, imbibing a whiff of his qi.

Their drinks arrive. The Sencha Daiquiri looks like a floral terrarium in a delicate beaker. Giovanni's whisky sits in a solid glass with copper accents. He noses the whisky as the bartender gives Emerald the lowdown on what's in hers: "Okinawan cane sugar rum, white peach, iced sencha, edible petals." Only now does it occur to Emerald that he ordered the most cloyingly feminine, oriental-presenting drink on the menu for her. The worst part is knowing he meant it as a thoughtful gesture.

"Mm," he says. "Looks like something a geisha would drink."

Emerald doesn't say anything. She reaches for his whisky. The amber glow slides down her throat. She'll feel it in her blood soon.

"Babe," Giovanni observes, "you mad about something?"

She shrugs. "This geisha just felt like having whisky."

"Take the compliment, hon." Giovanni waves a hand. Girls these days. "All I'm saying is, you possess a certain grace. An air of mystery, y'know? I would never call a white girl a geisha . . ." When she raises an eyebrow, he backtracks. "OK, OK. You're not Japanese. I get it, Asian chicks are *not* a monolith." He palms the small of her back. "You said you were born in . . . Hen-zoo, China, right?"

Emerald used to spin profuse lies about her background. But she's come to realize that Americans may be the last people to be able to tell truth from lies. From Hollywood razzle-dazzle to Silicon Valley Ponzi schemes, from himbotic-despotic elected politicians to charismatic cult mass suicides, Emerald finds the aspirational deceit and drama of the land of the free a convenient place for an immortal to let it all hang out. When everyone operates under the assumption that fake-it-till-you-make-it is the given, no one will be able to recognize the truth.

"I miss Hangzhou a lot, yeah."

"Don't you ever go back to visit?"

"Nope." Emerald can still recall that willow tree with the hollow trunk by the water's edge at West Lake. It seemed spacious for two snakes back then, but it would look so narrow to her eyes now. She wonders, not for the first time, if Su has been back to Hangzhou. It's been thirty or forty years—maybe more, she's stopped counting—since she last saw her sister in the flesh. Over time, the tight pang of missing Su has dwindled into a muted ache in her chest.

"Tell me, how old are you, really? I don't quite buy that you're twenty-five . . ."

That's Emerald's age on the app. "Now you've put me on the spot."

"You're younger, aren't you? Just look at your skin."

"I'm pretty ancient, to be honest . . ."

Giovanni smiles. "Sure, babe."

Emerald almost swats his hand away when it goes up her skirt, but it's not like she has a choice at the moment. She sits tight and smiles back at Giovanni grimly. In the past, you could live off qi and goodwill. A few hundred bucks went a long way. These days, things are different.

. . .

Six months back, Emerald's card bounced at the Sherry-Netherland. She'd been living it up in a sixth-floor suite, ordering coffee and carpaccio from Cipriani's. A couple of times, when she was too lazy to head out for qi, she hovered behind the poor sweet chambermaid and sucked a few breaths out of her when she was cleaning.

Emerald decided to call her sister for the first time in a long time. Emerald changed numbers often, but Su had kept the same number since cell phones were invented. No matter where she moved to, Su maintained the +44 British number, even if it incurred roaming costs. This time Emerald didn't even have any money left to top up her prepaid card. It was almost impossible to find a pay phone, but finally she stumbled upon a booth at Penn Station.

It took Su a long time to pick up the phone. She didn't say hello.

"You ran out of money, didn't you?"

"Hey." Emerald was hurt. "Can't I call to say hi?"

It was true, however, that every time Emerald called Su, she needed something from her.

How was any of this her fault, though? There are so many things that humans have decided they need in order to survive. Money. Property. Status. If survival isn't an issue, getting ahead comes into play. If you do get ahead, then you start mulling over your legacy. There's no end to all the striving. None of it makes sense to her, even after all these years. In the wild, you hunt when you're hungry, find a rock to hide under when you want to rest. You do what you feel like doing, when you feel like doing it. There's no one to answer to but yourself.

When they were snakes, they were as close as two willow boughs on the same tree. But being human is a torrid world of complications, and after the canker of centuries, it was easier now to let Su think the worst of her, to assume she was an irresponsible brat who didn't care about anything but having a good time.

The last time she'd called Su up, eight years before in Macao, Emerald owed the Venetian Casino ten million patacas. Su smoothed it over in forty-eight hours. Some slippery dude from Su's suite of wealth managers direct-deposited $50,000 into Emerald's account so she could start over. "I'm not going to do this next time, Xiaoqing," Su warned. "You're never going to learn if I'm always bailing you out." Emerald knew it was ungrateful on her part, but she found Su's tone condescending, given the amount—it was fifty grand, not five hundred grand, which would have better warranted the moralistic undertone.

Maybe she didn't want to learn, she wanted to say. Moderation was too human for her. Besides, it wasn't like Su couldn't afford it anyway. Su had taken to this gainful aspect of being human in a way that Emerald would never have been able to, even if time had been turned back. Women were not allowed on the trading floor of the London Stock Exchange in the 1850s, but Su bought Lloyd's stock at an inflated price from an illegal broker in Change Alley.

Time is a natural multiplier. The value of that bundle of shares had swelled into something astronomical. Over the centuries, Su continued to make judicious investments that snowballed her vast holdings across offshore accounts. In spite of this, Emerald knew Su still made careful projections of how long her assets would last, taking global inflation and such into account. Emerald didn't get any of it. Stock exchanges—now, cryptocurrency and non-fungible tokens—why would humans invent unreal shit like that? Su had long urged Emerald to have a "diversified portfolio" and to exercise "financial prudence," which made Emerald want to barf. But Emerald wasn't too worried as she let Su lecture her over the phone; Su had a hard mouth but a soft heart.

"Where are you these days, anyway?"

Su paused. "I'm still in Singapore."

"Really?" Emerald's voice went up by half an octave.

Emerald moved cities every two or three years. It broke up the monotony of millennia. She couldn't root in one place for too long. Flux suited her best. Emerald did the math: Su must have been in Singapore for about a decade by now. The last time Emerald called, Su was already living there. In the same time, Emerald had torn through Macao, Guanajuato, and Trieste before arriving in New York. It was her second time living here. The first was during Prohibition.

She could feel Su bristling over the line.

"It's wonderful here," Su said, a little defensively.

Emerald was deciding on what sum to request when she noticed a homeless man, asking for change by the turnstiles in a Yankees jersey, staring at her. "You have that regal kind of beauty," he declared, "just like Henry's first wife Zainab. It's a shame he had to divorce her."

Over the phone, Su remained cold. "I meant what I said the last time. For your own good."

"You can't be serious, Jie. I'm calling from a pay phone. I'm down to my final dollar."

"You are the daughter of kings!" the man boomed.

Su wasn't relenting. Emerald started to panic. "I can't just waltz into a Wall Street gig or a Flatiron tech start-up. People like us don't have shit like credentials, degrees, internships—"

The line beeped. The call was ending. "Wait!" Emerald dug in her pockets. They were empty. The man came over. She drew back, but he was picking two quarters out of a deli cup. He slid them into the pay phone. *Thank you*, she mouthed to him. He gave her a cool shrug.

"Start with waitressing," Su was saying. "They pay under the table."

"I'm not going to be a waitress, it's a waste of time—"

"What have you ever done with your time anyway, Xiaoqing?"

Su was being unreasonable. "How about you?" Emerald exploded. "Do you think your long line of deceased husbands and your Stepford-wife aesthetic will make you hate yourself less?"

The line went dead. "Fuck," Emerald muttered. She hung the phone back on the hook.

"Ooh, that was harsh," the man commented. "We should all be kinder than necessary, little lady." He gave her a sage smile. "Everyone you meet is fighting a battle you know nothing about."

In the week that followed, Emerald lowered her metabolic rate as much as she could, taking the 1 train after hours to feed on the qi of club kids, drunk drifters, and graveyard shift workers. Back in the wild, snakes could go months without eating. She wouldn't starve just yet. By night she rested in the twenty-four-hour McDonald's on Broadway; by day she visited the New York Public Library flagship down by Bryant Park, comforted by its warm chandeliers and dark wood reading rooms.

New York was a hotbed of niches and weirdos. With patience, persistence, and a bit of luck, you could find anything you wanted. It took Emerald less than a week of hogging free Wi-Fi kiosks at the library to find this under Craigslist sublets: "Free temp stay in G'point studio: Gay Pop Surrealist painter seeks femme life-model bff as he preps solo show. Day bed + healthy meals, this is not a scam I am wholesome AF!"

His name was Bart, but he wanted Emerald to call him Bartek. "I have Polish ancestry," he sniffed. She told him she'd spent some time in Warsaw. He'd never been there, but he was saving up for a big trip to connect with his roots. He reminded her of the bunch of dreamers she'd lived with in a student hall in Mokotów in the 1980s, how they'd started up an avant-garde café/bookshop/gallery in their basement after martial law saw the closing of numerous public cultural institutions. Bartek was working on a queer biblical rococo lowbrow series in which he spliced male and female body parts into hybrid forms on the canvas, like the X-rated gay love child of Jean-Honoré Fragonard and Mark Ryden. He had a word tattoo emblazoning his left palm:

THE ROLE OF THE ARTIST IS
TO MAKE REVOLUTION IRRESISTIBLE

"Toni Cade Bambara," he told Emerald. "I really believe that." He nodded at his ramshackle easel and modestly sized canvases. "I wanna start an antibinary revolution with my paintings."

Emerald had not lived with a housemate in a long time, let alone a millennial painter who believed he could make a mark on the world with his art. She found Bartek's chaotic coalition of irony, optimism, flippancy, and anxiety infectious and adorable. He was so oblivious that she could easily have fed on his qi every now and then, but she decided not to do him dirty. He cared for her, cooked for her. Bartek was vegetarian, and his chickpea alfalfa salad made her more, rather than less, hungry. For a couple of weeks, the poor-but-sexy artist life was fun—she could even pick up good cuts of raw beef that had yet to reach their expiry date when they went dumpster diving at the Bedford Avenue Whole Foods—but it soon wore her down. Maybe it was cute for a twentysomething, but Emerald only *looked* the part.

Bartek was the one who told Emerald about the sugar app.

He'd been fishing for his own daddy, but the showing had been poor. "It's taking a toll," Bartek complained as he temporarily disabled the app. "Y'all bi girls have it so much easier." Emerald, who'd dated men and women interchangeably since the seventeenth century, was too tired to get into a pan-femmes-are-queer-frauds squabble with a gay art boi. Bartek was looking at himself on his phone camera. "My hair's too limp. Maybe I should get that K-pop root perm?"

She pictured it. "Go for it, you have the right jawline."

"You think so?" he fished, but he was already googling "best Korean hairdresser" on his phone. "Hon, I love having you around"—he nudged Emerald's knee with his foot as he scrolled Yelp reviews—"but for real. You can do so much better than my dump. Just *look* at you!"

Emerald was in one of Bartek's thrifted tees, which he'd cropped and reattached with safety pins à la Vivienne Westwood, and not feeling particularly hot, but she appreciated the sentiment.

"Thotty baesians are in high demand," he said to her a little sternly. "Ride that yellow fever bullshit and profit off it, sweetie! Stop AAPI Hate billboards in Times Square aren't gonna pay for skyrocketing rent, am I right? Emmy, I bet it'll take you all of five minutes to snag a midlife crisis Midtown normie who thinks sriracha is exotic. Girl's gotta do what a girl's gotta do . . ."

. . .

Emerald's cheeks are flushed by the time she and Giovanni leave the bar. In his experience with coquettes who can't hold their liquor, if

Giovanni puts enough overpriced cocktails into their bodies, they'll seamlessly segue to a room upstairs in the Plaza. Emerald finished his whisky and capped it with a martini. So much for a girl who said she wouldn't be drinking.

He steadies her as she totters about in her heeled boots—best to make sure she looks sober, so it won't seem too predatory when they check in. But Emerald makes a detour for the exit as they walk into the lobby. "Let's take a walk in the park!" Her voice is bright.

"It's half past one in the morning."

"Are you my *daddy*—or are you my *dad*?" Emerald giggles, tugging him by the elbow.

Outside, the night air is balmy. A porter bids them a pleasant evening. She lets go of his arm, pattering down carpeted stairs, jaywalking across Fifty-Ninth Street. Cars honk, but they stop for Emerald. They do not stop for Giovanni—he tries once, twice, then sheepishly waits to cross at the light. She passes the fruit-laden bronze nymph topping Pulitzer Fountain as he tries to catch up. When Emerald reaches the sidewalk, she looks over her shoulder to make sure he's following—then vaults over the granite perimeter into Central Park.

"Whoa," he calls out. "Wait a sec!" He breaks into a jog, already beginning to perspire. When he looks over the stone perimeter, it's not flat grass or a flower patch, but a ten-foot drop on an incline.

Emerald waits for him on the path, not a scratch on her.

"Shoot, did I mention?" She skips ahead. "I'm not wearing underwear . . ."

Giovanni throws his tie over his shoulder and jumps the barrier, skidding down shrub and soil. They're at the southernmost edge of the Pond. He can't see Emerald, she's too far ahead. There's no one else around. He's never been to Central Park at night. The greenery is the same, surely, but it feels incalculably wilder. Fresh water babbles.

A nightjar makes its churring song. Giovanni follows the footpath to where the Pond narrows into a creek—still no sign of Emerald.

"Hon?" He notices one of her boots by the edge of the water, in the dirt. He gets off the paved trail. Tiptoes across the ridge. Another boot. She's leaving a trail. What is this girl up to?

He's never had outdoor sex before. It crossed his mind once, while walking the private nature trails of his Vermont country home with his wife. She was walking ahead when the thick strap of her nude bra slipped off her shoulder. He didn't mention it to Sloane because he knew she would shoot it down, instead of being grateful that he still had raunchy thoughts about her. It wasn't like she was getting any younger. Instead of doing something to make up for that, she was killing his drive by wearing only sensible underwear and cashmere sweaters. Some time back, in a moment of what he felt to be true vulnerability, he asked if she could dress sexy for him. Just once in a while. On federal holidays, maybe. "Sweetie," Sloane mocked him, "you want me to *dress sexy for you* when you pat your beer belly every time you belch? Why don't I get you a Planet Fitness membership for your birthday, buddy bear?" If she ever found out about his recent pursuits, he wouldn't obfuscate them. He'd tried to make it work, hadn't he?

He sees Emerald's leather minidress on the ground. Where is she, hiding in a tree in her panties? No, wait, she said she wasn't wearing underwear. Hold your horses, he counsels himself. There's thrills, and then there's trouble. Even on the app, his gut told him this girl was hot soup, but it was tempting to play with fire. He's reaching his limit, though. He turns to go.

"Aww!" Emerald's voice comes from behind. He turns to find her in the creek. Water up to her shoulders. "Are you gonna leave me out here in the dark on my own?" She pouts playfully.

He really doesn't want to have to get into the murky water, but just look at her—wet clavicles in the moonlight. A long string of duckweed catches on her. Dazzling smile. His heart melts. "Come here, you crazy, beautiful girl." He reaches out toward her.

"Come in and play." She swirls in the water with her hands up. "I'm, like, all wet!"

Blood rushes to Giovanni's crotch. He can't remove his shoes, belt, pants, and shirt quickly enough. At the last moment, he takes off his silk boxers too. To hell with it, he's all in this time.

He steps into the creek. "I'm right here, princess."

"We're just getting started!" She slips out of reach.

Giovanni's erection is shrinking in the water. He tries not to sound impatient. "Let's go, the Plaza's beds are something else. Sweet Jesus. Best in all of Manhattan for tailgating."

She looks over at him with an innocent expression. "Tailgating?"

"Doggy style. Rump pump. Or whatever you like to call it."

"You wanna fuck me like a dog?" Something hardens in her voice. He thinks it's hot.

"Bend over and take it, bitch," he growls.

"Ooh," she gasps. Glides to the other end of the scrabbly ridge. "I'm afraid we don't respond well to that word, Giovanni." As Emerald scooches up the shore, Giovanni sees that she's waxed, and he loses his shit completely. He follows, but when he pulls himself up to the riverbank, she's nowhere in sight. "Emerald?" he calls out as he clambers onto the embankment.

It's then that he sees the green snake at his feet.

For a moment, he's hypnotized.

Lithe and undulating, it's about six feet long. Thick as a young oak tree, jewel-green skin patterned with distinctive diamonds. Its lips part to reveal a forked tongue, flickering to taste the summer night. Before he can move, it twists itself around him, cool scales on his wet flesh.

He can feel the snake's muscles rippling powerfully beneath its skin.

Giovanni comes to his senses. He tries to kick it away, but the green snake wraps itself around his torso. Small, sharp fangs sink into the side of his neck. He grabs it with his hands, trying to tear it off, but the snake's body is lean and its grip is strong. The venom it has put into his body is making him weak and uncoordinated. The only thing he can do is scream. He is screaming as a man never expects to hear himself scream: like an animal, like a girl—

The snake rears up triumphantly, almost like it's dancing. Begins to squeeze him, slow but steady. It gets harder and harder to breathe.

"Over here!" An NYPD officer on patrol in night-vision goggles waves to his partner as he crashes through the bushes, wading into the water. "Sir, I want you to stay calm!" His deep voice, the presence of other men, gives Giovanni hope. He grabs something. A rock. Strikes at the snake. It skitters off his body. "Stay down!" Giovanni obeys.

A gunshot crackles through, hitting the snake as it writhes away into the clearing. All that's left is a trail of viscid blood, darker than ink in the moonlight.

2

Conformity Makes for Excellent Camouflage

Su stares at the two stark red lines on the pregnancy test stick. It isn't possible. Didn't she make sure of it a thousand years ago? There's no way there can be a baby inside her irreparable womb. Soapy water cascades across the shiny floor of the shopping-mall bathroom.

Su is crouched unceremoniously in a cubicle in Wheelock Place, clutching a teal Watsons pharmacy plastic bag. She wraps the stick as neatly as she can in a wad of toilet roll and is about to deposit the bundle into the blue bin when she notices the sign: *Strictly for Sanitary Pads Only.* Su stows the stick back in the plastic bag.

By now, she's been in Singapore long enough that it has become completely natural to obey public signage without thinking twice. Other than the soupy humidity and tropical greenery—both of which she loves, for they remind her of summertime Hangzhou—one of the first things Su noticed about Singapore when she got here was the profusion of overexplanatory placards.

Initially, the degree of micromanaging left her bemused: *No Durians on the Train. Do Not Feed the Pigeons. Press for Green Man. Beware: Is It Love or a Scam? Smokers Will Be Reported to Police. Please Don't Leave a "Surprise" for the Next Bathroom User.* After nine years here, she's used to these pervasive public service announcements, and finds them quite endearing.

She is startled by a cleaner auntie rapping repeatedly on the door. "Excuse me, miss, you never see the sign?"

Su saw the yellow *Cleaning-In-Progress! Floor Is Slippery! Do Not Enter!* sign, but she was desperate for an anonymous space in which she could administer the test. She would never have done it at home, in the immaculately appointed Bukit Timah bungalow she shares with Paul.

"I'm sorry." Su opens the door. The auntie glowers at Su. As Su moves to the sink to wash her hands, the test kit falls out of the plastic bag. The auntie recognizes what it is at once. Su freezes.

"Aiya." The auntie shakes her head. At first Su thinks she's being judged. Then she sees it's something else—some sort of woman-to-woman solidarity. "Sit," the auntie declares. "Sit as long as you need."

The auntie bends to help retrieve the box, but Su grabs it from the floor, stuffing it into the bottom of her bag before scrubbing her hands at the sink and hightailing it out of the bathroom.

On the spiral escalator at the back of the mall, Su catches her reflection in the glass of a window display. Not a hair out of place, she is immaculate in Chanel neutrals: an ivory lace A-line dress and white lambskin ballet flats with black-tipped toes. Slinging her Himalaya Birkin on her arm, she shields her abdomen, though there's no bump to hide, and goes through notifications on her phone. She sighs as she reads the text from her Swiss private wealth lawyer—a financier is offering to fly her out to the Mediterranean for the Monaco Yacht Show.

How many times does she have to reiterate that she is trying to tone down? She didn't think twice about splurging when she was living in Luxembourg, Geneva, London, and even Hong Kong, but now that she is in Singapore and wedded to a man who holds public office in a political party with socialist roots, she leads what she thinks of as a relatively modest lifestyle.

After replying to her lawyer, she decides to call Emerald. They've been giving each other the cold shoulder for the past couple of months, since Su blew Emerald off about the money. Su wasn't serious about cutting her sister off financially, and she'd already prepared a deposit of new funds—she just wanted Emerald to learn to be more responsible, and not expect things to be fixed with a wave of the hand. An apology for that unwarranted Stepford-wife remark would have been nice too. But they had never been the sort to say sorry, and it seemed too late to start now—the backlog would be uncontainable.

Unsurprisingly, the call goes to voicemail. Su isn't even sure if Emerald is still at this number. When Su really needed Emerald, she was never there. It was hard not to feel a sour pinch of resentment, when she had looked out for Emerald over the centuries.

Maybe I should cut her off for real, Su thinks. But even if Emerald picked up, what could she say? There's no way she would have told Emerald about the baby. She would probably default to the usual: *I hope you haven't been drinking, Maybe it's time you find a job, Have you thought about settling down—*

Su jumps when her phone rings.

It's Paul. She turns her phone to silent mode, slides it back into her handbag. But in a moment it buzzes again, and she feels guilty for pretending not to see his call. She picks up.

"Hi dear." His Singlish staccato soothes her. "Where are you?"

Every time he calls, he asks the same thing. If it isn't *Where are you?* it will be *Have you eaten?* Su doesn't find it annoying. Love is someone fretting over you. "I'm at Orchard Road." All roads seem to lead back to the gleaming facades of the central shopping belt. "Picking a tie for you." She crosses over to the Giorgio Armani store, so it isn't a lie.

"No need lah," he tells her, "I've got my suit for tonight's dinner."

"Not for tonight, Paulie." She steps into the boutique. The air-conditioning cools her down. "For Parliament." His colleagues don't seem to care what they wear to parliamentary sittings, but Su thinks Paul should look smart. He's being considered for Chief Minister.

"It's Parliament," he chides her gently, "not a fashion show."

It is widely agreed upon that Paul is the most good-looking politician in the Party. He's self-conscious about being too well dressed because of that, and wears glasses rather than contact lenses. "I know how you feel," Su tells him, "but I just want you to look your best."

"OK, OK. Whatever makes you happy. I have to run, some hoo-ha over a school uniform . . ."

In Armani, Su runs her hands across the soft silk of handsome ties, perusing patterns of fleur-de-lis and chain link. Luxury is her coping mechanism. By the time she swipes her card for a striped gray-toned tie so ordinary she could have picked it out in a department store for a fraction of the price, Su is feeling fine, absolutely fine. The two lines on the test stick grow faint in her mind.

· · ·

Su is ten minutes late to her facework appointment at the celebrity aesthetician's clinic, nestled farther down Orchard Road's unending mirage at Palais Renaissance. "Suzhen!" the aesthetician greets her. She clocks the Armani paper bag. "Squeezed in a spot of shopping?"

Su nods, then can't help but add piously: "For my husband."

"Minister Ong is such a lucky man." The aesthetician smiles warmly.

It took Su much courage to approach the aesthetician, but she's glad she took the plunge. Each time, the delicate handiwork makes her feel more comfortable in her own skin. The very first time, Su worried about what to say to Paul when he saw her. For one shining, destabilizing moment, she fantasized and catastrophized about telling her husband the truth—all of it—but as it turned out, Paul didn't even notice that she'd done anything to her face. Mixed deep into the relief was a touch of disappointment. Her secret, as ever, was her own to keep.

She'd explained it this way to the aesthetician: "I have an autoimmune condition that prevents my skin from wrinkling." It's not exactly a lie—the botulism in snake venom is a key ingredient in Botox. "I'm sure many women will see it as a gift," Su went on guardedly, "but my husband is with the Party. When I stand next to him, I want to look age-appropriate. I don't want people to think he's a skirt-chaser."

The aesthetician didn't bat an eyelid. Money can buy most things.

Su's lines make her feel more human. Wrinkles are proof. Time touches your face the same way it leaves a mark on everyone else.

It helps her to pass, and it is so important to blend in here.

Su loves Singapore. It's small, it's safe, it's shiny. Just like her, Singapore has a meticulous and cautious character. Everything runs like clockwork, and nothing is left to chance. Most of the city is densely built up, but the Party has been mindful to retain pockets of greenery. There are all sorts of rules and regulations, for matters large and small—Su appreciates this. If you know the rules, and follow them, you can't go wrong, and you can be just like everyone else.

Conformity makes for excellent camouflage.

Su is determined—inspired, really—to fit in. Here in Singapore, she has settled into the rosy modesty of the traditional-wife life.

They could have easily afforded a live-in helper or two, but Su values her privacy. The helper, along with a gardener, comes in three times a week. Their chauffeur is round-the-clock, but he doesn't live with them either. They could have had a private chef too, but Su likes to cook for Paul. Putting gourmet meals on the table with napkin rings and silver cutlery makes her feel secure and grounded. The world out there is a dangerous place, whether for a human or a snake. Bad things could befall you around every corner, but the kitchen is her domain: she knows where each soup ladle and spice jar is. As long as she follows a recipe with exactitude, she can serve up perfection. If a dish fails, she will beat herself up over it, despite Paul's encouragement.

"Why are you so upset, my dear?" he'll say as he pops whatever it is into his mouth. "It's just food. Don't waste, don't waste." He has the Singaporean habit of saying things twice for emphasis.

Paul doesn't have much of a palate, but he is a President's Scholar.

Picked out of the hoi-polloi from the impressionable age of eighteen, groomed by the state for exacting excellence and unswerving obedience. Su has the hots for bureaucrats. They're so serious, so dependable! And—she finds this terribly appealing—they are thoroughly dedicated to keeping others in line, for the greater good.

Singapore's steadfast commitment to staying in your lane is exactly what Su has always wanted for herself, and she's doing so well. Since moving here almost a decade ago, Su has not inhabited her snake skin, not even for her yearly molt. Nor has she fed on human qi in all this time. She's finally weaned herself off that infernal addiction.

At first Su itched so badly from refusing to shed her old skin that she went to a dermatologist for allergy steroid shots, but after the first year, she grew used to it. Every month she pays a handsome fee to a dairy farmer in Lim Chu Kang to supply her with a billy goat and leave her alone with it in the privacy of a shed, no questions asked. The goat's lesser qi has an unpleasant grassy aftertaste. Her immortal body needs qi to maintain itself, and human qi is top-grade, but animal qi seems less of a sin in her book. Abstaining from human qi has sapped her power, and the full force of her beauty, but she doesn't mind that. Her complexion is sallower than before, it's true, and her hair less shiny, but these days it's easy to compensate with makeup and treatments. It's all been worth it. She is the most human she's ever been.

And under the influence of the Spice Girls—the name that a gaggle of coiffed ladies with high-powered husbands, who brunched together in gentrified hamlets like Dempsey and Ann Siang, had given their WhatsApp group chat—Su has even gone vegan recently.

She isn't exactly sure if she can call them her friends, but the Spice Girls like to fawn over her, and she likes to hear them doing so. *Suzhen, you're so beautiful, it's simply unfair. Why do the rest of us bother? Suzhen, you and Paul are the perfect couple. Suzhen, your taste is impeccable! Suzhen, Paul is such an important guy I feel shy to even bring this up, but do you think he can help my daughter get into Raffles Girls' Primary School?*

The only perceivable difference between her and them is that they all have kids, and she doesn't. Of course, in a place like Singapore, the baby question reared its head early on. And despite her great fear that she might lose him, Su made it clear to Paul, right off the bat on their first date, that she was barren.

"Paul . . ." She looked at him nervously after the champagne cart pulled up to them; she said she would stick with Perrier, while Paul opted for a glass of Chartogne-Tallet rosé. "There's something I should be upfront about. I don't want to end up wasting your time."

They were at her usual table at Odette, Su's favorite restaurant in Singapore, which served mod-French cuisine in a blush-and-dust-accented space on the first floor of the National Gallery.

"Waste my time?" Paul touched his finger to hers across the table. "That's not possible."

The amuse-bouche was served, mushroom tea poured over a porcini sabayon topped with shaved black truffle. Paul marveled at the presentation. It was his first time at such a fancy joint.

"I have to tell you," Su blurted out, "I can't bear children."

Paul put down his cutlery. "What happened?" he asked, very gently.

In vague terms, Su mentioned an accident she had when she was younger, involving an abrasion of her womb. "I don't wish to relive it," she said. She was glad that he did not press her.

They were quiet as they started on the next course, a velvety egg-yolk ravioli. "I understand," Paul said in a low, soothing voice. "There are things in my past I don't wish to revisit either."

They had just finished trading mutual backgrounds.

As far as Su let slip, she was the deeply private daughter of a Hong Kong commodities magnate who'd migrated to London, where she grew up. Her parents had died in a boating accident in the Vaud Alps, leaving her oversight of a considerable fortune, partially in the form of a charitable trust, which she managed in lieu of a day job. Money begets money, but there was so much to take care of, she explained to Paul. It was a never-ending Rolodex of meetings with board members and potential beneficiaries, consultants and financiers.

Paul wanted to know what causes she supported. Su grasped for a name, but she was blanking. There were so many over the years. Her lawyers took care of these matters. She'd given perfunctory instructions to support organizations that uplifted women's issues.

"Period poverty," Su told Paul. "Equity for survivors, women in STEM scholarships . . ."

Paul said he was passionate about education. Singapore was pretty far along with women's rights, he opined, but there was still a lot to be done for the low-income who fell though the gaps. Then he revealed that he was an orphan too. He had grown up dirt-poor, with an absent mother and an abusive father. He was deeply grateful to the Party for the generous scholarship that had brought him so much further than he would otherwise have gotten in life.

"Who we were doesn't matter," he said decisively, smiling at her. "We're here now."

Su felt too bloated to finish the last savory course, Brittany squab served three ways: a breast coated with kampot pepper, a leg with the producer's name tied to it, a fried ravioli filled with meat. Afraid to meet Paul's eye, she stared at the beet puree on the plate.

"To be very honest," Paul said, "I'm not a fan of kids. Of course the Party pushes for and incentivizes citizens to conceive because, socially, we're worried about the low birth rate. But personally, I think that if two people really love each other, they're better off without children."

The waiter came to take their plates away. When Paul saw that Su's plate was still half full, he asked the waiter to come back later. Su felt a little embarrassed as he finished up her portion.

"I don't know about you," Paul went on, "but that's the sort of love I'm looking for." He leaned over and kissed her full on the lips, just as the palate cleansers arrived. Kyoho grape granita topped with aloe, verjus, Sauternes ice cream, oolong tea foam, and a raspberry sugar tuile in the shape of a maple leaf. A few patrons in the Michelin-starred establishment turned briefly to stare at them.

Su blushed. "Shouldn't we be more discreet?"

"You're too beautiful for that," Paul said, and then he kissed her again.

. . .

By the time Su steps out of the aesthetician's clinic, she's put the pregnancy test behind her, for now at least. Nothing like a couple of artfully etched crow's-feet to make her feel more at ease. It could be a fluke result. She'll schedule a blood test before jumping to any conclusions.

She boards her white Porsche SUV at the Palais Renaissance pickup area. Su learned how to drive in the early nineteenth century, but she doesn't think a real lady should be seen behind the wheel. Their chauffeur takes care of weekdays. Paul drives on weekends.

Su looks out the window. A throng of brands passes her by in a whirl. Gucci. Nike. Apple. Prada. Starbucks. The chauffeur drops Su off at her next stop: an elegant mansion tucked away at Grange Road.

A valet buzzes the gate open. They pull up to the foyer of Singapore's first private Christian Dior haute couture boutique. Closed to the public, it serves the brand's top-spending clients. Su is greeted by her personal consultant, whom she has been liaising with for the fittings. "Welcome back to the salon, Miss Bai. Your dress is ready." They go past archival racks, gleaming with classical pieces suffused with that conservative womanliness that Su admires. Up the stairs to a mirrored attic atelier flooded with natural light, a few mannequins, a sewing table.

A French couture seamstress in a white chemise and a neat bun smiles at Su. She nods to the garment on a mannequin behind her.

"C'est le plus élégant, madame."

Su steps up to the mannequin—*her* mannequin; Dior made it to Su's dimensions—prim and full skirt, nipped-in waist, wide shoulder straps, a debossed floral bodice.

When Su emerges from the fitting room in the full outfit, the consultant swoons. "Miss Bai reminds me of Audrey Hepburn in *Roman Holiday*." It's true—Su's doe eyes and swan neck recall Hepburn's delicate femininity and timeless sophistication.

In an adjoining room, a beauty artiste fusses over her: minimal makeup—Su barely needs it; just a hint of blush, a touch of liner, a swipe of gloss. She sweeps Su's silky, jet-black hair up in a high chignon. "We shouldn't have favorites, but you're the most beautiful client I have in Asia . . ."

Su's personal security officer is waiting for her in the foyer. Tik's eyes are alert.

Her short hair is slicked back neatly. She holds the door open for Su. "Mrs. Ong, mind your step." Su notices that Tik is dressed more formally than usual, in a white long-sleeved men's shirt, black pants, leather brogues.

"Mr. Ong wants me to tell you he will be delayed," Tik reports. "He will see you at the ball."

"Do you think this is too much?" Su smoothes down her skirt as they wait for the chauffeur.

Tik glances at her respectfully. "You look perfect, Mrs. Ong."

They're headed to the Red and White Ball, an annual dinner and charity auction the Party hosts at the historic Raffles Hotel. Attendees include politicians, high-society fixtures, and celebrities, as well as prominent members of the legal and business communities. Auction proceeds go to diverse causes: cancer research, a bursary program for low-income students, a regional think tank.

"I thought Paul was making sure not to work late tonight?"

"There's been a situation in a junior college, if I heard right."

"A situation?" Su is worried. "He's not in danger, is he?"

"Oh," Tik assures her immediately, "no, ma'am, nothing like that at all. From what I heard, I'm not very sure, but it's something about a student not wanting to wear the school uniform."

That sounds below Paul's pay grade, but Su figures she'll hear it from him later. The car pulls up. Tik opens the back-seat door for her, then goes around to the front. Before Tik started working for them, the air-conditioning was always too hot or too cold. Now the temperature is just right. There's a bottle of Evian in the cupholder, and the radio is tuned to classical music.

Tik has only been assigned to them for a couple of months.

Like all cabinet ministers, Paul is issued a security detail at public events, but he hasn't been high-profile enough (*yet*, he told himself) for a dedicated full-time bodyguard. That changed after the incident outside their bungalow a few months ago when someone spray-painted in big red caps on the timber of their gate: EAT THE RICH!

Su was starting on her morning yoga at the garden patio when she detected the acetone smell. She stepped out onto Coronation Drive, and was pelted with a red paint bomb by a masked assailant who whizzed by on an e-scooter. Graffiti is a criminal act in Singapore. The Party tried to hush up this transgression in the mainstream media: they had a long history of close ties with the company running the one-and-only local newspaper and broadcast station. But with the slew of independently run social media accounts that claimed to call truth to power these days—halfway between sensationalist tabloid and scrupulous fourth estate—it was harder to conceal gossip from the masses, even though the wall was scrubbed clean in less than two hours.

The police commissioner assigned Paul and Su their own elite security officers after this incident. Paul's security officer was Cheng, a burly Chinese man with protuberant eyes. Su's was Tik. When they were introduced, Paul and Su were told that Tik had graduated top of her cohort, as the sole female and the only Malay officer. Su wondered if it might be inappropriate to single Tik out in this way, but Paul gave Tik a genial pat on the shoulder.

"One in a million, huh? Good job."

Paul acclimatized easily enough to Cheng's presence: though he grew up poor, he had been groomed for success from boyhood. There was an inherent arrogance in the way he took for granted a pecking order in which their chauffeur operated in the front as they lounged in the back, in which Cheng and Tik walked behind them, watched as they ate, opened doors. Su felt a little self-conscious in the beginning, but she's grown used to it as well, and Tik is so discreet.

Outside Raffles Hotel, Tik gets out of the Porsche and comes around to open Su's door. "I'll see you inside, Mrs. Ong," she says, stepping aside tactfully.

. . .

In the hotel, everyone is dressed to the nines. Su sees more socialites than politicians at first glance—the former's gowns are louder. The Spice Girls, loudly bantering over a cocktail table, spot Su at once.

Ping, the editor in chief of the local edition of *Vanity Fair*, sashays up to her. "Oh my goodness, Suzhen," Ping gushes. "Mamma mia! Is that Lanvin—no, wait, it's *Dior!*"

Ping turns to her right and left dramatically, batting her eyelids at her posse for affirmation. Hanis, a designer of Nusantara-inspired loungewear, is married to the Public Utilities Board's CEO. Amrita, a celebrity florist, has a husband high up in GIC, the state's sovereign wealth fund.

Amrita sighs. "I'm still trying to get into that couture salon, but they won't have me!"

"Aiyo, sayang," Ping chastises her, "you know it's invite-only, you mustn't chase them—"

"How come we are all on the same diet, but only Suzhen looks *so* good?" Hanis chips in.

"Ya, when are you going to agree to let my beauty columnist interview you?" Ping demands.

Lady cliques speak like a Greek chorus. When Su first met these women, she didn't know which to respond to first: they spoke back-to-back, leaving no room in between. But over time she realized that she barely had to speak: they hardly noticed what anyone else said.

Su spots Divya, the Minister for Health, coming toward her. Su respects Divya, even if she can't identify with a woman who is a leader herself, who can withstand the spotlight alone.

"Suzhen." Divya pulls her aside, speaking in a low tone. "Could you pass a message on to Paul?"

"Of course." Su leans in closer to Divya.

"I heard about the trans student case. There's overlap between Health and Education . . . I don't know how much Paul's aides will tell him, so I want him to know that the student has been diagnosed with gender dysphoria by a qualified doctor. But an Education department head hounded this doctor until he stopped the student's hormone replacement therapy . . . I think there's room for Paul to act with empathy, to set the direction for policy. This is a health-care issue, and I'm worried it will get politicized in a way that disregards the actual lives at the heart of this matter."

Su is still trying to understand what Divya is talking about when Riz cuts in.

"Div! Our very own vaporizer crusader." Riz smiles mockingly.

Divya refuses to dignify this with a response. Vaping is illegal in Singapore, and Divya has suggested it be legalized, subject to age restrictions, arguing that it doesn't make sense to stop adults from using e-cigarettes—they're adults, for god's sake. That hasn't gone down too well with the rest of the Party.

Riz turns to Su. "Suzhen! How are things with Paul?" Su hears the vaguest taunt in his question, but surely she's being too sensitive.

"Things are well," she says, keeping it generic and placid.

Riz and Paul are both in the running for Chief Minister in the upcoming cabinet reshuffle. Currently, Riz is Minister for Defense, and Paul is Minister for Education. Both were President's Scholars under the Public Service Commission, and they've forged similar career paths. They're now neck and neck for the position of Chief Minister.

Each has a social disadvantage that is politically incorrect to point out: Paul is Chinese but childless; Riz, though a father, is a minority Malay. Su knows that Paul thinks he might be passed over because he doesn't have children, and can't embody the Ideal Family Nucleus the way Riz does, with two boys, one more on the way.

"Still *trying*?" The smile never leaves Riz's face. The baby-making jibe is intentional.

"Aren't we all?" Su says as lightly as she can. Looking around for an out, she sees Tik stationed diligently at the other side of the room. "Oh, there's Tik. I left something in the car," she lies. Noticing Su's attempt to make eye contact right away, Tik starts to move toward her.

"You know, Suzhen," Riz drawls, watching Tik cross the room, "I must say, I'm not sure if it looks good for Paul to have a little mat butch following him around." Su is shocked by how he spits the words *little*, *mat*, and *butch*. Either Riz doesn't notice, or he wants her to be repelled. "Some things are hard to say, man to man. But think about the optics, especially now, with this pondan problem."

"Pon-dan?" Su isn't familiar with the Malay slur for trans.

"That male student who wants to wear the female uniform to school . . ." Riz trails off when Tik stops in front of them. "Good evening, Minister Rahmat," Tik says. He nods at her without making eye contact. "Mrs. Ong." Tik checks in with Su. "You need something?"

Su lets out an involuntary sigh of relief as they exit the crowded ballroom.

"I can get whatever you need from the car, Mrs. Ong," Tik offers. "Then you don't have to walk all the way to the car park?"

Su shakes her head. "I just need a break."

"Ah." Without another word, Tik shows her to a cloistered-off section of Raffles Hotel's lushly planted grounds, a quiet corner with a wrought-iron bench under a palm tree. It's just what Su needs. She sits, then realizes that Tik is standing behind the bench.

"Please"—Su gestures to her—"I insist." Tik sits down, looking a little awkward. Su notices Tik absently reaching for her cigarette pack—but in a moment she catches herself and slides it back into her pocket.

Su bites her lip. "Actually, can I have one?"

Tik is surprised, but she takes her pack out, giving it an expert tap so a cig pokes out at the end. She shrugs apologetically. "I only have Sampoernas . . ."

Su takes one. Tik lights her up. "God," Su exhales. "It's been ages since I had a smoke."

Clove-scented smoke hangs languidly in the evening air.

"You used to smoke, Mrs. Ong?"

"Not exactly." Su had a military commander husband with an opium habit a century ago. "Well, a puff or two, here and there." She smiles sheepishly. "Don't tell Paul, OK?" They smoke in comfortable silence until Su's phone pings with a Google Alert. She's set it to filter news on "green+snake" in the United States—three to five hits a day on average. She glances through.

Critter of the Week: Maryland's Two Varieties of Green Snake
Green Snake Bites 6-Year-Old California Boy in Mojave Desert: 42
Vials of Antivenom Needed

Su frowns, clicks on the second link. She's pretty sure Emerald hasn't moved to the West Coast, and her venom isn't powerful enough to require that much antivenom, but it's good to be safe. She reads the article on *Desert News*—a pit viper, not Emerald. She goes on scrolling.

4xAlpha Snake Boot 16" Xtra Green
Green Snake Attacks Forbes 400 Billionaire in Central Park

Su clicks on the last link. A grainy video on the *New York Post* website, pulled from a security vid from a streetlamp's vantage point, shows a white man being attacked by a green snake with diamond-shaped patterns. Su doesn't have to watch it twice to recognize Emerald.

Then, a gunshot. Heart pounding, she drops the cigarette onto her pleated white skirt.

Tik jumps up and stubs it out at once. "Are you OK, Mrs. Ong?"

The cigarette has burned a hole in the expensive fabric. "Yes." Su tries to steady herself. "Just a little dizzy." She notices Tik's concerned face. "Oh, no, it's not the cigarette. I haven't been feeling good all day," she lies. "Could you send me home, Tik?"

"But Mr. Ong—"

"I want him to have a good time at the ball. It's important for him to be present." She smiles convincingly at Tik. "Don't worry, I'll text him that I'll see him at home. He'll understand."

By the time they get back to Bukit Timah, Su has bought a ticket for the next flight out.

The plane is scheduled to take off at 11:30 p.m. Su is on autopilot as she peels off her gown, changes into a simple dress. Methodically she puts together an overnight bag and leaves a note for Paul: *Family emergency in New York, will call when I land.* Places the gift-wrapped Armani tie beside it. Instead of texting Tik or the chauffeur, she books a cab to Changi Airport.

At the Singapore Airlines counter, the ground staff hands back Su's passport in its handsome Hermès holder. "Have a pleasant flight." Passing through immigration, Su turns her phone off.

. . .

A pretty stewardess in a tight-fitting kebaya uniform brings champagne around the first-class cabin after takeoff. "Miss Bai, may I offer you some Dom Pérignon?" Su shakes her head; she'll stick to sparkling water. She has just started on *North by Northwest*, which she saw when it first came out in 1959, dubbed in Japanese at a Tokyo cinematheque, when she starts finding it hard to breathe.

The grainy video of the green snake darting away after the gunshot. As she imagines the worst, the thin red lines of the pregnancy test come back to her at the same time. *No, please—*

Suddenly, she can smell the spermy miasma of catkins again, can see their pendulous form moving in the wind. Her throat constricts, her breath grows shallow. She feels the awful sensation of having her head held down. *This body itself is emptiness. Emptiness itself is this body.* She isn't even sure what the mantra means to her by now, but she still uses it to calm down. This time, it doesn't work.

She's starting to hyperventilate. She couldn't be pregnant, after what happened—

Su was trapped in a mating circle more than a thousand years before, in the early 800s in the Tang dynasty. It was the first week of spring in Hangzhou. Catkins were starting to bloom. She was still a white snake then, fresh out of hibernation, enjoying the scent of budding daffodils. A banded krait came up from behind her. He pushed his chin against the back of her head. Of course she knew what that meant, but she ignored him. She was not going to raise her tail for someone she didn't even know.

She went on her way, moving faster than before. She could feel him following. Two other male kraits appeared in front of her.

Breathing frantically, she tried to make a run for it, but they hurled themselves onto her, trapping her in a tangle. When she managed to loosen the grip of one, another took his place. Each of them mounted her, trying to force their way in. She resisted. Their spiked penises were out, but she would not open her cloaca. One of them rubbed his chin all over her, but it wasn't courtship behavior. He was mocking her. Then the banded krait took hold and squeezed her so tight she couldn't breathe. Because she was suffocating, she lost control.

Her cloaca opened up. He dug himself into her.

She stared at the catkins swaying on a branch of the poplar tree as he sacked her body. He did not seal her up when he was done. Upon ejaculating, male snakes secrete a gelatinous substance to plug the female's cloaca, so no other snake can have its way with her. But this krait left her raw, and the others took their turns. After they left, she dragged herself to a rock. She did her best to ruin her womb, abrading herself on its jagged edges so she wouldn't bear any of their children.

She might have bled herself dry then, had a younger green snake not passed her way, and nudged her head hesitantly with its own.

Su hissed back as fiercely as she could. She did not want to be perceived. She did not want to be helped. She wanted only to die.

The green snake recoiled in alarm and was about to go on her own way, but their eyes met.

When the white snake felt the green snake's warm and open gaze, she could not hold back any longer—she let herself crack open in front of this stranger, who made her feel like it was safe to break. She couldn't stop shaking, even as the green snake coiled itself around her body, bringing her into the hollowed-out trunk of a weeping willow. As gently as she could, the green snake packed soft moss around her wound to stanch the bleeding, then bedded down beside her.

When she woke the next morning, the green snake was no longer by her side. The white snake assumed she had left. Snakes are solitary creatures, after all. She hugged her tail about herself and sniffed the hollow—the green snake had left a fresh, citrusy yuzu scent. She should have thanked her while she was still around.

A while later, she was surprised to see the green snake returning with dewdrops on a waxy leaf and a field mouse. Over the next week, the green snake brought back prey in the day, and curled up around her at night to steady her sobbing body.

A fortnight later, when she was well enough to venture out of the hollow, they made a pact, awash in the mellow glow of the sunrise by West Lake. *Sworn sisters?* the white snake signed.

For as long as I live, the green snake readily signed back.

It was after this unspeakable violence, which she tried to push away into the darkest recesses of her mind, that the white snake began to spend much of her time under West Lake's bridges.

Before, she had avoided humans, but now she observed them. Hunched grannies selling steamed dumplings, masterful painters dousing ink over silk canvases, giddy lovers tossing lucky coins into the water. Most of all, she found herself drawn to the scholar poets who frequented the bridge, drawing inspiration from the lake's bucolic, expansive waters, composing pretty paeans, and mulling over public policies. Those male kraits had been animals, driven by the basest of impulses. These upstanding men, with their scruples and sciences, their courts and schools, were different. They concerned themselves with higher endeavors, carried themselves with logic and noblesse. If she could only be human, she would be part of that world too.

"Miss Bai, are you OK?" The pretty stewardess hovers over Su, concerned by her shallow breathing. "Can I get you a plastic bag? A warm drink?" There's nothing Su loathes more than being witnessed in a moment of weakness. "I'm OK," she gasps. "I'm OK." She tries to bring her breathing under control, but she could be pregnant, her sister has been shot at, and she's boarded a nineteen-hour red-eye from Singapore to New York, the longest flight in the world, without checking with her husband. She clutches the leather armrest.

"Miss Bai, should I page for a doctor?"

The stewardess is so close that Su can hear her breathing. In, and out. Her qi has a sweet, strawberry-cream smell to it. Su feels swimmy in the head. Her breathing starts to ease as she imagines the dewy breath congealing in the stewardess's mouth.

She catches herself. "No," she manages. "That won't be necessary."

Su pops a Xanax and doesn't look up until *North by Northwest* ends. "If we ever get out of this alive," Thornhill says to Eve on-screen, "let's go back to New York on the train together, all right?"

Su rubs her temples. The remaining flight time pops up in a corner. Sixteen hours to go.

3

Humans Are Scum But I Can Make You Come

The first time she lived in New York, during Prohibition, Emerald did not stay in Chinatown but up in Harlem, where things were lit. Right away, she fell for Jean-Baptiste, a Francophone Haitian poet swanning down 133rd Street in leather loafers and a velvet-collared Chesterfield coat with only tighty-whities underneath.

Every Friday night they went around the corner to Clam House, where they watched the magnificent Gladys Bentley, who often called on Emerald to straddle her lap as she played piano in a white zoot suit. The crowd went wild as Emerald twirled her feather boa around Gladys, who replaced the saccharine lyrics of the day's popular tunes with her own raunchy inventions.

Emerald was happy in New York until the gator craze.

It was February 1935 in East Harlem. Some boys were shoveling snow when they spotted an eight-foot alligator in a storm drain. They lassoed it with a clothesline. When it started to snap at them, they hit the gator on the head with their shovels until it died. A picture of two proud boys holding up the bloodied creature appeared in the *Daily News*, and led to a frenzy: boys wanting baby gators as pets.

Not much longer than a dinner fork, they could be purchased by mail order for $1.50 from Florida, sent to New York in corrugated cardboard boxes with holes in the side. But once the baby reptiles grew too large or began to show their teeth, they would be flushed down a toilet or dumped into a street drain. Rumors of a growing gator colony down in the sewers began to spread. When a pale two-foot alligator showed up on a Lower East Side subway platform, a police squad armed with raw chicken and hunting rifles was sent into tunnels to exterminate them.

Emerald was enraged. How did the police have any right to shoot alligators dead when it was humans who had brought them here in the first place? "Humans are scum," Emerald said to Jean-Baptiste. He had a faraway look in his eyes as he mumbled: "But I can make you come." He hastened to scribble it down on the back of a napkin, as the final line to one of his poems: *Humans are scum / but I can make you come.*

. . .

After the gun goes off, Emerald barely makes it to the creek. Murky water gushes around her. Too weak to fight the current, she is pulled under as one of Central Park's storm sewers sucks her in.

It's dank and dark. Her body grows heavy.

When Emerald sees two pale alligators swim up to her, she's not sure if they're really there, or if she's made them up to stay awake and save herself from drowning. She's back in her human skin now. Something feels raw and angry around her abdomen, where the bullet grazed her.

One on each side, the gators nudge her between them, draping her arm across their ridged backs, silently taking her down a series of labyrinthine sewers. The air goes from musty to fresh. They've emerged into a gushing canal connected to the East River. Emerald almost loses her grip on the gators, but one of them gently clamps its jaws on her elbow and drags her to the shore.

Emerald winces as her naked body is pulled up over gravelly rock.

She flicks her tongue to read the air, bringing it back into the roof of her mouth. Uncut grass and polluted water. Fresh paint and old brick. The gators push her as far up the breakwater as they can with their long snouts, then recede into the river. With a flick of the tail, they're gone.

Emerald is disoriented. She sees the world in blues and greens. She has no idea where she is. Her heart is pounding so hard her ears are throbbing. She tries to stand, but her body flops on the rocks. She pushes her head against cold stone, teetering on the verge of consciousness. If only Su was here, she would know what to do. She would make everything OK.

The meth head perches on his haunches. That buzzy warmth in every cell of his body has cooled by now. His last hit was oral, parachuted down with cigarette paper. He was so horny he could have pegged a cantaloupe with a hole in it, but that sensation has passed, and now he can think again. "Matter causes space to curve, and I'm the king of fender benders," he mutters, wishing someone was around to record the messages coming out of his mouth. He's been awake for forty-eight hours, maybe more. He picks at his forearm. His dog tries to nose his hand away from the sores he's making, but he can't stop scratching at what feels like dozens of gummy worms burrowing under his flesh. "Shoo, Cheeto." He picks up a branch, tosses it toward the river.

Cheeto goes after the branch, then barks ferociously in the distance. "Cheeto?"

It's hard to walk when it looks like there are hundreds of fire ants on the ground, and he must avoid stepping on them. That's what he's focusing on when he sees the naked Asian chick. Not a stitch of clothing on her! He's got to tell her to be careful of the ants. She's crouched over like she's cramping, but it looks like she's got a dope bod. Maybe if he protects her from the ants, she'll lie with him under the stars, and he can point out constellations to her? He can take his clothes off too, and hey, they can just lie side by side, he won't make a nice girl do anything she doesn't want to. Unless she wants to, hehe. He's got a couple of grams left. They'll get off on that. Jack her up, bam!

"Heya lil lady," he says politely. "It's not safe for you here."

She is on her knees, bending over something. When she hears his voice, she straightens. Not to be rude or anything, but he's a total boob man. His eyes go straight to her chest. Great tits. Now he is ready to look at her face. Yellow contact lenses, green buzz cut, as edgy as an anime character—he's really lucked out this time. She sticks her tongue out at him. He's taken aback, but he sticks his back out in case it's, like, a cultural thing? Her tongue looks forked. No way, she's into body mod? This is the girl of his dreams. Only thing is, she's rubbish at makeup—her red lipstick is smeared all around the lower half of her face. He blinks when he notices the unmoving, beige-and-black mass at her knees—Cheeto. He turns to run.

In a feral haze, a snake's tongue is its most important organ. Each time it flicks its tongue into the air, receptors pick up minuscule chemical particles, perceived as scent. Chemical information is sent to the brain so the snake can act accordingly: feast, flee, fuck. A snake's tongue is split so it knows which direction to move, left or right, based on the prevalence of chemical particles on either side.

Emerald's tongue flickers in the night and registers two mammals. The first is a large, sinewy mongrel with raw-chicken-smelling qi, coming toward her with its hackles raised. The other is a bumbling beanpole of a human, still some distance away. When the dog bares its teeth and launches itself at her fiercely, she strikes out by instinct, tearing her fangs into its neck. It growls, still trying to snap at her, as she takes its qi. When the human reaches her and then starts to run away, she leaps at him, biting him on the ankle. He screams, falling to the ground.

She clambers over him, drawing his qi in a translucent, silvery stream. He tastes of Windex.

Strength seeps back into Emerald's body. Her blue-green dichromatic snake vision returns to full human color. The guy before her is skinny, missing some teeth. The acne on his face isn't too bad, but there are sores and scabs on his arms. She takes his bony wrist in her hand to pace herself. The moment Emerald feels his quickened pulse slowing, she stops feeding on his qi. He slumps onto her, murmuring something about sandworms and spice and global warming.

She drags his body to the ruins of the old hospital behind them, slips his hoodie off. It is emblazoned with a picture of Megan Fox holding up a lighter to her tongue in *Jennifer's Body*, with the dialogue caption: "I'm a god." After watching that film, Emerald tried burning her forked tongue on a lighter. It gave her a blister, and she was low-key worried she'd damaged some of her receptors.

"You'll be fine when you wake up," she tells the guy as she puts on his hoodie. She feels terrible about the dog, but it would have torn her to shreds, and sheer animal instinct had taken over. Sliding her hands into the pocket in the front of the hoodie, she finds twenty bucks, some seashells, a soggy pepperoni Hot Pocket wrapped in a paper towel, an Alcatel phone. The phone still has a sliver of battery life.

Emerald starts to dial the +44 prefix—Su's number.

It's a quarter to six in the morning. It's evening in Singapore, on the other side of the world. As she pictures Su pristinely dressed and setting a table for dinner, she deletes the digits. What could she say to Su—that she is sick of sugaring for cash, that she got annoyed with her date for being a stupid prick who thought he was so suave, that she just wanted to scare him and ended up in this mess? Su already thinks she is a fuckup; she doesn't want to give her evidence that she *has* fucked up. She can imagine Su storing it up, to be used as future ammunition.

Emerald winces as she lifts the hoodie to peek at the wound on the left side of her abdomen. Still bleeding—but it feels like a graze. She's lucky the cop missed. Snake spirits can maintain their internal essence and youthful looks as long as they take in qi, but their physical bodies can be torn apart just like humans'. They can still be mortally wounded. She shouldn't have been so reckless, she knows, but that's what immortality has done over time—given her a taste for danger, for pushing it further, so the endlessness feels more alive.

Biting her lip, Emerald decides to dial Bartek's number instead.

. . .

The number is unknown. Bartek has canceled the call three times. It isn't even seven. A text message notification vibrates through his pillow, but he keeps his eyes resolutely shut, groaning. When the phone rings a fourth time, he picks up. "This better not be a booty call."

It's Emerald. There is no more battery, she says, but come to the smallpox hospital.

"Smallpox?" He's so confused.

"Please just come," she says, and the line goes dead.

He sits up in bed and checks his texts. Emerald has texted him with this number. *B, it's E. I got into a mess and I'm at the abandoned smallpox hospital on Roosevelt Island.*

The Uber ride from Greenpoint to Roosevelt Island isn't cheap, but Bartek reminds himself that Emerald cabbed to the Highline Ballroom to get his drunk ass off the dance floor at a leather party a few months ago. He peers curiously out the window. He's lived in New York for years, but has never been to Roosevelt Island. He's imagined it to be an island-island, but it feels more like a college campus suburb. Nervously, he heads into the ruins of the old smallpox hospital.

"Barty?" He hears Emerald's voice faintly from inside. She is curled up in a corner in an oversize hoodie, hugging her elbows around her knees. She is so pale her skin looks translucent.

"Emmy!" He rushes over to her. "What happened?"

Emerald winces, and Bartek feels like he's in a movie: he sees the bloodstain on the hoodie, and her hand applying pressure on top of it. She lifts it to show him. There's an angry laceration of raw red on the left side of her rib cage.

Bartek blanches. "Oh my god." He doesn't have a clue what to do; the only thing he feels capable of right now is changing the emphasis placement of what he's saying just to calm himself down. "*Oh* my god, oh *my* god, oh my *god*!!!" He takes his phone out. "I'm calling nine-one-one . . ."

Emerald stops him. "I don't want to go to the hospital."

That's when Bartek spots the half-naked guy asleep in the corner. Bartek jumps. "Did he—"

"No, no, it's not what it looks like . . ."

Bartek stares at Emerald, trying to make sense of everything. "What is going on, girl?"

"Barty," she says softly. "I'm going to tell you something about myself, OK? And then you can decide if you still want to be my friend. If you're uncomfortable, I'll move out . . ."

Without thinking, Bartek backs away from Emerald. He sees the hurt in her eyes, and remembers how he tried to come out to his best friend in junior high. It had taken him a long time to get there, to even be OK with himself—he'd thought about whether he should tell Maude for months. They'd grown closer ever since he shielded her period stain during PE class when she forgot her tampon, and he thought it would be safe to share with her. It was over MSN Messenger. He'd typed "I'm gay," then backspaced and changed it to "I've kinda been questioning my sexuality, just curious do you ever think about this stuff? Haha." Hit enter before he chickened out. Maude didn't even say anything, just logged off. He thought about offing himself, searched online for "best ways to die painlessly," but he was too afraid to do it. When he showed up at school, his chair had a paper stuck to the back. It read: I AM A FAGGOT AND I WILL BURN IN HELL.

Bartek scooches back to Emerald till they are shoulder to shoulder.

"This is where you tell me you're part of the East Asian mafia illuminati, right? Hit me with your best shot, come in like a wrecking ball. Mami's got an open mind, no judgment, no shade . . ."

. . .

OK, just breathe. Bartek picks up gauze pads, rubbing alcohol, antibiotic ointment at the Walgreens around the corner from Peter Pan Donuts back in Greenpoint. *My bestie is a mo-fo man-eating snake!*

The cashier is bored and unbothered, but Bartek flashes a jumpy smile as she rings him up.

Back in his apartment, Bartek tries to sound more confident than he feels: "Doc B is in the house!" He ices the wound; it's no longer bleeding. He cleans what he can with the gauze. They google to figure out her injury. Emerald was right. There is an elongated abrasion, but it's not an entry or exit wound. The bullet must have struck her skin at a shallow angle, perforating the epidermis and subcutaneous tissue. Opinions differ over whether to close the wound or leave it open. Since there's a flap of skin attached, it seems best to close it up. Bartek is surprised: there are already threads like "Can normal sewing thread be used to stitch wounds?" on Reddit. After scanning the forums, Bartek digs into his art supply stash. Boils a curved needle and a spool of cotton thread to sterilize them. He is going to try out a YouTube video titled "purse string suture technique."

Bartek puts on Patti Smith's covers album *Twelve* for sonic company as he sews Emerald up. His hand is surprisingly steady. He finishes just as that dark folk take on Nirvana's "Smells Like Teen Spirit" hits, nothing more than the truth in Patti's voice and a guitar and a banjo, as she strips Kurt Cobain's anthem naked to its pure essence, ad-libbing her poetry into the bridge: "*Forgotten, foraging mystical children . . .*"

Bartek gets teary. "I just want to say, I love you like Patti Smith loved Robert Mapplethorpe. I love you like an angel loves another angel, like an axolotl loves another axolotl . . ."

"Aw, Barty." Emerald reaches out to him for a hug. "I love you too."

Emerald drifts in and out of sleep on the sofa, feeling safe as Bartek checks her temperature at regular intervals to be sure there isn't an infection. Now he is making her golden milk, with turmeric, ginger, and cinnamon. "Drink it all up. Is there anything else you need?"

The fastest way for her to heal is for her to have some qi, but she'll wait till she can head out for that. The next best thing is to eat the way she would in the wild, live feeders, but she doesn't want to freak Bartek out, so she asks if he has any eggs.

"Yeah! Scrambled or poached?"

She shakes her head. "Can I have them raw?"

Bartek brings the carton to her. She lets him see her tongue flicking out of her mouth. She opens the carton. Takes an egg out. Swallows it whole. When it reaches the back of her throat, she flexes her neck vertebrae into her esophagus to break the egg. She eats the whole carton in front of Bartek, egg by egg. She notices how he tries not to flinch as he hears the crack and sees the shape of the eggshell collapsing as it slides down her throat. Emerald knows Su would never let anyone see her feed like a snake; it is an immense loss of status in her view, tantamount to self-sabotage. "Once they see our animal sides," she warned Emerald, "they won't treat us like humans."

Emerald could have fed privately, but she wants to be vulnerable before Bartek, after all he's done for her. But maybe it's not fair to expect people to accept you wholly. Maybe it's better to show them only the ways in which you're like them, to keep the rest to yourself—

"I'm sorry," Emerald says. "I don't know why I did that."

Bartek shrugs. "You're basically paleo. No big deal."

"Honestly, you don't think I'm a freak?"

"So what if you're a freak?" Bartek demands. "As long as you're *you*, that's what counts, no?"

Maybe Su is wrong, Emerald thinks. Maybe it's OK to be visible, as long as you're being seen by the right people. Even if it were possible to choose, why is normativity the way to go?

Biodeterminism is so 1920s. Emerald unloosed herself in the Damenklubs of Berlin around the fin de siècle and was a connoisseur of Anita Berber's qi—it tasted like morphine and white roses. She crashed in the Charlottenburg attic of the editor of the lesbian periodical *Die Freundin* and attended Magnus Hirschfeld's lectures at the World League for Sexual Reform. Much of Hirschfeld's argument for mainstream acceptance came from hinging empathy on the nascent scientific theory that homosexuals did not choose to be gay but were born as such and should not be persecuted for something they could not change. But whether it is a genetic truth or a personal choice, Emerald does not see why anyone should dictate how someone else lives. Su always maintained that life had dealt them dirty as snakes; they had to fight against their base instincts and strive to be as normal, as human, as possible. But why was that the only way to live?

Su was always coming down on her for standing out, for not fitting in. Emerald wishes Su could see her the way Bartek does: simply as someone who chooses to be herself. She tears up.

"Emmy," Bartek moans theatrically, "I had to deal with your blood, don't make me mop up your tears. No more leakage of bodily fluids, OK? Love you for who you are. You're a freak, I'm a freak. Ride or die, baby. You're a queen, I'm a queen. We don't need *saving*. We're out here, *thriving*."

4

A Self-Possessed Woman Can
Turn Your World to Dust

This body itself is emptiness. Emptiness itself is this body. After swallowing the lotus seeds in 815, the white snake and the green snake slithered into West Lake to meditate upon this mantra. Self-cultivation—the Taoist practice of bringing body and mind into the eternal cosmology of nature, in order for the authentic self to transcend form, corporeality, and destiny—was an elusive art. There was no guarantee of manifestation. Others had tried and failed, only to revert to their original forms.

The white snake was made for self-cultivation. She had the natural discipline to empty her mind with ease, chanting sutras silently in her heart till she melted into shapeless succor and fathomless light. The green snake struggled to keep up. Her eye wandered with every yellowed leaf and wilted petal that fell into the water. Her head hurt from contemplating the same cryptic line over and over—what could it possibly mean? Many a time, she felt as if she could take the seclusion of introspection no more. She wanted to give up. But the white snake was a loving companion and a steadfast guide. Every time the green snake faltered, her sister steered her back on course.

They were in this together, and each would always have the other's back. Existing side by side in this liminal state for centuries, they grew closer than they had ever been before, fortifying each other silently, waxing and waning under the moon's lucent glow.

Like a seed splitting irresistibly through its sac, under the full moon on the night of Mid-Autumn Festival in the year 1615 in the Ming dynasty, a woman broke through the water's surface.

She was naked, and she flailed her arms desperately, looking for all the world like she was drowning even though she was in the shallows. Her breath came in urgent gasps as she learned to inhale, as she kept her head above the water. Quickly she realized that she could paddle her arms and kick her legs to keep afloat. With utmost apprehension, she slowed her kicking—only to find that her feet could easily touch the ground. A burbling sensation began in her stomach, vibrating up through her chest and rising through her neck before it spilled out of her mouth.

Laughter. She was laughing. It was pure euphoria.

How many times had she heard that unfathomable and gorgeous sound? Trembling, she reached out—*her very own fingers! Five of them on each side, ending in assorted lengths*—to touch her parted lips, pleased by their protruding softness, followed by the wondrous bridge of her slender nose. Almond-shaped eyes, on either side of that. Her lashes tickled her fingertips when she blinked. Tears came to her eyes, leaking out of their tight corners in tiny droplets. She wiped them away in wonder. Placed her fingers in her mouth. Salty.

She was enjoying their briny taste when she was pulled under by another pair of hands, clinging tight around her neck. Underwater, bubbles came out of her mouth. She struggled to open her eyes. The thrashing, naked body of a beautiful young woman came into view—it was her sister. She pulled them both toward the shore.

Her sister coughed water out of her lungs. She had the instinct to pat her on the back, admiring the curvature of her spine. It was no longer bendy, like before, but solid and rigid.

Breathe, she tried to sign with her tongue, but what tumbled out of her mouth were the Mandarin words, an ethereal sound. She was so shocked that she said it again, suspending the vibration between her lips: "Breathe." Breath by breath, her sister calmed down.

She reached out to her. No more tails—it was their hands that touched. First palm on palm, then finger to finger. The electricity of having a human body fizzed through her. Soft skin, no longer scaly. Long black hair flowing from her head. Limbs that bent at angles. Ears on either side of her head. An adorable, useless little belly button!

"Isn't this everything?" Her tongue was much shorter. She would have to get used to it.

"It's another way of being." Her sister had a steady and melodious voice, a little lower than hers. "But that doesn't mean it's *everything*. We shouldn't forget who we are, where we came from."

"Well," she said obstinately, "I'm already forgetting."

"A snake can shed its skin a hundred times, but it will always remain a snake."

This was the last thing she wanted to hear right now. She felt her face darken, her features pulling into a scowl. She realized, with astonishment, that what she was feeling was being displayed on her face, faster than she could control it. She understood that to possess a face, with features tightly knitted to feelings, was both convenient and bothersome. How sophisticated this was! But how vexatious as well, to not be able to hide how you felt till you were ready to show it. She didn't want to spoil the buoyant mood, so she hastened to replace the scowl with a smile, and picked up something soft and good-smelling beside the pointy bone of her elbow.

"Look." She touched its petals. "A flower."

She held it out to her sister, who tried to smell the bloom with her tongue. "Here, silly." She held it under her sister's nose instead. She inhaled, sighing pleasurably. They lay on their stomachs, cheeks against damp earth, staring into each other's now-round eyes.

All of a sudden she jerked upward, frightening her sister.

"Are you all right? Does something feel wrong?"

"I'm fine, but get up, quick." She gathered her legs together, trying to imitate a cross-legged pose. "Humans don't flop about on their bellies," she went on anxiously. "We must pay attention to posture. Have you seen the lords and ladies? They have impeccable carriage."

"Let's go slow. We've been humans for less than a candle hour."

She tried to stand up, but her ankles were soft and her knees wobbly. Her center of gravity, used to being evenly spread across the horizontal length of a sinuous body, had not yet adjusted to the vertical orientation of the human form. She fell chin first, landing back on her stomach. Her sister laughed. The sound tinkled in the air, flowing through her ear canals.

She held on to a tree trunk as she hoisted herself up. The view was marvelous. Standing straight, she could see all the way to Broken Bridge. How had they spent their lives slithering on their bellies? "Come." She reached for her sister's hand. "There's so much to see."

Her sister rose to join her. "The view is pretty, but you are prettier."

She felt her cheeks prickle as she blushed. The moon was heavy as an overripe melon in the sky, and a night breeze pulled forth the scent of seven-mile azalea. Her sister leaned over to whisper: "I'm glad we'll have all the time in the world. To be sisters with you in one lifetime is not enough."

The white snake named herself Bai Suzhen. Bai for white, and Suzhen sounded like just the sort of name the virtuous wife of an honorable scholar poet would have. Her sister found formality stifling, so Suzhen gave her the diminutive name Xiaoqing, for the pretty green hue of her snake skin. Much later, the green snake called herself Emerald, but Suzhen would never change her name.

. . .

"Miss Bai?" Su startles at the sound of the stewardess's dulcet voice. "May I know if you'd like to have breakfast? There are Asian and continental options on the menu . . ."

Su blinks awake in her fully reclined bed to see the stewardess proffering a leather-bound menu with a bright smile. The Xanax sent her into a slumber so deep that it was not a dream but a walk through the vault of her memory. Dazed, she sits up. "How long till landing?"

"About two hours to go." The stewardess helps her to set the table.

Su nurses a cup of hot coffee, trying to hold on to the fast-fading edges of the half memory, half dream. She can almost smell the azaleas. She's never been able to relive that night in such detail. This reverie makes her feel like she is right there again, feeling everything for the first time. Many times, over the centuries, Su has wanted to return to West Lake. But she could never bear the thought of being back in Hangzhou without Emerald. What would the point of that be? She doesn't know what Hangzhou is like anymore. So much time had passed. She and Emerald are around four hundred human years old by now, but they've spent eight hundred years in self-cultivation, and ten years as snakes—how does the existential math add up?

Su's breakfast tray is cleared away, and she puts on a news program to distract herself.

"Good morning, ladies and gentlemen," a friendly baritone cuts through Su's thoughts. "This is Captain K. J. Lee from the flight deck.

We are currently cruising at an altitude of thirty-three thousand feet. The weather looks good, and with tailwind on our side, we expect to land at JFK fifteen minutes ahead of schedule. The local time in New York is five thirty a.m. Weather in New York is clear, with a high of twenty-one degrees Celsius and sixty-nine Fahrenheit. We'll get a great view of the city as we descend. Until then, sit back, relax, and enjoy the rest of the flight. Cabin crew, prepare the cabins for arrival, thank you."

Su is about to reset the time on her Rolex, every hour denoted by a diamond, when she realizes that it appears to reflect the correct time: New York is exactly twelve hours behind Singapore, so her watch already points to half past five. She has hurtled a sliver back in time to be with Emerald.

The air pressure in Su's ears pops as the plane greases the runway. "Ladies and gentlemen, welcome to New York City." Su takes her phone out. Her finger hovers over the power button. She slides it back into her bag, so she can sit with the peace of this feeling a while longer.

Over the course of the long flight, Su should have turned her phone on, connected to Wi-Fi, and updated Paul, who must have been worried sick to come home to an empty house and a perplexing note, but she didn't want to do that. Once she calmed down, she began to feel a little thrill of disconnection. Because no one knows where she is and what she's doing, she's been warming up to an unfamiliar sensation: that she belongs solely to herself. She knows she will no longer be able to feel this way once she turns her phone back on, speaks with Paul, gets assailed by a volley of notifications. She is in constant communication with her three private wealth lawyers. One is in London, and also takes care of her Swiss assets. There's another guy in Hong Kong, while the third is based in New York.

Part of why Su moved to Singapore was its favorable tax structure. She didn't expect to stay put there, but she met Paul eight years before by chance at the Botanic Gardens. She was in the hothouse admiring the orchids when a man came up from behind her.

He was tall and broad-shouldered. He had a handsome face and wore frameless glasses.

"Good afternoon," he said, a little boldly, a little awkwardly. "Your beauty inspired me to . . ." He unfurled his closed palm to show her the purple bloom he'd plucked off a potted orchid.

"Oh." She was flattered but flustered. "I don't think we're quite supposed to—"

"It's Vanda Miss Joaquim," he cut in, reaching his hand out tentatively. When she didn't stop him, he slotted the bloom behind her ear with a gentle touch. "Our national flower."

She laughed a little. "I'm not Singaporean, I'm afraid."

She looked at him looking at her and saw that he was deeply, instantly smitten. His Adam's apple bobbed as he swallowed. Then he threw caution to the wind: "Well, would you like to be?"

They were married just over three months later. Paul had told her he knew the moment he glimpsed her that he wanted to be with her, and how uncharacteristic this was for him. From as early as he could remember, he had been careful to think through and weigh out his options. Growing up poor, he understood that a governmental scholarship was his best way out. He mugged his brains out to get into the elite Raffles Institution. He participated in extracurricular activities not as a pursuit of what he liked, but in accordance with what would look best on his future résumé—debate to sharpen his speech-giving skills; badminton singles so he could win alone.

But he'd fallen for Su at first sight, Paul told her, without his usual caution and calculation. He had seen her among the orchids and thought unequivocally: *I'd like to make her my wife.*

Su was swept away not by Paul's good looks but by his propriety and political ambition, mixed inextricably with his humble background. On their first night in the swanky, spacious District Ten bungalow she'd bought without a loan, she laid her head on his chest and told him she empathized with how hard he'd striven to get to where he was. She really understood that.

Paul gave her a strange look, both scornful and admiring.

"Why would you?"

He was referring to the ease he must have imagined her to have grown up with. She, on the other hand, was thinking about how difficult it had been to transition from snake to human.

For a cloudy moment, as she listened to the steady beat of his heart, Su pictured Paul sizing her up in the orchid hothouse and placing an easy bet. He didn't know anything about her right then, it was true, but her wealth was plain to see: the elusive Sac Faubourg Birkin bag, the Maybach sunglasses with diamond-encrusted corners.

Then she blinked, and she was in love with him again.

As she steps out into the terminal, Su is reminded of how ugly John F. Kennedy Airport is. Absolutely dull, no frills. It's not in any way befitting to the global city that New York is. JFK does not care to make any impression on the traveler whatsoever. Singapore's Changi Airport is the polar opposite. With its cascading ferns, spotless carpets, soaring skylights, art sculptures, ergonomic rest areas, and designer stores, Changi is thoroughly determined to wow anyone passing through.

Su respects that about Singapore—how much thought and effort it puts in to dress itself up. She can relate. Ever since the first luxury brands established themselves, Su has relied on haute couture as a soft armor against a hard world that isn't made for her, a world she is worried will call her bluff. Fashion helps to ground her in her own body. It makes her feel perceivable.

Su turns her phone on, scrolling past the avalanche of Paul's missed calls and her ever-increasing unread-email count to call Emerald. She prepares herself for no answer, but to her utter surprise, the call goes through. "Hey Jie." Su feels the knot in her chest soften into something more elastic. Her sister is fine. Did she misrecognize Emerald's snake skin in the video? She didn't think she could mistake her sister anywhere, but it's been a while.

"Hi." Su tries to match Emerald's casual tone. "Sorry to call so early, did I wake you up?"

"All good. I haven't gone to bed yet . . . What's up?"

"I'm in New York."

"Oh?"

"Last-minute mortgage broker meeting," Su lies. "Let's grab a bite?"

"Sure," she hears Emerald mumbling noncommittally, "maybe."

"Later tonight?" Su tries to pin Emerald down before she reaches the front of the immigration line. There's an incoming call—it's Paul. "I have to run. Pick a place and text me, OK?" She takes a deep breath before she picks up Paul's call. "Paulie? I'm so sorry—"

"Suzhen, where are you?"

"JFK. My flight just landed."

"What happened?"

Su had thought it over on the plane. "I'm very sorry I never told you, but I have an estranged sister who lives in New York. We haven't spoken in years. She got into an accident, so I— I got on the first flight out." She braces herself for anger or incredulity. She's never pulled something like this on Paul before. But he only asks, "Is she OK?" Su is so relieved that he isn't mad. "She's fine. A gun went off, they're still trying to piece things together . . ."

"This would never happen in Singapore." It's beside the point, but she hears the pride in Paul's voice. Singapore has extremely strict gun laws, and very few violent crime cases. This is another reason that compelled her to stay: Singapore is profoundly secure, often ranked as the safest city in the world by global indexes. Even late at night, Su sees teenage girls jogging in skimpy sports bras, expensive headphones jammed on their heads, the latest iPhones bright in their hands, with a total lack of fear of theft or molestation.

"You're right," she says, without telling Paul that the gunshot came from the NYPD. She's next in the immigration queue.

"Ma'am"—an officer snaps his fingers—"no cell phones!"

"You better go," Paul tells her. "Call me later."

Stepping out of JFK, Su feels the cool, dry air of New York hit like a palate cleanser. Her head—so used to Singapore's sweltering humidity—feels lighter, refreshed. She expected to go straight to searching for Emerald, but that isn't necessary now. "St. Regis," she tells the driver.

Fiddling with her phone, she rewatches the video in the cab. It's Emerald, for sure. She's glad nothing untoward has come of it, but how have they reached this point, where you put on a nonchalant tone instead of telling your sister that you've been shot in the stomach? Su places a hand over the floaty fullness in her own abdomen. She's not coming clean either. For a moment she imagines confiding in Emerald, telling her that she suspects she's pregnant, and doesn't know if she wants to keep the baby.

She sighs. She can't imagine saying any of this out loud.

It wasn't always like this. Su has tried to be there for Emerald over the years, but sometimes the distance between them is necessary. They are completely different by nature. Emerald is a green viper, Su a white krait. Vipers are impulsive, never hesitating to strike when provoked. Kraits are reluctant to bite. When agitated, they coil up to keep their heads concealed, their bodies flattened. Once, in a fight, Emerald reminded Su that despite all appearances, kraits are far more poisonous than vipers, and while vipers feed on small mammals, kraits primarily eat other snakes and reptiles. "Let's face it, Jie," Emerald said. "Underneath it all you're a cutthroat cannibal. You're way more ruthless than I could ever be." The remark stuck with Su.

The St. Regis suite is timeless and ornate. Chandeliers and velvets. Su slides her stockinged feet out of her shoes, nestles into the eiderdown pillows, and stares blankly at the ceiling.

A text comes in from Emerald. *Union Pool, 8pm.*

There's a full day ahead. Su decides to look into the Forbes 400 man from the video. Emerald can be imprudent and loose-tongued. Su wants to figure out what kind of guy they're dealing with, in case he knows too much. She contacts her New York lawyer to dig up info—the monthly retainer Su pays is handsome enough that he's always happy to run the occasional errand. The man's name is Gabe, or Giovanni on the app. Married with a kid in college, he's the cofounder of a medical cannabis start-up. He's been admitted to Mount Sinai for the snake bite.

When Su goes through Emerald's profile on the app, it breaks her heart a little. Emerald is in a push-up bra, with this bio: *You can't choose your father, but you can choose your daddy. The only hair between my legs should be your beard ;)*

Su is racked with guilt. Emerald only turned to this because she didn't send the money. She puts her phone away. I'm sorry, Xiaoqing, she thinks. I'll take better care of you. I'll make it up to you.

. . .

In Midtown West, Gabe's convalescing in Mount Sinai Hospital's premium wing. The ward is spacious, with a view of Times Square. Tucked in a tartan robe, he's rifling through *Newsweek* when a well-dressed Asian woman walks in. She introduces herself as Emerald's representative. "Representative?" He isn't sure what that's supposed to mean, but he's wary. She is older than Emerald, but still a total knockout. Great gams, uptight strut. "How did you find me here?"

"I won't take up too much of your time. Tell me what you know about Emerald."

"This is a misunderstanding," he lies. "She propositioned me at the bar. I bought her a drink, that's all. That girl was so desperate for dough, even a ho has more dignity—"

The woman flinches. Dark fills out her eyes. Her pupils enlarge. Her irises grow narrow. She glides up to him in a supple motion, so quickly he is unable to react. It's only when she tears off the bandage on his neck that he yawps: "What the fucking fuck!"

Gabe tries to jab at the call button, but she bends over, and he sees a flash of fangs. She strikes where the green snake bit him, without making any new puncture marks. His arms grow heavy. He can't lift them to defend himself as she leans over his mouth. There is a sharp, windy pull in his throat. Gabe spasms. He gets a mad sense that she is taking his breath, his brightness, right out of his body.

He groans. She lets go, but it is too late—Gabe's vital signs are going haywire on the diagnostic system. He sees her unhooking him from the machine. He wheezes, mouth opening and closing like a gaping fish. Standing over him impassively, she licks her lips. There is no fear or satisfaction, no mercy or benediction, in the way she's regarding him. Her gaze is so neutral, so removed, that for a moment Gabe feels calm too. Even as his heart seizes up from the lethal neurotoxins, he can't look away from her eyes.

How fresh and cold and endless they are. A carefully concealed well of the clearest water.

. . .

Times Square is a gladiator arena. Survival of the fittest, where nothing is sacred. Chonky pigeons flap their weakened wings to get out of the way of a yellow cab, whose driver is honking furiously and leaning his entire upper body out of the window to flip the finger at an intrepid Spandex-clad cyclist, who screams right back into the hot cloud of sputtering diesel, "Screw yourself, asshole!"

Su moves nimbly through the aggressive gridlock, blending into the madding crowd. She stops before a hot dog vendor.

"Can I have a bottle of sparkling water, please?"

He grabs her a chilled bottle. "One dollar."

She passes him a tenner. When he turns back with change, she's gone. "Sheesh, OK lady."

Half a block down, Su takes a cool drink as she tries to keep Gabe's qi down. After she's abstained for so long, the raw intake of human qi is a shock to her system, impossibly delicious.

She wants to throw up. She wants to spin around.

She's jacked. How did she forget just how shiny, pungent, and thrilling the world out there could be? Su lets the unrelenting throng of the crowd carry her forward as her senses reach a fever pitch. She is seeing with her eyes lit up. The sky is electric blue, the edges of clouds are sharp. Colors on billboards are so vivid they hurt. Textures pop out at her, highly defined. She can smell everything, how wonderful and awful: pizza, weed, hot coffee, roasted peanuts, sewer gas. And at the back of her throat: metallic earth of blood, powdery aftertaste of breath, sweetest umami of qi.

Her eyes are bright. Her pulse is quick. A man is dead.

Su is pressing the cool bottle against her hot forehead, sidestepping away from the Midtown Tetris of tourists, hustlers, buskers, corporates, crazies, and cops, when she sees Saks Fifth Avenue. She steps in, dazzled by the intricate patterns of the terrazzo floor.

The ground floor is dedicated to luxury handbags—Balmain, Bottega Veneta, Burberry. She breezes past the enriched smell of treated leather toward the iridescent escalator in the diamond-shaped atrium. Takes a gander at the beauty department on the second floor, where she is coddled by a cheerful cadre of salesgirls. She spritzes perfume after perfume to catch the high of every note with her heightened sense of smell: patchouli, musk, vanilla. Picks up random items—a fragrance here, a scarf there, a pair of sunglasses—like any other well-heeled lady on a shopping spree. As she heads to the payment counter, she passes the Christian Louboutin section. Spots a pair of adorable peach-pink satin baby ballet shoes, finished with a tiny bow on each side, iconic red soles in calfskin leather on the underside. The smallest size fits in her palm.

Su swipes her card at checkout, goes down the escalator, smartly beribboned Saks paper bag on her arm. She is passing through the doors when the security alarm beeps. The guard reverse-racially profiles her—such a beautiful, well-dressed Asian lady—and bows apologetically.

"I'm sure there's been a mistake, ma'am." He bids her pass back and forth once more, and frowns when the machine is set off again. "Gotta be a stray tag somewhere. Do you mind?"

When he finds the tiny pair of satin baby Louboutins in her bag, the woman laughs. It is a winsome sound he could have easily listened to all day. "I'm sorry, ma'am," he finds himself saying, "they must have forgotten this one." Wanting to leave an impression on her, even if he'll never see her again, he disables the security tag in one macho crack. "There we go. All set." Holding the door open for her, he can't help but add, gruffly: "My name's Bryan."

"Thank you, Bryan." Her smile is radiant. His knees go weak.

Then she is gone, twirling out the door, as light as a breeze.

He watches as she drifts down sunlit Fifth Avenue.

Something mesmerizing in the way she moves. More like gliding, less like walking. As if her feet are kissing the air that covers the ground, without touching the sidewalk. He cranes his neck as she turns the corner, disappearing around Madison Avenue. Now he laughs at the broken tag in his hand. At how a self-possessed woman can turn your world to dust with little more than a smoky look in her eyes, a liquid sway in her hips.

5

Apex Predator Femme Queen

Emerald takes off and puts on fit after fit: various configurations of tops, bottoms, dresses, shoes. It's a few minutes to 8:00 p.m. "Nothing works!" she exclaims to Bartek. She sits in her undies on the bed, blasting a playlist going from Arca to Tzusing to Easter to Doon Kanda to Alice Glass to Aphex Twin to Eartheater to Jenny Hval to Anohni to Björk. Emerald bites her lip. "She's gonna be so mad at me."

"*Girl.*" Bartek is amused. "I've never seen you like this."

Emerald rolls her eyes at him.

"Not even on a big date," he adds.

"It's just, I haven't seen her in a long time," Emerald counters. She's irked because it's true: no one gets under her skin the way that Su does. A hook in the flesh, slowly reeled in. Bartek runs a spindly finger over the clothes. "All right, tell mami the energy you're going for."

"Not trying to impress, I rolled up like this."

"Hmm." Bartek flicks through their shared wardrobe. "I'm sensing a low broil of unresolved seismic tension from past trauma bonds?"

Emerald snorts. "You can't tell that from sartorial choices."

Bartek drops his jaw like: *Umm, hello? That's my superpower?*

"OK, *you* can," Emerald concedes, "but can we stick with the brief? Accessorize, not therapize. Dark colors please, in case it bleeds through and she finds out . . ."

Bartek pulls out a well-worn black Bikini Kill band T-shirt, silky bright red Sandy Liang track pants with slits and ribbon ties at the sides, and Hieronymus Bosch Doc Marts.

"Hold up, Emmy. You're not going to tell your sister you got shot?"

"No way." Emerald puts on the pants. "She'll think I can't take care of myself." Bartek gives her a pointed look. "She already has a savior complex, I don't want to lend any weight to that."

"Are you, like, sister-sisters?"

"We're not related by blood, but we came up together in this world."

"OK, so like, chosen family. Oh shit, wait." Bartek stops dramatically. "Is she also a . . ." Emerald nods as she pulls the top on, wincing as she moves her arm.

"Fuck me dead." Bartek jumps up. "How many of you are there?"

Then Emerald remembers that Su would never tell.

"If you meet her, don't ever let her know that you know, OK?"

Bartek ignores Emerald. He is whistling Nicki Minaj's "Anaconda" and shaking his booty.

"You idiot." Emerald bursts out laughing. "But for real, Barty, she's super sensitive about it."

"She sounds like a party pooper." Bartek looks Emerald up and down. "All right, finishing touch . . ." He removes the cute cherry drop earrings from his own lobes, his favorites, realistically crafted from wine-red resin, dangling on dainty gold stems, helps Emerald put them on.

"She has hang-ups about being a snake," Emerald says, "which lead to prudish ideas about being the perfect woman. Chaste and refined and modest and domestic and long-suffering . . . Kinda funny how she always seems to find the place and time for it. Confucian China. Victorian England."

"Victorian England?" Bartek's jaw drops. "Babe, you were alive in the eighteen hundreds?"

Emerald had been a good two hundred and fifty human years old by then. 1868 was the second time she and Su tried to live together, and the first and last time Emerald allowed herself to be wedded. "This is a golden opportunity," she could still recall Su telling her. "Two of us, in the same noble household."

Su had caught the eye of an English marquess who called her his "Sugar Pearl of the Orient." Duncan the marquess had a younger brother, Arthur, styled with the courtesy title of a lord, who was also interested in an Asiatic concubine. "Concubine?" Emerald blinked. Naturally, the men already had English first wives.

Su tried to impress upon Emerald how this—a willingness to take a Chinese bride—was an unusual attitude for an Englishman of the times, and that as the spouses of the landed gentry, they would not have to worry about food on the table, a roof over their heads. They would wear fine furs and heat their hands over a cozy hearth, Su said. They would have seedcake and sherry. England was booming with multifarious colonies, and these astute brothers had a stake in the British East India Company. First dibs on tea, silk, porcelain, tobacco.

Emerald didn't see what could possibly be so good about being someone's concubine.

Returning to the same quarters to sleep every night and being fussed over by servants didn't sound like a luxury, but a limitation. She was a snake spirit with venom and fangs; she didn't need the brittle protection of some mortal marquess. Besides, all the fine goods were items they had savored back in Hangzhou. Why on earth did she need an Englishman's extraction to enjoy them?

But she went along with it because it meant she could be close to Su, and she'd missed her.

The small things made it worthwhile, Emerald tried to tell herself. To be able to wake up and see Su sitting across from her at the breakfast table, to exchange a smile as their fingers touched when she passed the salt. To trail behind Su on a walk in the topiary maze, watch her tuck a stray strand of long dark hair behind her ear. Su was lovelier than ever, but she'd changed in many ways. No sway in her step, no sibilance in her voice. She spoke the Queen's English, and knew what cutlery to use for each course, how to hold a fork with its tines pointing downward.

Su seemed contented, but nineteeth-century London didn't sit well with Emerald. The British Empire was burgeoning, but women's status was still scraping rock bottom, even for the rich. They could not vote, sue, or own property. They were expected to devote themselves to the household and submit to their husbands.

The quintessential woman was passive and powerless, same as it had ever been in Confucian China, where the adage of the day went: "The talentless woman is the most virtuous." Emerald was shocked by how similar the popular English poem *The Angel in the House* was to Confucius's ideas about women: "Man must be pleased; but him to please / Is women's pleasure; down the gulf / Of his condoled necessities / She casts her best, she flings herself."

It was the most boring year in Emerald's life, even though (or because) they were waited on hand and foot, even though the feasts were fulsome and the manor was magnificent. The pièce de résistance was the drawing room, which boasted a tropical mural. In the middle of the handsome room hung a gilded cage with two pure-yellow Harz canaries. They were prized for singing with their tiny beaks closed, issuing a soft, sweet song that blended into the background, unlike more strident songbirds. Each time she heard their muted melody, Emerald felt sorry for the birds—and herself.

Emerald hardly had two words to say to Arthur, nor he to her, but he liked to spank her ass with a riding crop in bed. She took her revenge by stealing his qi, which tasted of damp cows, but there came a time where he smacked her so hard that she bit him by instinct, right in the jugular. Thankfully for Arthur, her venom wasn't lethal. After a slight fever, he was off hunting fowl and fox again. He kept a distance from Emerald after this, preferring to patronize the local whores.

This suited Emerald fine, but Su's take was: "You're lucky he didn't punish or banish you."

"*I'm* lucky he didn't punish me? *He's* lucky he's not a rotting corpse in a cypress coffin!"

Each day, Emerald looked forward to the languid hours between lunch and dinner, when she and Su had some private time to themselves, often taking tea in the gazebo by the duck pond.

The tea service was made of the finest bone china with a gold fleur-de-lis pattern, and the household had an endless supply of coveted tea leaves from India and China. Once they drank a sweet, mellow green tea that made Emerald swoon. She asked the maid to open the teapot. Emerald stuck her finger in; Su told her to cut it out and behave with civility before the servants. But when Su saw the smooth, spearlike, light-green leaf that Emerald was spreading out on the tip of her finger, she too recognized it as Longjing tea. It was an early cropped green tea variety cultivated exclusively around the steppes of Longjing Village, close to West Lake, in Hangzhou.

They were heartsick for home that afternoon, as Emerald listlessly tossed her cucumber sandwich ends to the fat white ducks.

"Are you even happy here, Jie?" she asked Su in Mandarin, but Su refused to answer. Emerald knew that Su didn't like her to speak Mandarin, here in London.

One morning there was a flurry in the household at breakfast.

There was but a single canary left in the gilded cage in the drawing room. The other had vanished. The elderly duchess, mother of Duncan and Arthur, burst into tears—the precious birds were so dear to her.

The servants were lined up and questioned. Finally the housekeeper brought a young parlormaid before them. She reddened, afraid to speak. "Go on, Milly," the housekeeper said.

The young maid went on her knees. "It was before dawn. She was standing on a chair . . ."

"Of whom do you speak?" the duchess demanded.

The parlormaid looked up. "It was one of the oriental ladies."

"And?" the housekeeper prodded. "Tell the duchess what you saw."

The parlormaid shuddered. "She brought the bird to her mouth . . ."

The duchess glanced at Emerald. But Emerald had been in bed at dawn. Surreptitiously, she looked at Su. Su froze, and could not hold her gaze. Everyone's eyes were trained tight on Emerald.

Emerald smiled nervously. "I was just playing with the bird, and it flew out of my hands—"

"Ma'am." The housekeeper cut in, directly to the duchess. "That's not what our Milly saw."

The duchess turned to the parlormaid. "What did you see, Milly?"

The parlormaid broke down, sobbing, terrified. "She ripped it to shreds with her teeth!"

Emerald could picture it clearly: her faultless sister with blood dripping down her chin.

"You." It was Emerald the duchess turned to. "You crazy savage!"

Su said nothing as the duchess railed at Emerald. Emerald took it all in silence too. After Emerald had been humiliated before the entire household, Su came to look for her in her room. "I'll talk to the duchess," Su said calmly. "Duncan can easily get her another Harz canary—"

Emerald's insides turned cold. She stared at Su.

"Is that all you have to say, Jie?"

"Well." Su's tone was composed, but her eyes were pleading. "What do you want me to say?"

Emerald headed for the stables, where she climbed onto her husband's Shire stallion—the women had only been given ponies—without a saddle. She squeezed his flanks with her heels, and they flew off into the woods. Emerald had only intended to blow off some steam, but she found herself riding farther and farther, all the way to the docks of London. When an eastbound steamship sounded its horn, she decided to stow aboard on the spur of the moment. She ended up in Delhi, where she fell for Rani, a hard-nosed tawaif actress who was using her theater basement as an ammunition collection point for the sepoy mutiny against the British East India Company. "I will lay down my life for the freedom of my people," Rani told Emerald in Hindi as they lay in a sorghum field in each other's arms.

When Rani was captured, Emerald managed to escape in her snake skin. She watched from a tree as Rani was executed alongside a row of freedom fighters: not by hanging, but tied over the mouth of a cannon and blown to pieces when the cannonballs were fired. She did not turn away as their blood spurted and limbs shot into the sky.

Emerald wanted to remember the cruelty of humans. But she was younger back then. She did not know there was no need to memorize the atrocity of authority. It was bound to rear its head—sometimes more violently, sometimes more quietly—over and over again across time's arrow.

. . .

Union Pool is just two subway stops away, but it's 8:40 p.m. by the time Emerald gets there. She gets carded at the door; she's forgotten to bring her fake ID. "Trust me," she teases the bouncer, "I'm a fossil." She passes the dinky dance floor to the garden patio with the taco truck, where mismatched tables and chairs are laid out under fairy lights.

Emerald catches a note of that floral lightness—Su's jasmine scent—before she sees her. Following her nose, she spots Su from the back. There she is, in a corner. Su's hair is in a neat, low chignon. She is dressed in a cream tweed bouclé jacket with a matching skirt, carrying one of her expensive bags, nursing a glass of sparkling water. The slender nape of her neck is lily white.

Emerald's heart is pounding as she watches her sister from across the yard. How long has it been?

Sometimes, when she hasn't seen Su for decades, Emerald tells herself that the only thing still binding them together is their secret. Rather than any real currency of feeling, it is the empty immensity of their history that keeps them together. But every time she lays eyes on Su again, she is jolted by an inevitability so sharp it makes her wince.

This is her person, across time and space.

She wants to take Su in, without Su perceiving her, for just a few seconds longer. Su sticks out in this janky yard of hipsters guzzling craft beer, but then again, she's so stunning you wouldn't miss her anywhere. Su turns. The outdoor bar is crowded, but her eyes fix on Emerald's right away.

Whenever Su looks at her, Emerald has a sense that she is getting appraised, rather than being seen. Emerald tries to shake off this feeling as she walks over, feeling gangly and self-conscious as her poised sister observes her. For a moment she feels bad for making Su meet in a dive bar. She didn't want to make a big deal of Su visiting, but at least she could have said Pete's Candy Store, not this hookup spot where she once walked into a throuple having sex in the bathroom.

"Hey stranger." Emerald stops in front of Su. "Is this seat taken?"

Now that she's in front of Su, she can smell that delicate jasmine fragrance more clearly. Emerald breathes it in, trying to hide how much she relishes the familiar smell. As always, Su looks impeccable, but Emerald isn't sure how she doesn't get bored of her own style—she has been wearing Chanel and carrying Hermès since the 1900s.

"Xiaoqing." Su smiles. She looks a little tired, like she's had a long day. Emerald sees Su's eye flick to the Rolex on her wrist.

"Sorry I'm late," Emerald says. "Have you eaten? There's tacos here."

"I'm not hungry." Su leans forward in her seat. "How are you?"

"Good," Emerald says as vaguely as possible. "And you?" New York has inured her to the usage of "How are you" as a generic greeting, rather than a genuine question. The USPS mailman says it, the bodega guy says it. It's a sure sign of fresh-off-the-boat naïveté to provide an earnest answer.

"Good," Su returns just as opaquely. "I'm good."

Then they're both quiet. Before an awkward stillness sets in, Emerald says: "I'll go get a beer."

Su looks concerned. "Have you been drinking?"

"It's just a pilsner." Emerald tries to keep the irritation from her voice. What does Su think she drinks when she's gone, fruit smoothies? "Five percent. Don't get your panties in a twist."

She returns with pissy pale pilsner. Su sips primly at her sparkling water. "Your hair," Su notes circumspectly, like she's been holding back judgment so far about the buzz cut, but must make a comment now. Su is the sort of woman who keeps only one hairstyle her whole life: long, silky, cascading down her back, never shorter than her shoulders or she'd feel "naked." Emerald changes up her hairstyle every season, the more dramatic the change, the better.

"Yes?" Emerald feels her voice rising. "I like it." Why is it so easy to slide right back into the same stupid dynamics with family? She shouldn't even have to defend this. She tries to divert the conversation before it goes downhill. "How was your day?"

"I settled some business, then I lost myself a little at Saks . . ."

Emerald knows vaguely that Su runs some foundation that supports various global causes. She suspects that Su does it for the charitable deductibles, though she doesn't understand any of that—Emerald has never filed a tax return in her life. She doesn't even know what a mortgage broker does.

"Saks?" Emerald makes a face. She hates malls and department stores, has gotten by picking up all of her wares in thrift shops, indie boutiques, and flea markets the entire twenty-first century.

Emerald notices the showy diamond on Su's ring finger.

She raises a brow. "Got hitched?"

Su nods, hesitant.

Emerald makes a face. "How much am I gonna hate him?"

"I've actually forgotten how rude you are," Su says dryly.

Emerald bristles. "You're fudging, so I know he's gross. What is he, another pale, straitlaced bureaucratic nerd who's afraid to moan in bed and writes nature poetry in his free time?"

Su tries not to laugh at how spot on some of this is.

"Three out of five," she admits.

"Ugh," Emerald groans. "A pale, non-moaning bureaucratic nerd?"

"Kind of." Su smiles. It feels wrong, but liberating, to talk like this. "And Paul likes poetry."

"Ah, fuck it." Emerald shakes her head grimly. "I swear you have the *worst* taste in men."

They're quiet for a moment, then Su says: "God, I've missed you, Xiaoqing."

Emerald softens, but she fights to keep her face impassive. She doesn't want Su to know how much she misses her: all the time. She fiddles absently with one side of her cherry drop earrings.

"I want to ask you something." Su lowers her voice. "And I want you to promise not to say no right off the bat."

Emerald's stomach turns. She's less concerned about Su finding out about the gunshot than she is about Su learning the reason behind it, that she's been sugaring for cash—

"Will you come stay in Singapore with me?" Su asks.

Emerald is thrown off. She's so surprised she bursts out laughing.

"I'm serious," Su says.

Emerald stops laughing. "You know how that always goes, Jie." Emerald plays with the beads of condensation on her glass and smiles a little sadly. "We'll be at each other's throat in no time."

"Maybe this time it'll be different." Su's gaze is intense as she leans across the table and looks searchingly into Emerald's eyes. She touches the back of Emerald's hand. "Just for a while?"

That warm note of jasmine lingers in the air. Everyone has someone they can't say no to. Emerald wishes it wasn't her sister. How do I always end up behind you, she thinks, even when I'm running away from you? In the backyard of Union Pool, under the sulfur glow of twinkly fairy lights, with Mitski's "Washing Machine Heart" blasting over the speakers on this balmy night, Emerald feels a familiar, syrupy feeling, so thick it's cloying, rising from her chest to her throat as she looks at Su.

"OK," she whispers. "Just for a while."

. . .

Bartek's having himself a self-care evening—boba, art-house film, scented candles, DIY hand job—when Emerald calls. He sighs.

"*Hihi.*" Her voice is bright. "What're you up to?"

"I'm wanking off to Alain Delon manning a boat in tighty-whities on the Criterion Channel, aka *Purple Noon*, aka *The Talented Mr. Ripley*, aka I'm a Patricia Highsmith bipolar lesbian stan. Sup?"

"Wanna come for a farewell stayover?"

"Farewell?" Bartek is confused. "Where're you off to?"

"Singapore!"

"*Pardon?*" He enunciates it the French way to emphasize his surprise. "When?"

She laughs. "Tomorrow." Bartek sits up straight and snaps his laptop shut on his bed. Emerald's always been unpredictable, but this is a total one-eighty. She was reluctant, had almost seemed afraid, to meet her sister. Now she's absconding halfway across the world with her?

"Uhh, babes," he probes, "are you OK?"

"Huh?" he hears Emerald saying. "What?"

"Emmy," Bartek says cautiously, "if you're in trouble, just say Jesus Christ superstar."

He hears another woman's laughter, soft and sophisticated.

"You're on speaker, Barty. Look out the window," Emerald is saying. "Do you see a Bentley?"

"What's that, the name of the neighbor's pug?" He shuts up when he sees the huge, slick luxury car idling outside his apartment. "Uhh, whoa, is this a kidnap? Because I consent . . ."

The Bentley pulls up on Fifth Avenue. Bartek steps through the golden doors of St. Regis, dazzled by the Renaissance-style mural ceiling of cherubs and clouds. He heads up to the suite number Emerald gave him, knocks on the door. Emerald opens it in a fluffy bathrobe.

"Barty!" Her pupils are bright and dilated.

"Are. You. High?" Bartek mouths urgently at her.

She giggles, pulling him through a corridor with gilded light fixtures. "I hope she likes you."

Bartek has never seen Emerald jittery as a schoolgirl. He decides he does not like this shady lady and the destabilizing effect she has on Emerald, even if she's her sister, or whatever.

But when they enter the silk-wallpapered parlor and he sees the stunning woman on the chaise longue in her classic Chanel skirt suit, he feels himself being pulled into her aura. Quiet, but potent. Her face is carefully made up, her features delicately striking. Lustrous black hair spills over her slender shoulders. She smiles slightly but doesn't get up when Bartek enters the room.

"Bartek?" When she looks at him, there is a dark, compelling depth in her eyes that suggests she knows one or two secrets about him that he doesn't yet know about himself. "I'm Suzhen." Her voice is so soft, but the feeling that Bartek gets is that she is completely in control.

Bartek can't help but compare the two sisters. If Emerald is prosecco, Su is whisky. If Emerald is spring, Su is winter. If Emerald is Matisse's *Dance*, Su is Rothko's *Black in Deep Red*.

Su is so flawlessly composed, so quietly magnetic that the air around her feels denser than usual. To be proximate to her is to be subtly elevated to a different plane. Time is a beat slower.

And instantly Bartek is thirsty for Su's approval. He offers his hand, and his voice rises. "Pleased to make your acquaintance." He tries to say her name the right way, fails: "Susan."

"Just call me Su," she says crisply.

"Sure, I can do that," Bartek chirps. "Su."

In the unwittingly careless way of those who are born ridiculously beautiful, Su doesn't notice the effect she's having on Bartek, but Emerald clocks it immediately. Bartek gawks at Su as she picks up her glass of ice-cold Perrier with a slice of lemon. He has never seen anyone make sparkling water look smart and sexy, and he immediately wants to start drinking Perrier too.

"Emerald tells me you're an artist," Su is saying to him. "What sort of art do you make?"

"Oh, god." Bartek feels unprepared to talk about his *practice*. He's proud of his work but self-conscious that it may come off as pretentious. "Umm, rococo lowbrow paintings of antibinary bodies, like, femmebots with male appendages frolicking in amorous encounters amid biblical references. I guess they're aesthetic sublimations of my raised-and-lapsed Catholic guilt?"

"And that's not just a fancy artist statement," Emerald chips in. "They're actually good. I've been modeling for some of them." She whips out her phone and shows Su pictures.

"The lighting's a bit off." Bartek downplays it in case Su doesn't think it's any good.

Emerald swipes to another work. *Ye Shall Not Surely Die* depicts a female form with multiple scrota for eyes slaying a monstrous serpent with legs, who is tempting them with bright red apples.

Bartek is jolted when he notices the potential faux pas. "Oops, I swear I completed this before Emerald came out to me." Emerald is shooting him dagger eyes. He nods—he's got this. "I just want to say that, for me, the snake in the Garden of Eden is, like, the one speaking truth to power. I don't see snakes as a shorthand for evil, not at all, but as an arbiter of knowledge—"

Bartek hears the crystal crunch of glass shattering.

He's confused for a good five seconds before he figures where the sound came from: Su's glass has broken in her hand. "Whoops!" He thinks it's an accident, and passes her a napkin, but Su doesn't put the glass down. That's when it hits him, Emerald saying: *She's super sensitive about it.* "Oh—" Bartek panics, "shit shit double-fisted shit!" He looks frantically at Su. "I won't tell anyone. Scout's honor! And," he adds, "for what it's worth, I think you're, like, the perfect woman!"

Su's face remains expressionless. An impassive and impenetrable quality comes over her skin itself. She is as beautiful as before, but her uncanny stillness makes Bartek's skin crawl. There is a dark flicker in her eyes. Emerald slips in front of him protectively. Bartek shrinks back as subtly as he can. Emerald angles her body between Bartek and Su, just as she lunges forward—

"Waouw!" Bartek yelps like a puppy that's been stepped on.

But Su is just picking up a shard of broken glass. "Careful, behind you." Bartek is so relieved he could piss his pants. "I'll get housekeeping to tidy up," she says. "Do either of you need anything?"

"Jie . . ." Emerald is eyeing her, trying to decode her. "Bartek isn't like Bjørn—"

Su cuts her off. "Of course he isn't." She turns to Bartek. "You're a heathen, aren't you?"

Bartek has no idea who Bjørn is, but he bobs his head to show deference. "Good." She smiles tightly. Bartek can't help but check Su's teeth. Nothing pointy, all pearly. She picks up the phone. "Can I get you some hot cocoa?" she suggests. "Or some chamomile tea?"

Bartek is flummoxed by her erratic shift—from the silent rage of breaking a glass in hand to this hospitable facade of offering a warm drink. "Uhh, chamomile?" he bleats. "Dairy makes me bloated."

Su dials the hotel concierge. "Can we have chamomile tea, some cake, and fruit? Two of everything." She puts down the phone, turns back to them. "My jet lag is setting in, but please enjoy yourselves."

"G'night," Bartek squeaks as she rises from her seat.

Su seems to float out of the parlor. Once the door clicks shut, Bartek clutches Emerald's knee. "Babes. Who's Bjørn?"

Emerald swallows. "Just somebody that I used to know." Bjørn was a pastor she'd grown close to in seventeenth-century Finnmark, when she was in her mystic era. In a bout of feverish confession, Emerald had told him what she was. He stuck her in prison, and she went to trial, where she was convicted of satanic heresies. She would have burned at the stake if Su had not got there in time. Su left

Bjørn's body hanging from the highest beam in the church, entrails swinging.

"Somebody you *used* to know? Maybe I should just, like, leave?"

"Trust me on this, you've got to at least make it look like you ate some of the stuff she ordered."

"She won't know. She's gone off to bed, hasn't she?"

"She'll come out to check later. She used to go through my trash."

"Am I supposed to *eat cake* when I'm afraid she's gonna *off me*?"

"If she was going to off you, she'd have done it already."

"Hey." Bartek's eyes bulge. "You're not serious, are you?"

The bell buzzes. They both jump. It's the butler. He sweeps up the broken glass without batting an eyelid, arranges the fresh spread of dessert and drinks. The hot cup of chamomile tea calms Bartek down.

He looks at their reflections in the mirror opposite, touching his neck and chin. "I think I would be a llama spirit. Maybe an ostrich. Fuck, that's not sexy, is it?"

Emerald smiles at him. "Llamas are cute . . ."

"Are there other, uhh, types out there? Or are you, like, the apex predator femme queen?"

"There are others." Emerald has met a few along the way—an animal spirit can always sniff out another who is passing as a human—and tried being friendly, but she was taken aback by their awkwardness, their hostility. There was a sparrow spirit who told Emerald she didn't appreciate being outed. "Outed?" Emerald hadn't said it in front of anyone. She merely followed the sparrow's twiggy scent on the night train from Siliguri to Darjeeling and sat discreetly in her cabin, waiting till the other passengers alighted before approaching her excitedly.

"But there's no one else here!" Emerald pointed out.

"*I'm* here," the sparrow spirit said.

Emerald slunk back to her own cabin and thought about Su. She knew Su loved her, but sometimes she felt that Su couldn't stand to be around her. Maybe this was part of why they had to spend so much time apart. The way they approached their humanness was fundamentally different.

The only other animal spirit Emerald met who danced between both skins with uninhibited fluidity was the monkey guy, a Ming dynasty situationship in Suzhou. Three hundred and sixty years or so later, in 1982, Emerald could not believe her eyes when she spotted her ex's face on a poster in the Mokotów student hall. She learned that he'd put out a dark synth pop album called *Flower Fruit Mountain* under the moniker Sunny Kong and attracted a cult following. He was wearing Ray-Bans and had waxed his facial hair, but she'd recognize that impish mug anywhere.

"This is probably gonna sound stupid," Bartek says, "but you can't turn me into one, can you?"

Emerald laughs. "Umm, I don't think you get it. You're supposed to be the end point, dude!"

"You're a super-slaying everlasting animal goddess. Why would being human be the goal?"

"You wouldn't believe how hard we worked for it," Emerald tells him. "It took hundreds and hundreds of years of self-cultivation. People these days can't even focus for more than five minutes!"

"Self-cultivation?" Bartek deadpans. "How Goop of you. Just tell me how many oil pulls, crow poses, juice fasts, yoni steams, and meditation apps it'll take me to get to where you are."

Spirituality has long been ruined—Emerald bears witness to how humans continually find new ways to make such a commodity out of transmuting nonmaterial wellness into the marketable.

She sighs. "Y'know, I'm not sure I'd wish it on you. The ennui and anomie are real."

"The ennui of not aging? The anomie of fucking hot guys forever?"

"I know it sounds like that in theory, but in practice, it's not all it's jumped up to be."

"Check your undead privilege!"

"Hey!" Emerald yelps. "I'm not an undead, that sounds awful. I prefer to go by immortal."

"Go on, rub it in. Salt in the wound, blood in the cut, while I'm out here like a sitting duck . . ."

"Don't worry," Emerald says. "You'll be OK. I'll go talk to her."

6

Whatever Happens in New York Stays in New York

The nausea has been making unwelcome overtures all evening, but it's coming to a head now. Su barely has time to bolt the bathroom door before she's hurling bile into the marble bowl. She isn't sure if it's Gabe's qi, or morning sickness.

"Jie?" she hears Emerald outside. "Can we talk?"

Su runs the bathwater to mask the sound of her throwing up. "I'm about to take a bath," she calls out.

"Please?" Emerald says. Su softens. She puts down the toilet seat, gargles her mouth, spritzes the air with perfume, splashes her face with water. She realizes she is exhausted. She opens the door.

Emerald sighs. "I know what you're thinking . . ." No, Su thinks, but I wish you did. How to tell her about any of it? Where to even begin? That she's been worried sick about Emerald, that she was so happy to see her she wanted to crush her in an embrace at Union Pool, that she almost got caught shoplifting at Saks, that she cut down a man for calling her a ho, that she might be pregnant, and she didn't know what to tell her husband?

"But Barty gets it, you know," Emerald goes on. "What it's like to have to hide. It was real hard for him in high school. He was, like, the only gay senior in a Catholic school in the suburbs . . ."

This is all very minor to Su. She holds off the nausea. "Look, I'm really tired right now."

Emerald bites her lip. "Does that mean we're all good?"

"What do you mean?" Su looks at her. "Of course we're good."

"We are?" The *we* feels heavy. "Then what was the glass about?"

Su doesn't want to talk about it. "Like I said, I'm really tired."

"OK, because you were being kinda weird out there . . ."

Su is offended. "I haven't been out of this skin in ten years. And," she adds primly, "I'm now vegan, actually." This does not have the effect Su intends at all. Emerald bursts out laughing.

"*Vegan?* We weren't even vegan in the wild."

"I'm not like that anymore."

"C'mon," Emerald says. "Of course you are!" She recites an old Mandarin idiom: "A snake can shed its skin a hundred times, but it still remains a snake."

Su flinches. She hasn't heard it in centuries. "I disagree," she says. "We evolve in order to transcend that which no longer serves us—"

"*OK, OK.*" Emerald reaches out to give Su a hug. "Sometimes you just have to relax a little . . ."

Su freezes for a moment, then hugs her back. It feels good. "You still smell like citron, you know?" Su murmurs.

. . .

Back in the parlor, Emerald plops down beside Bartek on the leather couch. "I never thought I'd say this, but I think she's mellowed. Something's different about her." She picks up a teacup. "Cheers?"

Bartek clinks their cups. "See, I knew she wasn't as bad as you were making her out to be." Now he digs into a tiramisu with gusto. "But for real, she's scary, posh, and hot."

"I know," Emerald agrees. She's not even jealous.

Bartek lowers his voice. "Isn't it annoying, though, how hot people get away with anything?" He gives Emerald a meaningful look. "Remember the time you said Ed had me on a leash and I needed to get away from him? You've got that same lapdog energy around your sister."

This hits a nerve. So much of Emerald's life has been spent trying to minimize the impact Su had on her, still has on her. She's been doing just fine, but once Su orbits back into her life, things get thrown out of whack. "I mean," Bartek prods, "do *you* want to go Singapore, or does *she* want you to go?"

"*I* want to go," Emerald says, a little too forcefully. "Singapore sounds cool."

"What do you even know about Singapore?"

Emerald has a vague impression of a small, affluent island in Southeast Asia, with street food endorsed by Anthony Bourdain, gleaming skyscrapers she's seen as a futuristic *Westworld* backdrop, a lush, high-tech park with *Avatar*-esque trees and an air-conditioned glass dome.

"Not a lot," she admits. "Amazing food, tall buildings, clean streets, blah blah . . ."

"I matched with a Singaporean guy on Hinge. We went for drinks, and he said that up until recently there was a law criminalizing consensual gay sex, and it was illegal for women to freeze their eggs. There's capital punishment for peddling drugs. You can be fined for feeding pigeons."

"Why would it be illegal for women to freeze their eggs?"

"Social engineering, babes. They think that if they give women access to those sorts of options, they'll put off having kids. Nanny state, one. Bodily autonomy, zero. Yikes, if you ask me."

Emerald wrinkles her nose, but she doesn't take Bartek seriously.

Liberal Americans have a penchant for magnifying authoritarian quirks without taking a good hard look at the gutted state of populist democracy in their own backyard. She asks: "Have you been there yourself?"

"Just in transit, when I was going to Bangkok. There's a butterfly garden inside the airport. At first I thought it was cute, then it started feeling creepy, I don't know, like some tropical dystopia . . ."

"Honestly, B?" Emerald decides to come clean. "I don't care what city it is. It could be Oslo or Hanoi, I'd still go." She pauses. "My sis and I have messed each other up in the past. We didn't mean to, but it happens. But this time, I wanna see if we can move past that baggage."

"Girl, I get it." Bartek pats her on the shoulder. "Family is a Greek tragedy. Can't live with them, can't live without them. Can't let them in, can't cut them out. It's real nice, until it sucks."

"Yeah." Emerald looks glum.

Bartek notices, and feels bad for raining on her parade. "But you know what? I get this feeling she cares about you a lot more than she lets on."

Emerald tries to keep her voice casual. "What makes you think so?"

"It's obvious." Bartek shrugs. He's starting to see why it's hard for Emerald. It's clear to Bartek that Emerald worships her sister, but she doesn't want Su to know. She's just trying to play it cool so she doesn't get hurt, because she doesn't want to need Su more than Su needs her.

"It's a simple equation. You *both* need each other. Why're you so afraid to show it?"

"I dunno." Emerald throws up her hands. "I don't know that things between people really change. Or if we're all stuck in the same vicious cycles or karmic relations or trauma patterns or whatever for the rest of our lives. Know what I mean?" She reaches for Bartek's hand; they interlace their fingers. "Things between us are *easy*, like this. Things between Su and I—it's complicated. I want to say that she's a difficult person, but probably, to her, I'm the difficult one, you know?"

"There was never a good time?"

The best time was when they were still snakes, back in Hangzhou. Emerald still carries those simple, tactile memories—swimming in the river, sunning on the shore—around with her like an emotional support pebble in her pocket, edges smoothed from years of touch. "There were good times, for sure." She doesn't tell him that it was only after she and Su took on human skins that things became hard.

Bartek checks his phone. It's coming to two in the morning.

"I should head home. I'm modeling for a nine a.m. life-drawing class, and I get morning wood when I'm underslept."

"OK, too much info, dude . . ."

"Emmy." He gets a funny feeling as he pulls her into a hug. "You'll be back, right?"

"Of course I'll be back. Don't get too used to having the bathroom to yourself, k?"

"Ahh . . ." Bartek fans his eyes like he's wearing mascara. "I don't know why I'm crying!"

"Ugh," Emerald tells him, "you're gonna make me cry too."

"Remember, babe," he whispers, "I love you the way you are."

. . .

Puking her guts out helps to calm Su's stomach. Everything is settling back to normal: dull-sheened colors, one-note smells. She takes a warm bath to ground herself, then video-calls Paul. He's at work, but he picks up. She lowers her voice when she lies about Emerald, describing her as an artist type who went to New York for a BFA and lost her footing, mixed around with the wrong crowd.

"Oh." Paul looks concerned. "I hope it's not *drugs*?" He whispers the word. Su knows that even weed is a Class A drug in Singapore, which means you could be executed for trafficking the stuff. She assures Paul it's nothing like that. He nods thoughtfully. "So she's just—artsy-fartsy?"

Even Su cringes at the way bureaucrats cotton on to corny terms like that, how they're so pleased with themselves when they use them. "I guess you could say that," she says. "I want to keep her close for a while. I hope it's OK I invited her to spend some time in Singapore."

"Of course. I'm glad to finally meet someone from your family."

"Things between us are a little tricky, but I really care about her, and I want her to be safe."

"Well, then, there's no better place for her to be." Paul smiles. "Anyway, I'll see you girls when you get back, I've got to troubleshoot this completely unnecessary situation now—"

"Is it something to do with a uniform? I saw Divya and Riz before the dinner—"

"I don't want you talking to Riz. He's out to get me."

"Divya was saying something about acting with empathy, and it's a health-care issue—"

"Divya can talk a big game." Paul looks annoyed. "They didn't arrow the Ministry of Health. It's an Education problem now, and I'm the sucker who has to deal with it. This boy, he's been turning up to school in the female uniform. The principal told him to show up in the right uniform and cut his hair, or he won't be allowed in class. He refused, so the principal told him to stay at home, do online learning. Whenever he decides to follow the rules, he can return. Fair, no?"

Su knows not to contradict Paul, it could set him off. "Right," she says uncomfortably. "But Divya wanted me to let you know that the student has been diagnosed with gender dysphoria—"

"If everyone decides to identify as this or that and wear whatever uniform they want, won't there be chaos?" Paul sighs. "What happens in schools isn't just about the present, but the future . . ."

After they disconnect, Su lies down. The bed is so comfortable she's lulled into a series of intermittent naps. She's verging on a deeper sleep when she jolts awake all of a sudden.

The pregnancy test kit in the teal Watsons plastic bag.

She jumps up and checks in her Birkin. Still there, tucked under her Altoids mints and Aesop hand cream. Not a bad thing, she thinks, to have accidentally brought this detritus all the way to New York. More traceless for her to discard it here than in Singapore, where CCTVs spawn by the moment, robot dogs patrol public parks, and government apps track your movement. Su finds it interesting that most Singaporeans don't seem bothered by privacy concerns, and voluntarily download said apps. Paul has told her it's a straightforward good-faith equation, repeating the Party's line of reasoning: If you're not doing anything wrong, why would you be afraid to be watched?

She shudders slightly, almost glad to be away for a while. She looks out the window at the bright gleam of a fully lit but empty office building. Brazen graffiti on some scaffolding: IF I'M TOO MUCH FOR YOU GO FIND LESS. A fire hydrant that's been wastefully gushing gallons of clean water since she checked in this afternoon, still unfixed hours later. And just around the corner, a disheveled man pissing on what's left of a half-stolen locked bicycle: just handles and a frame.

Su puts a white coat on and jams the test kit into one pocket. Then she digs out the baby Louboutins, stuffs that into the other pocket. Maybe she did it for the thrill. Maybe she wants to have this baby. She shakes her head, trying to clear it. All of this is so unlike her, it makes her sick to the core. Gabe—one moment she's getting worked up, listening to him humiliate Emerald. The next, she's bitten him, overwhelmed by the smoky, meaty smell of his qi. When she inhaled that raw essence of human qi for the first time in so long, she lost control. She wanted more and more of it. Su startles at the pang in her abdomen. This gaping, primal hunger she's managed to push down for so long. A shame so red, a want so deep. Is it the baby, or is it just who she is? She goes to the bathroom, splashes water on her face.

Whatever happens in New York stays in New York.

New York: the brightest lights, the hardest concrete, the keenest rats, and, at its molten core, the purest id. A city that places its bets on all who pass through to act on their wildest dreams and innermost desires. All this licentious grime must be left here. She will take none of it back to Singapore.

She steps into the parlor. The lights are still on, but Bartek has left, and Emerald has fallen asleep on the couch. They've finished the cake, the tea, the fruit. Good. Silently, Su exits the suite.

Out on the street, Su jams her hands in her pockets, clutching the test kit and the baby shoes tight, like she's afraid they'll spill out. At first she thinks to dump them in the very first trash can she sees, on the corner of Fifth Avenue and Fifty-Fifth Street. But there are a few people milling around, and it feels too close to the hotel. She goes down one block, then another. The night air is crisp, so different from Singapore's humidity. Walking down Fifth Avenue, it's soothing to go by the exact same brand names she's used to passing on Orchard Road: Gucci. Nike. Apple. Prada. Starbucks.

On the corner of Fifty-First Street, she stops in front of a LEGO flagship, with a splendid castle made entirely out of tiny, colorful plastic bricks in the window. How nice it could be: to do up a nursery with adorable things, to buy picture books and a bunch of toys. A tear slides down her cheek. She wipes it away and crosses the street to St.

Patrick's Cathedral. Su has never been one to pray, but now she stops in front of the Gothic spires, and steeples her hands together for a moment.

Please please please let my baby be a human, not a snake.

She reaches for the tiny Louboutins in her pocket. Hangs them by their pink ribbons on the iron fence of the cathedral. She spins around, heading back uptown, tossing the pregnancy kit into a trash can outside a Dunkin' Donuts. In the morning the garbage truck will come and crush it all up.

. . .

Bartek emerges from Duane Reade with a paper bag chock-full of fun but practical goodies. He was walking to the Fifty-First Street 6 train on Lexington Avenue when he passed a Japanese confectionery with the prettiest sweets in the window, packed in gracious gift boxes. He wished something was open so he could get Emerald a little farewell gift, but everything on the street that isn't a bar was closed—well, except the Duane Reade on Fifty-Second and Madison.

He is pretty pleased with his selection: echinacea vitamin C gummies, sanitizing wipes, a blackout sleep mask with a panda eye design, SPF 100 sunscreen, a dark plum lipstick named Avarice in Aubergine (he always buys lipsticks not for their colors but for their snazzy names), and a Tetra Pak of coconut water. There is even a greeting card aisle he's never noticed in drugstores before. There are all sorts of cards for the usual milestones: birthdays, valentines, weddings, baby showers, retirements, funerals. But there are no cards for the lifesaving wonder that is everyday friendship. He picks a card with pink roses and a looping, cursive font.

For My Sister on Her Engagement, it reads. *You deserve all the love in the world.* He signs off with multiple XOXOs, grinning at just how much Emerald will hate it.

He is strolling back to the St. Regis to leave the care package for Emerald with the concierge when he sees Su standing alone, very still, outside a LEGO store on the corner of Fifty-First and Fifth.

She peers furtively at the toys in the window. She turns—Bartek hides in the shadow of an awning—and crosses the road, coming to a stop outside St. Patrick's Cathedral. Bartek is surprised when she raises her hands, briefly but unmistakably, in prayer. She leaves something dangling on the fence.

Bartek holds his breath and gives it a good minute, lets her put half a block between them, before he goes to check out what she's left on the fence—a pair of pink satin Louboutin baby shoes.

Huh. He takes his phone out and snaps a picture.

There's no one else on the street, just a tipsy couple ducking into an Uber. Su is a whole block ahead now. She stops outside a Dunkin' Donuts, tossing a teal plastic bag into a trash can.

Bartek waits for her to disappear down the street before he approaches the Dunkin' Donuts.

The teal plastic bag is right on top of the trash. His pulse races as he reaches for it, and finds a pregnancy test kit inside. He opens the box, unravels the wad of tissue, gingerly holds up the stick.

Two red lines. Holy shit. Su is pregnant.

A breeze swirls the leaves at his feet. Bartek is about to snap a pic of the wand and send it to Emerald when the entire row of streetlights goes out. He hears a low hiss: *Sssssssssssssssss*—

Bartek's body is lifted up and slammed against the Dunkin' Donuts storefront, so fast there isn't even time to scream. In the dark, a cool scaly length sweeps across his legs. He holds his hands to his chest, where a knot of air is coalescing uncomfortably in his diaphragm.

He bends over, gasping. It's as if his very breath is being summoned irresistibly away from the oxygenated fibers of his body. When Bartek feels the knot rising through his windpipe, he tries to push it down, but it keeps moving upward. He is choking now. The breeze has turned into a sudden, howling wind.

He sees it—for one brief, terror-stricken, metaphysical second as his life force is expelled, against his will, through his mouth—a color-less ball no larger than a chicken egg or a calamansi lime, twitching and wavering, on the verge of dissipating into the torn velvet of the night.

Someone, or something, leans over his spasming body, swallowing the globule of qi into their own embodiment.

Bartek's head lolls back against the Dunkin' Donuts door.

Scattered around the sidewalk are the contents of his paper bag. Sunscreen. A greeting card. Echinacea gummies dot the concrete.

All is still and staid but for a trace of jasmine in the cool night air.

7

His Erections Are as Lackluster as His Poems

Emerald whines like a mournful old bloodhound as the duvet is pulled off her warm body. "Morning sleepyhead," she hears a sweet voice murmuring. Emerald peels open an eye. Plush leather couch. Damask curtains. Crystal chandelier. The smell of coffee. Wait, what the hell, where's she again?

St. Regis. With her sister—Su is fully dressed in a well-cut dress, sitting on the side of the couch with a takeaway cup of Blank Street Coffee in one hand and a petite Bulgari gift bag in the other.

"How was your sleep?" Su seems chirpier than usual, more solicitous. Maybe she's become a morning person, Emerald thinks. Snakes are mostly nocturnal, but people change over time.

"Good," Emerald croaks as she sits up, bleary-eyed. Su passes her coffee. "Thanks." She takes a sip.

Su waves the gift bag. "I went for a walk, saw this in a shop window, thought of you . . ."

Emerald would have liked to brush her teeth first, but you don't say no when your sister is spoiling you, even if she's being a bit pushy about it. Knowing that Su is watching keenly as she unboxes, Emerald feels herself trying to perform excitement. "Oh, wow wow, what's inside . . ." She rattles the box and feels slightly idiotic. It's not unlike the way she felt on a date with Giovanni: being expected to react in a certain, prescribed way to a provider's generosity.

Emerald releases the monogrammed ribbon, opens the box. She gasps, for real. It's the iconic Serpenti necklace in white gold, set with emerald eyes and pavé diamonds.

"*Whoa*." Emerald looks at Su. "It's gorgeous, but this is extravagant, you didn't have to—"

She bites back saying something about how whatever Su had spent on the necklace would probably be enough for her to live off for a year, so why couldn't she just have given her the cash? It would have saved her a whole lot of trouble. Emerald starts to wonder if there's something similar about Su and someone like Giovanni. One moment they're spoiling you silly. The next they're holding money over your head. She wipes the correlation from her head.

Su is smiling serenely at her. "I didn't have to. But I want to."

Su lifts the necklace out of its velvet bed. She slides off the couch, waits for Emerald at the vanity table. Emerald settles on the pouf. Behind her, Su unhooks the clasp. Slips the white gold chain around Emerald's neck. The snake pendant falls exquisitely in the concave of her wishbone. "It looks so good on you," Su says. "I could never carry something like that off."

"Please," Emerald snorts. "With your bone structure? You just don't let yourself, that's all."

In the mirror, for a second, they look into each other's eyes.

Su smiles enigmatically. Emerald smiles back, trying to reach the place that was once so easy between them. Maybe Su senses it too. Unexpectedly, she places her palm on Emerald's head, running her hand back and forth over the poky intimacy of her buzz cut without saying anything.

. . .

In the car to the airport, Su fastens her seat belt in the back seat. When Emerald doesn't follow suit, she prompts: "Seat belt?"

Emerald gives her a look. "This is New York, Jie. No one puts this crap on."

"Well, can't you just do it?" Su asks. When that still doesn't work: "It's not so hard, is it?"

"Fine." Emerald doesn't want to get off on the wrong foot with Su. The seat belt cuts in at her shoulder. She pushes it under her armpit.

Emerald has always found it a crying shame that Su is so nervy. She can't understand why Su lives out of an uneasy feeling of fear and lack, rather than a bright sense of possibility and abundance.

If Emerald didn't take a chance back then, they would have lived and died as snakes eons ago. As traffic slows to a crawl in the Queens-Midtown tunnel and Donna Summer's "I Feel Love" plays on the radio, she thinks about the day they were slithering under Broken Bridge, the day they heard the minstrel's song.

He had a Cantonese twang and was accompanying himself on wooden clappers. Centuries had passed but she could still recall the ditty ever so clearly—

"Attention, one and all!

Bard or broad, creature or phantom,
This is your chance, hear my song:
Tonight a magic flower blooms
Shape-shifting, youth-bringing,
Karma-breaking, god-making!
By the light of the mid-autumn moon,

Ride the whirlpool to Coral Cave
Where the great Nüwa herself
Sowed the Lilac Lotus of Transcendence
Herald of dreams and desires!"

Did you hear that? The green snake's eyes widened.

The white snake looked doubtful. *Surely he's a drunkard who made up a nonsensical song.*

The green snake surged ahead to peek at the minstrel. Dressed in rags, he'd rouged his lips and cheeks. Minstrels typically had a repertoire, but this one repeated the same song untiringly. No one paid him any heed till a finely robed old man with bushy brows and a long white beard stopped by. "How do you do, Old Lan?" he chortled. "Heaven's secrets in open sight, eh?"

The minstrel clicked his clappers. "Is that you, Old Lu? I sing to exalt the mother goddess . . ."

The green snake slid back, deep in thought. A snake could live up to twenty years in the wild, if it was extremely lucky. They were already pushing ten. Besides, she knew how much the white snake yearned to be human. Yearning doesn't make things happen, she wanted to tell her.

That night, the green snake signed good night to her sister, curled up, and pretended to sleep. As soon as she heard the white snake's breathing slow into an even slumber, she slithered quietly out of their tree trunk.

It was the night of Mid-Autumn Festival in 815, which marks the moon at its roundest and brightest. The moon was so full it appeared swollen, so bright it hurt to look at.

She slipped headfirst into West Lake. The water seemed murkier, or was she afraid? They bathed in West Lake often, but she'd never encountered a whirlpool. The green snake was a strong swimmer. She pushed toward the deepest part of the water. She was keeping parallel with the undertow when a dark churn came out of nowhere, dragging her into the depths of a swirling abyss. She struggled hard against the current, but a vortex formed around her. She was drowning.

She squeezed her eyes shut. Should she perish here, she hoped the white snake knew how much she loved her. The water had stopped churning. If she was dead, at least her last thought was pretty.

It was then that the green snake realized she could breathe again.

She opened her eyes. She was in a limestone cave whose walls were studded with coral, lit by bioluminescent algae. This must be Coral Cave. Shuddering as she got out of the water, she slithered onto an uneven stone precipice. Cautiously she made her way forward. There was yellow coral, soft as a fern. Mushy pink coral with the texture of diseased fruit. A wall of ridged bloodred coral, hard as marble.

Then she caught the aroma: sweeter than honey, with a marshy undertone. Following her nose through the cracks through a rocky passageway, she noticed a violet glow. At the end of a cavern, no larger than a human fist, was a luminous lilac lotus in full bloom, on a gold stem poking out of a fissure in the wall. Quietly, she moved toward it.

"Shameless creature." A disembodied voice echoed around the cavern. "Who are you to deserve the lotus of alchemy and immortality?" The green snake leaped back, but saw no one. "You are lucky enough to be a snake." The voice spoke old Mandarin, courtly and classical. It had a low, menacing pitch that could have belonged to a male or a female. "Nüwa promised me a body when the Shang dynasty fell. It has been thousands of years since I last saw the sun."

The green snake did not fear a wraith if it could do her no harm. She slid forward.

"One seed turns bone to flesh, or beast to human," the voice went on tauntingly. "Two seeds give everlasting youth. Three seeds for karmic enlightenment. And four seeds, a deity's ascension."

The green snake was barely a few feet from the pale-violet glow of the lotus. Her tail tingled. Up close, the lilac petals were ripe and heavy, unfurling to reveal a golden seedpod within.

"*This body itself is emptiness. Emptiness itself is this body.*" The voice articulated this line with a certain reverence, which made the words stick in the green snake's mind. Then it gave a hollow laugh. "But how would a lowly snake like you have the will to self-cultivate upon this mantra for eight hundred years? You will never rise beyond your destiny."

Staring at the lotus, inhaling its honeyed aroma, the green snake was mesmerized. One of its petals fell, shriveling to purple ash when it hit the ground. Now she could see the four shiny gold seeds embedded in the pod. Boldly she stuck her head forward, severing the pod from the stem.

The walls of the cave began to rumble. The voice let out an anguished shriek. The green snake gripped the lotus between her lips as she darted out, trying to find its entrance again. One wrong turn and she could be stuck in here forever. As she passed the wall of bloodred coral, relief flooded through her—she was on the right track.

Right then a huge orange crab jumped out of the coral, catching her tail with its mighty pincer. She struggled, but it pinned her viciously to the wall. She would have bitten it, but the lotus was in her mouth.

With its other claw the crab vied for the lotus, making a grab for the golden seeds. She turned her head away, trying to wriggle free, but the crab twisted its muscular claw through her scales. She winced in sheer pain, then swung her body around, sending the crab off-balance as she wrapped her tail around it and threw all her weight against the wall, smashing its claw with an awful crack. Freed from its iron grip, she darted out of the cave, surging forward, then upward with all she had, till her head broke through the water's surface—

Her breath was ragged. The moon was bright. Heart hammering, she checked the lotus. All four seeds, perfectly intact. For a fleeting moment, the green snake wondered what would happen if she consumed all four seeds—but she was neither greedy nor grasping, and she wanted only to share these treasures with her sister. She was exhausted, but adrenaline brought her back to the hollow.

The white snake was fast asleep. Her tail swayed slightly, dancing in a far-off dream. The green snake took a beat to compose herself, then roused her sister casually with a mid-autumn greeting.

Once they swallowed the seeds, a hot glow surged through them from head to tail. Recalling the mantra, the green snake signed to the white snake: *This body itself is emptiness. Emptiness itself is this body.*

. . .

After takeoff, the stewardess serves Emerald a Tropical Fizz mocktail with pineapple and bitter lemon while Su sticks with her Perrier. Clinking drinks with Emerald ten thousand feet up in the air, disconnected from the world down below, buoyed up along fluffy white cottontail clouds outside the window, Su feels the tight swathe of tension in her skull subsiding.

They're flying in Suites, the cabin category above First Class. She is glad to be able to spoil Emerald, who looks on in amazement when a steward comes to join up the double bed. Su watches as Emerald sprawls on the Lalique bed linen, mocktail glass in hand. "Salut, Jie."

"Can I get you anything else?" the steward asks.

"Hmm." Emerald tries her luck. "Caviar?"

"Of course." He bows. "And anything for you, Miss Bai?"

"I would like a slice of lemon for my Perrier," Su tells him.

Su wants to flush out the taste of Bartek's qi. She's been popping mints, hoping Emerald won't notice anything. A snake's sense of smell is its most powerful faculty, and she knows Emerald has a good nose.

Back at the St. Regis in the wee hours of the morning, Su carefully stripped off her clothes, tossed them in a laundry bag, and asked a chambermaid to dispose of it. She scrubbed her skin with a loofah till it reddened under the hot shower. She laid on moisturizer and perfume so thickly it was as if she'd bathed in the stuff. Emerald was snoring delicately on the couch. Su took the duvet from the bedroom and with a light touch covered her sister, then crept back into the bedroom, lying wide awake on the four-poster bed.

She had killed one man. And then another. One was her sister's sugar daddy. The other was her sister's best friend. Gabe's qi had a char-broiled quality, like the darkened edges of roasted meat. Bartek's had a milky aftertaste, with the mealy texture of cereal gone soft in milk. And this time Su did not try to expel it from her body. As she lay in bed, a warm, clammy sensation prickled over the skin of her lower abdomen. Something was growing, imbibing the qi she had taken in. Right then Su knew, with dead certainty, beyond any tests, that she was pregnant.

Su excuses herself to the bathroom. Looks for mouthwash in the amenities drawer. She gargles, spits, gargles, spits. Stares hard at her reflection in the mirror.

Everything is going to be OK, she tells herself. Emerald is coming to Singapore to live with you. Isn't that just what you wanted? Singapore is an ideal place for a family of means to come together. Slowly but surely, she will find tactful ways of conveying to Emerald the importance of fitting in. It wasn't so pronounced the last time she saw her, but Emerald clearly hasn't been putting much effort into maintenance. Just as one example, Su can spot the slither in her stride.

It embarrasses Su, though she knows that logically, no one else will see what she sees: the *snakeness* of it all. Even if a human noticed anything, they'd perceive it as a sensual confidence, an easy sway in the hips. To Su's eyes, however, this is a regression of form that must be nipped in the bud. If it's left unchecked, what might Emerald do next? Writhe about on the sidewalk?

On the night of their transition in 1615, when they stepped out of West Lake after eight hundred years of self-cultivation, Su found an abandoned courtyard house they could hide themselves in. She was adamant that they should polish up their mannerisms before they ventured anywhere near humans. There were so many things to learn about being human, Su felt nervous just thinking about it. How to pick up a brush, pour a cup of tea, speak without sibilance.

Emerald didn't see why they should have to conceal themselves at all. She could barely hold her body upright, but she wanted to head out right away. "Look, this is incredible!" She grinned at Su, spreading her fingers and her toes like they were paper fans.

Su chastised Emerald for her naïveté. Someone would notice they weren't doing things the proper way. She didn't want to appear wayward and demonic. At worst, they could be arrested and executed. And even if not, they would still be ridiculed and laughed at.

Emerald disagreed. All those years under Broken Bridge, hadn't Su seen how loopy humans could be? Besides, they could always just say they were drunk. Even court officials slurred their idioms and walked sideways when they had knocked back too many cups of wine.

Su checked inside a bamboo cabinet, and was glad to find simple robes they could cover their naked bodies with. She passed one to Emerald, who had difficulty figuring out which end her head should come out of. "You've got it backward." Su helped to adjust the garment.

Emerald pounced on something. The way she leaped, Su thought it was alive. But it was an old rouge pot that had rolled onto the floor. Mesmerized, Emerald dipped her finger into the red.

"I thought the world was definitive and beautiful in blue and green," Emerald mused as she painted her lips. "How could I have known it held so much color we were not equipped to see?"

Emerald reached out to rouge Su's lips, bringing her stained, insolent thumb to Su's mouth, spreading the color into a crimson smudge. "There!" she exclaimed, pleased with her handiwork.

And with that, Emerald wanted to go paint the town red.

"It's not safe, Xiaoqing," Su cautioned. "Let's settle in first."

"It's *never* going to be safe anyway. Come on, let's go!"

Emerald lifted her sleeves and danced her way into town. Su followed behind her cautiously. It was the night of Mid-Autumn Festival. Hangzhou was so beautiful in the fall. The pendulous moon was missing just a fingernail's sliver at the top. Emerald tripped and fell a couple of times along the way, but she simply laughed, picked herself up, and went on her way.

A finely decorated sedan chair was parked by the edge of the town. As Emerald passed by, she stuck her head in. Su signaled to her to cut it out, but Emerald was already striking up a conversation with the person in the carriage. Su caught up to them, and saw that it was a famous scholar poet. Her heart fluttered. She'd seen him crossing Broken Bridge a few times, and even heard him composing one of his well-regarded poems. *A civil servant's life passes like a cursory dream / Clumsily I raise a wine cup to the wilting peony.*

"That's the silliest simile I ever heard," Emerald was saying with an insouciant swagger. "The moon is as ample as a wet nurse's bosom? You've done injury to my ears. Reparations are in order."

The scholar poet was not offended but amused. "What do you suggest?"

"A taste of wine from your calabash."

"Feisty women are in short supply. What else may nature have endowed you with?"

"Balls." Emerald grabbed his calabash, pouring the wine into her mouth like a bandit.

Watching them, Su wondered if she might have been wrong about her sister. Was it naïveté or confidence? It came from deep inside Emerald, and drew people to her. Su felt a prick of envy.

"That's enough, Xiaoqing." Su stepped in, bowing before the scholar poet, not daring to meet his eye. "I apologize on my sister's behalf. She had a little too much to drink over supper."

The scholar poet looked at both of them. "It isn't safe for two ladies with such fine faces to be out on their own so late. Might I offer the use of my sedan chair to escort both of you home?"

With that, he unfurled his outer robe and threw it to the ground before them. "Let's not get your feet wet." Su felt her heart keening as she stepped onto the fine embroidery he'd laid across the puddle, while Emerald hung back, unwilling to board, annoyed that this man had cut short her night of revelry with her sister. She just wanted to have a drink of wine and stroll up to the lantern parade with Su, not sit in the fancy carriage of some boring bureaucrat.

It's not hard to guess what happened next. Su fell for the scholar poet, who was already smitten with Emerald. Emerald didn't care for the scholar poet, but enjoyed his attention all the same. Given how opaque Su was, and how poorly Emerald regarded him, it came as a huge surprise to Emerald when Su eventually let loose, a few months down the road, in a quiet rage, calling Emerald's loose morals and easy romps with the scholar poet the betrayal of a lifetime.

"*The betrayal of a lifetime?*" Emerald said. "His erections are as lackluster as his poems!"

Su said nothing. "Why didn't you tell me?" Emerald asked. "I didn't even want him. You could've had him." Of course Su's pride prevented her from saying that this was precisely why she had kept silent for so long. "Let's take some time off," she said, her words pelting Emerald like flinty ice in a hailstorm. "I want you to move out."

They had repaired the old courtyard house with their own hands, scrubbed its floors, painted its walls, hand-sewn curtains and bedspreads, dusted spiders from corners. It was simple but very cozy. Every day they took in dried wood to kindle a warm fire. It was home.

Emerald glowered. "I'm not going anywhere."

Su set off the next dawn. She didn't say where.

Emerald could not believe her sister was gone. They had spent barely a quarter of a year together as humans. She'd loved every minute of it. There were so many new things to do—braiding up each other's hair with flowers, walking down to town and sharing a bowl of sweet soybean pudding. Su carried a waxed paper parasol to shield them from rain or shine, which she had decorated with trailing pieces of red ribbon for luck. They'd not yet learned to properly digest human food, and it gave them the runs, but they tried it anyway—Su because she wanted to look like she was eating like a human, and Emerald because she liked the funny tastes of the things humans ate. Emerald's favorite snack was candied haws, fresh red hawthorn berries dipped into caramelized rock sugar.

Emerald was sure Su wouldn't stay mad for long—she'd be back in no time.

Winter came. Emerald turned back into a green snake and huddled under their bed, sticking her tongue out from time to time, hoping she would get a hint of her sister's jasmine scent. She wasn't eating enough. Lack of energy and bitter cold slowed her into brumation.

When she woke, it was spring. Crocuses were pushing through the melting snow, and still no Su.

The house grew dusty. The roof fell in again. Spiders took up residence in every corner.

Emerald waited all summer, with no inclination to partake in village life. Where was the fun in doing this alone? When she saw the colorful lanterns hung up around town, she realized that a year had passed: Mid-Autumn Festival was here again. It was 1616.

She wandered out of Hangzhou, ending up in Suzhou Creek. She was bathing in her human skin one morning when a golden monkey stole her clothes and ran up a whitebark pine tree, chittering at her. Emerald chased him to the highest branch. When she fell out of the tree, the monkey turned into a caddish but irresistible young man with a shock of gold hair, grabbed her by the waist, and spun her around. By the time their feet touched the ground softly, he'd clothed her again in the robes he'd stolen.

She shook her fist at him as he dipped her back. "You stinking piece of cow dung."

"Forgive me"—he bowed—"I was just trying to make an impression on a beautiful girl."

They indulged in several years of mayhem and debauchery in Suzhou before going their separate ways—he was looking for his master, and she was searching for her sister. "I don't know why I'm looking for him, really," he admitted, "the only thing he ever does is punish me."

"Well," Emerald asked him, "do you like to be punished?"

"Do you?" he asked. "Maybe we're sick fucks."

They wished each other luck. Emerald went through Central Asia and Russia, to no avail. It would be decades before Su found Emerald instead, saving her from the gallows in Finnmark.

. . .

When the in-flight meal service begins, Su and Emerald move to the leather armchairs. Attentive stewardesses serve up sticks of lamb satay with peanut sauce and finely sliced onion as an appetizer. For the main course, Emerald orders lobster thermidor. Su is barely able to finish a Niçoise salad. The milky taste of Bartek's qi rises in her throat again, making her want to gag.

"OK," Emerald says. "Time to spill the tea."

Su almost chokes. "Tea?"

"Give me the lowdown on your man."

Su pushes her plate away in relief. Emerald is asking about Paul, not Bartek. "Paul is a minister." She adds with a swell of pride, "Actually, he's being considered for Chief Minister . . ."

"Minister?" Emerald frowns. "Like, a church kind of guy?"

"Oh," Su says, "no, a minister is like"—she reaches for the US equivalent—"a senator, maybe, or a secretary of state. Paul is the Minister for Education."

"Was he an educator before?"

In Singapore, it is unlikely for a rank-and-file teacher to climb to a ministerial position, or even to become a Party member. "Paul was a President's Scholar." Su's voice melts like butter in the sun. "In Singapore, they earmark promising students at eighteen. It sets them up for life."

"Hmm, sets them up for life?" Emerald observes. "Doesn't that depend on what they want to do in the first place? Eighteen is embryonic. To sign your life away at that age—"

"For these men, serving the country is a great honor."

"These men?" Emerald looks suspicious. "Aren't there women in politics?"

Su could count all the women in the Party on one hand, and come to think about it, only Divya was a full minister overseeing her own ministry. "Of course there are women," she says.

"Good," Emerald deadpans, "I was all ready to start a riot."

"Ha." Su is nervous. "Don't use words like that in Singapore."

"Words like what?"

"Like *riot*," Su says. "Words like *start a riot*."

"Jesus." Emerald laughs. "You can't be serious."

Only now is Su jolted by a sharp prick of fear. *My sister is going to hate Singapore, and Singapore is going to hate my sister.* Su's love for the island state, her desire for her sister to be near, her conviction that the former will exert a positive influence on the latter, have converged to create a blind spot, gassy with wishful thinking. It truly had not crossed her mind that Emerald in Singapore was, potentially, a man-made disaster. Su's eyes flick to the flight navigator at the top of the screen. They're ten hours away from Singapore. She says carefully, "I've worked hard to build the life I have there. I have a husband, he has a job in the public eye, we have a home together—"

"Right," Emerald quips. "Is that why you went vegan?"

"I'm serious. You've got to follow the rules there."

"Relax. I'm, like, a tourist!"

"You're also my sister—and Paul's sister-in-law."

Emerald stops chewing and stares at Su incredulously. "That's a lot of projecting—"

"I'm not projecting. I'm worried. About you."

"Me?" Emerald looks miffed. "What are you worried about?"

Su shakes her head.

"Go on," Emerald goads her. "What is it, my hair?" She runs a hand over her green buzz cut.

"Fine," Su says at last. "I think you could improve on your walk, for example."

"My *walk*? You've got to be kidding."

Su stands up and shows her, exaggerating in the privacy of their cabin. "You're swaying from side to side, like this. It's not how humans move, it's reptilian. You're backsliding."

"*Reptilian?*" Emerald stares at her. "*Backsliding?* What's with all these euphemisms?"

"Fine." Su draws herself up. "I'll say it plainly. You're not passing."

Now Emerald is riled up. "Maybe I don't *want* to pass. And what does passing mean to you anyway?" She narrows her eyes at Su. "Want to tell me where you got those wrinkles? Got a derm to doodle on your face? Have you thought about how stupid that is, when humans pay for Botox?"

"I haven't activated my glands in ages," Su lies blatantly.

"Hurray for your dried sacs." Emerald turns away from Su. "Assimilate all you want, but don't pass your self-loathing on to me." She pushes her half-eaten food away, jams headphones on, closes her eyes.

. . .

Su spends the rest of the flight following the flight path navigator, eyes glazing over as they pass mountain ranges on the Chinese border. Why did she ask Emerald to come to Singapore? But then she recalls Emerald's wan smile across the table in that backyard bar with the lights behind her. What if that bullet had hit her? She could have lost Emerald.

Su falls into a deep sleep as GMT − 4 turns to GMT + 8.

She wakes right before the final descent, missing breakfast.

Heading to the bathroom to wash up, Su brushes her teeth, washes her face, moisturizes, reapplies makeup. She is just about done when she feels something warm and wet on her thigh. She touches the seat of her pants. Her hand comes away sticky, dark, red. She's bleeding from the inside. Cold fear sieves her guts as she pulls her garments down, afraid she's going to see some bit of her baby sticking out, but there's nothing other than spotting. She takes a deep breath, counting to ten.

"Ladies and gentlemen, please ensure your seat back is upright and your seat belt is fastened as we begin our descent," she hears the smooth voice of the stewardess over the PA system.

Su cleans herself up. Puts on a sanitary napkin from the amenities drawer. Washes her hands, heads back to her seat.

The cabin has been readied for landing. In her seat, Emerald looks out the window. Su isn't sure if she's deliberately ignoring her. Below, stationary ships dot the South China Sea. Singapore's croissant-like shape comes into view as they descend.

Soon the plane is slowing to a halt on the tarmac.

Su looks at Emerald. She doesn't know how to begin to ask for help. "Xiaoqing—"

"Is this going to be London all over again?" Emerald cuts in. Her eyes are defiant.

"London?" Su has not thought about that in such a long time. "What about London?"

Emerald recoils like she's just slapped her. "What about London? Are you serious?"

Su feels a daub of blood trickling out of her. "I don't have time for this right now," she says, pulling herself together. "I need to meet with a shareholder, but I'll send someone to pick you up. See you at dinner, OK? I'll book us a nice place to eat."

"Fine," Emerald says icily. "Whatever."

Su shoots out of the airplane and the immigration hall with the singular purpose of an arrow, getting straight into the back of a cab in record time. She sends Tik a message: *Tik, can you do me a favor?*

Tik responds quickly: *Of course, Mrs. Ong. What do you need?*

Could you get the car from the chauffeur and pick my sister up at the airport? Take her home if she's tired, show her around if not? She sends Emerald's number and picture to Tik. *She can be a bit of a handful . . .*

No problem, Mrs. Ong. I'll take care of her.

The cab lets Su off at a private hospital with an ob-gyn ward.

The first elevator comes up from the basement and is almost full. Su tries to step in, but the weight-limit alarm buzzes angrily. Someone clicks their tongue at her for trying to squeeze in.

As Su waits for the next one, a stranger behind her taps her on the shoulder. "Ma'am . . ." She points at Su's leg. A thin, gloopy streak of blood, dribbling downward.

8

One Hundred Percent Prepared
to Go Full Death Metal

The fuck does she take me for? Emerald brushes back angry tears. Her sister convinced her to fly halfway across the world, they fought before touching down, and now she's being abandoned because some shitty, schlocky shareholder is apparently more important.

Emerald's first impulse is to buy a ticket right back to New York. Is it possible to do that, turn around and get back on a plane without passing through immigration? That would show Su.

But then she remembers that she has no money, and it's a nineteen-hour plane ride.

She receives a text message from a +65 number. *Hi, I'm Tik. Mrs. Ong sent me to pick you up.*

Emerald sighs. Changi Airport reminds her of the opulent casinos of Macao, busy around the clock. High-ceilinged, well lit, plushly carpeted, with a host of amenities and brands. Louis Vuitton, Paris Baguette. Emerald notices a sign that points to the Butterfly Garden. Looks like Bartek wasn't shitting her. She makes a detour, follows the directions, and steps into a luscious garden with a louvered skylight, a waterfall, a timber boardwalk. Hibiscus and ixora are part of the landscaping, but the butterflies are concentrated around a stainless-steel feeding plate, on which juicy, uniformly one-inch-thick pineapple slices have been laid out for their consumption.

Butterflies of various types and sizes flit about unhurriedly.

Emerald doesn't recognize them, but no matter! Educational signs in big fonts are ready to point out varying species: red admiral, monarch, painted lady, zebra longwing, cabbage white—

A thick, creamy orange painted lady drifts right by Emerald.

There's a pair of parents in the corner of the garden cooing over their toddler; no one's watching. In a split second, she flicks her tongue around the painted lady and swallows it whole.

It tickles as it goes down Emerald's throat, leaving a fine, powdery dusting on the roof of her mouth. She wipes it clean with her tongue—a pleasant nutmeg aftertaste. Flashing a victory sign, she snaps a selfie with a black swallowtail on the feeding plate, and sends it to Bartek.

Immigration is a breeze. Emerald doesn't ever travel with checked luggage, and this time is no different—just a black duffel bag.

She steps out into the arrival hall. There's a verdant vertical wall that Emerald assumes consists of fake ferns. When she takes a closer look, she realizes that all the plants are real. How do they maintain this? Not a vine out of place, nor a dried leaf in sight. Something about this strikes her as excellent, but sinister. The airport floor here is highly polished granite. Every inch sparkles—this public space is way cleaner than Bartek's place.

Emerald sends a text to her chaperone: *Hi, I'm below Léa Seydoux.*

She waits below a three-story-high LED screen with a Prada perfume ad on repeat: Seydoux in luxe locales, eye-fucking the camera. Emerald is amused by a robot cleaner moving toward her with a flashing sign that announces: *Please don't obstruct me, I'm just doing my job!*

"Go right ahead, buddy," Emerald says to the machine.

Behind the robot cleaner is a cute brown girl, who on first sight Emerald mistakes for a guy. She's got a crew cut, she's wearing a loose-fitting Adidas jacket, she stops in front of the Prada ad.

"Miss Emerald?" Her voice is husky.

Ooh yes, Emerald thinks. She tries to keep a surprised yet smug smile from showing up on her face. "You're Tik?" Tik nods. They shake hands. Before letting go, Emerald can't help but spill: "I thought you were going to be, like, umm, a toady middle-aged Chinese man."

Tik looks thrown off. She tries to recover, but blushes instead. Cute.

"How was the flight, Miss Emerald?" Tik takes her duffel bag.

"Too long." Emerald stretches her arms as they start to walk off.

Two auxiliary police officers stop in front of them. "Ma'am." The taller one nods at Emerald. "I need you to come with us."

Tik steps between them. "Is there a problem, sir?"

The two officers sit Emerald down in a security office. The air in here is stale, and the furniture is spare. Overhead, cold fluorescent lights shine harshly. The taller officer replays security footage on one of the many screens: Emerald in the butterfly garden, looking around. The painted lady flies by her shoulder. The next moment, the orange butterfly is gone.

The officer folds his arms. "Can you explain this?"

"Hmm?" Emerald stalls.

The shorter officer plays the video again, this time in slow motion. Almost imperceptibly, Emerald's tongue seems to flick out around the butterfly, pulling it into her mouth.

He places his hands on the table. "Did you consume a butterfly from the garden?"

"Of course not," Emerald tells him. "It's the angle." He plays the video again. "It flew right in front of my face, and gave me a shock," Emerald insists. "Why would anyone eat a butterfly?"

"We need to take down your particulars." The taller officer takes out a form.

"You know what, I don't think so," Emerald says. "I haven't done anything wrong."

The officers are galled by her bold way of speaking. This isn't how it usually goes. "If you don't cooperate," the shorter one threatens, "we can investigate you for obstruction of justice."

Emerald rolls her eyes. "And just what am I being investigated for?"

"Willful removal of public property."

Emerald goggles at him like he must be kidding. The guy is less concerned that she may be chomping butterflies than that she may have taken a piece of this public garden away with her?

"Sir," Tik speaks from behind. "I think this may be a misunderstanding. Miss Emerald is in Singapore to visit family—"

"Please, ma'am," the officer says to Tik, "I'll have to ask you to leave the room—"

Tik holds out a badge. The officers peer at it. "Minister Paul Ong is waiting to receive Miss Emerald," Tik continues, "and we are running a little behind schedule at the moment."

An awkward pause. The officers register the name. Emerald senses the air shifting. "I see," the taller one says finally, still trying to sound authoritative. "I see."

The shorter officer replays the footage. "Yah, could be the angle," he parrots Emerald now, before holding the door open for them.

. . .

The humidity hits Emerald like a wet dishcloth as they exit the air-conditioned bubble of the terminal and walk to the adjoining car park. The air presses against her skin, hugging it uncomfortably. When she breathes in, the sensation is thick and damp. She glances at Tik, who is walking behind her, rather than beside her. Tik's face is stoic, her gait deferential. Emerald slows down till they're at the same pace—but Tik immediately adjusts so she's still a step back.

"So, he's a big deal, huh? This Paul dude? My sister's husband?"

Tik refrains from comment.

"What's he like?" Emerald prods.

"Mr. Ong has a lot of responsibilities," Tik says vaguely. "He's a very busy man."

"That's not really saying anything, is it?" Emerald turns to look at Tik directly.

Tik is not afraid to hold her gaze evenly. She gives nothing away with her eyes. "Discretion is a big part of my job," she says.

When they reach the car, Tik holds the back-seat door open. Emerald goes around. Opens the passenger door on her own. "I'll ride up front with you."

"I'm afraid that's against protocol, Miss Emerald." Mr. and Mrs. Ong always sit in the back seat. It's how Tik has been trained to ferry Party members and their spouses.

"I'm allergic to protocol." Emerald slides into the passenger seat. "You coming?"

Tik has no choice but to follow. As she starts the car, she sneaks a look at Emerald in the side mirror. She isn't sure how to handle her—Emerald is so different from Mrs. Ong. They're both incredibly beautiful, but Mrs. Ong's impeccable composure puts her at arm's length; it feels like nobody can get near her. Emerald is a live wire. Her unpredictability pulls you in. It makes you feel like today isn't just like any other day. You have no idea where you're going to end up with her; are you in for the ride? Tik's fingertips buzz as she maneuvers the Porsche out of the carpark.

"Would you like to go home and rest, Miss Emerald? Or do you want to see the city a little?"

"I'm hungry," Emerald declares. "Let's grab some food? I'm easy, I eat everything."

Tik isn't sure what to recommend. "When we come to a stop, I'll google something for you."

"I don't want a machine's recs," Emerald says. "Take me someplace where you're a regular."

Tik hesitates. The places she eats at are very different from the ones that Mr. and Mrs. Ong frequent. "I'm not sure if you might find those places to your liking, Miss Emerald."

"Why wouldn't I?" Emerald looks at Tik. There's a certain cockiness in her tilted chin.

All right, Tik thinks, let's see. She speeds up suavely, overtaking three cars to filter off the highway.

Tik turns out at the Rochor exit and parks the Porsche at Kampong Glam. "God, I'm so hungry I could eat ten more butterflies," Emerald says as they get out of the car and walk to Minang. "Actually, they'd be great in tempura batter, no? Flash-fried butterflies." Tik has no idea if she's kidding.

"Atika!" The auntie behind the counter spots Tik. She cringes to hear her full name, but she still manages to smile at the makcik.

"Is this your new *friend*?" the makcik says slyly, in Malay.

Ever since she was a teenager in oversize pinafores, trying to make the school uniform baggy enough not to feel like a skirt, Tik has brought all her girlfriends to this popular nasi padang establishment. When Tik is out with a girlfriend in public, they never hold hands for fear of being spotted by relatives, but with this makcik, things are easy. Tik knows this is only because she isn't family.

"Don't anyhow say." Tik lowers her voice, even though she's speaking to the makcik in Malay. "She's my boss's sister. Just came in from New York."

"Eh." The makcik lights up, like it's her dream destination, a picture postcard. "New York!"

"Hi!" Emerald says brightly to the makcik. "Everything looks delish." She gawks at the array of Indonesian food—spiced curries, marinated beef cooked over a slow charcoal fire, cassava leaf sprigs in coconut milk, fish steamed in banana leaf, pickled long beans, tender chicken in green chili, squid in a tangy gravy. "Would you pick out your faves for me?"

The makcik doesn't hesitate. Confidently she ladles beef rendang, tahu telur, botok-botok, begedil, gulai nangka, and acar onto a bed of jasmine rice for Emerald. "Specially for you."

Emerald sits at one of the plastic tables and digs in. "Oh god." She covers her mouth reverentially at the explosion of flavors. She had cottoned on to human food quickly, was enjoying the flavors within weeks of taking on her human skin—it took Su much longer to taste and hold down the stuff. "Sooooo good," Emerald exclaims. "Oof!"

The makcik beams, radiating pride.

Tik stands around by one of the pillars, the way she always does when Mr. and Mrs. Ong are having a meal or otherwise engaged.

Emerald waves at her. "What are you doing? Have a seat."

"Mr. and Mrs. Ong—"

Emerald gives her a look. "Coffee or tea?"

Tik turns to the makcik, who knows her regular order. "Teh tarik?"

"Make that two, please," Emerald says as Tik joins her at the table.

Taking a postmeal smoke by the pavement, Tik looks on in amazement as Emerald and the makcik huddle at a table, chatting with intensity over cups of hot teh tarik that have gone cold.

They've been at it for the last quarter of an hour, after Emerald wolfed down the food and complimented the makcik on the cooking. The makcik is now telling Emerald they've been family-owned since 1954. Tik is surprised. "Hey, I didn't know that." Minang has been around longer than Singapore has been independent. In this newfangled town that moves at breakneck speed, it's difficult to find establishments that have existed, in the same spot and in the same hands, for anything more than a decade. "I tell you," the makcik says animatedly, "so many things you young people don't know. Last time, in the sixties, auntie was a backup dancer for Anita Sarawak—"

"Who is Anita Sarawak?" Emerald asks.

"Adui, you don't know Anita Sarawak?" The makcik thinks of how to explain it. "Anita was the Beyoncé of Southeast Asia!" The makcik looks over at Tik. "Correct or not, Atika?"

"Correct," Tik goes along with her. There are things you simply do not disagree with makciks about. The makcik nods, pleased. Another regular customer greets her, and the makcik heads to an adjacent table, but not before winking at Tik: "Bring your *friend* back again, OK?"

Tik blushes and quickly salams the makcik's hand as she leaves.

Emerald asks: "Is there anywhere to hear Anita Sarawak's music?"

Tik almost says no right off the bat. Anita Sarawak was big back then, but no one's listening to her music anymore, and besides, there won't be a single pub open—it's not even noon. But there's something about Emerald that makes Tik want to make impossible things possible.

Tik takes out her phone. "Give me a moment." Tik doesn't expect Ploy to answer—given her job's hours, she's a late riser—but she picks up. "Hello," Tik says, a little awkwardly; they haven't spoken in a while. "How are you doing? Yeah, so I have a guest who wants to visit the lounge . . ."

Ploy works in a Thai disco with a karaoke lounge at Golden Mile Complex. Though it's only open from 5:00 p.m. onward, Tik knew that Ploy and her friends often use the space in the day.

"Guest?" Ploy asks. "What kind of guest?"

"My boss's sister." When she started, Mrs. Ong gave Tik a credit card for any expenses she might incur on the job. "You can just open the place up, and we'll tip . . ."

"Arai wah," Ploy says wryly. "Money fall from sky?"

Tik met Ploy when she was doing a stint with the Anti-Vice Enforcement Unit four years before. She headed a team to raid Club Nana on a tip-off. Several hostesses were taken back to the station. Most had entered Singapore as tourists, and were working at the club illegally.

Ploy was coolly unfazed as she flashed her legal entertainer visa in Tik's face. "Per-for-ming Ar-tiste," Ploy read off the visa with pride. She crossed her gamine legs and held Tik's gaze. Ploy was cleared, but the others were to be deported. She waited outside the station for the rest of the girls. When the investigation ended, Ploy demanded that Tik send all of them back to Club Nana in her patrol car. "Let my friends pack things na." Ploy rustled imaginary dollar bills between her fingers. "And pick up salary, from boss, before they go . . ."

This was very bold of her, but Tik relented. She accompanied them back to Club Nana and their dormlike quarters, an apartment on the tenth floor of the same building. Told them they had half an hour to gather their belongings and salaries. Some of the girls were crying. Watching Ploy comfort her friends and help with their bags, Tik felt a guilty twinge in her heart.

A week after the raid, Tik showed up at Club Nana in a baseball cap.

Stage lights went up. P'Bee, the manager, pointed her laser at the girls onstage one by one, soliciting tips from the otherwise all-male audience. Fifty bucks earned a hostess a pink sash. Five hundred bucks got her a silver cape. A thousand bucks bestowed upon her a tiara.

Tik raised her hand when the red laser beam hit Ploy's sternum, like a gun sight. "Tiara," she told P'Bee.

. . .

Emerald and Tik walk through the ground floor of Golden Mile Complex. Emerald peers at fat garoupas in the fish tanks of Double Happiness Steamboat, at the outmoded speaker sets in JJ Hi-Fi Electronics, at the ginseng in the shopfront of Ba Xian Friendship Herbal Dispensary. Tik takes her up a flight of old-fashioned spiral stairs.

They emerge into a mosaic corridor that leads to a corner unit.

The entrance to Club Nana is bedecked in tinsel fringe, lit by pink neon. Inside, a petite Thai girl in black-and-red cowboy boots and tiny shorts that show off her butt cheeks waits for them. She is fresh-faced, sans makeup in the daytime. This must be Ploy.

"Tiki-tik," she greets Tik lazily. From the way she says it, Emerald can immediately sense that Ploy and Tik have a history.

"Ploy, this is Emerald." Tik introduces them. "Emerald, Ploy."

"Funny." Ploy peers at Emerald. "Why you wanna listen to Anita Sarawak?"

In a karaoke lounge with a mirror ball, Ploy pulls up Anita Sarawak songs in the system, picks out "Sophisticated Lady." Emerald is surprised that it sounds like a funk classic straight out of Dayton. Tik explains that as Anita's fame in Singapore grew in the 1960s, she was courted by Caesar's Palace, and ended up performing in Vegas for twenty years. Tik picks one of Anita's earlier songs, when she was still singing in Malay, a song called "Joget Sayang Disayang." Anita is perfectly proficient in English, but when she sings in Malay, though

Emerald doesn't understand the words, there seems to be a difference that is hard to explain. It isn't technical, but emotional—it feels like she is singing straight from the heart.

Ploy is dialing up Blackpink's "How You Like That." She palms one mic expertly, tosses the other at Emerald. Throws a tambourine onto Tik's lap. Ploy winks at Emerald. "You ready, sis?"

After an hours-long karaoke session, Ploy and Emerald taking turns on the mic, they eventually manage to goad Tik into joining. "Just one song," Tik relents. Ploy is already inputting the selection.

"You wait and see." Ploy turns to Emerald. "Once the music start, she like a different person."

Emerald isn't sure what Ploy means. Then Tik starts to sing David Bowie's "Heroes." Her voice is richly timbred, keying up into a resonant falsetto growl: "*We can be us, just for one day.*"

Ploy pulls on Tik's hand, forcing her to get up. They start to dance.

Ploy is lithe with K-pop moves, and Tik somehow knows how to shimmy her hips like a matinee heartthrob. At first Emerald gets up to join in, but there's a thick and sweet familiarity between them, and she settles back down to give space to that. The song ends. Emerald whoops.

"See what I mean?" Ploy nudges Emerald.

"Totally," Emerald agrees.

Ploy takes them to a hole-in-the-wall resto in the basement where a resident ginger cat with a stumpy tail lazes before a bodhisattva altar. They share dessert: red ruby sago and mango sticky rice. The restaurant is chilly. Tik gets Emerald and Ploy small glasses of warm water.

"I like her na," Ploy says about Emerald to Tik, in front of Emerald. "You not like other people here." Ploy struggles to find the exact words. "You are very . . ." Then she lands on it, "you."

Emerald thinks it's the highest compliment. "Thank you." She smiles. "You're very you too."

Singapore—or at least Tik's Singapore—isn't what Emerald thought it would be.

It is all so real, and realness is the thing she has come to find most lovely. Nothing like the sheeny, synthetic, superficial image of the city she's come to expect from popular media. It's the little things: the goodness of the makcik's food, the random mishmash of Golden Mile's shops, Ploy opening up the lounge for them in the afternoon, Anita Sarawak switching effortlessly between English and Malay in her songs, this silken fresh mango paired so simply and assiduously with sticky rice—and Tik.

There is something deliciously old-school about Tik's masculinity, like she learned how to be a gentleman off Turner Classic movies. Tik really knows how to make a woman feel like a woman. The way she makes eye contact, holds a door open, gets you a glass of warm water in a cold restaurant. Tik seems to be out of sync with time and space, in a way that feels specific and special for Emerald—as the decades pile on, it has been rare for her to meet anyone or go anywhere without being haunted by a vague sense that they remind her of someone else, some-place else, sometime else ago. People and places are compressed and flat-tened into washed-out mosaics and toned-down facsimiles of those she's known in the past, and this is part of what depresses her as an immortal.

She smiles at Tik when she returns from settling the bill.

"Thank you."

"It's not me," Tik deflects. "Mrs. Ong gave me the money."

"It *is* you, actually," Emerald tells her. "My sister has the money, sure, but I bet you she's never eaten at Minang, or heard an Anita Sar-awak song, or stepped into Golden Mile Complex."

Having been Mrs. Ong's bodyguard for the past few months, and having served other ministers before Mr. Ong, Tik can confirm this to be true. As far as she's seen, members of the Party stick to affluent enclaves like Orchard Road, Marina Bay, Holland Village, King Albert Park. If ever they have a meal at a hawker center or a street stall, it tends to be a planned photo op to show that they, the ruling class, can eat like the masses too. But she's a loyal civil servant, so Tik shrugs as she tells Emerald: "It's not so convenient for the ministers to do regular things . . ."

. . .

It's late in the afternoon when Tik drops Emerald at Coronation Drive, so she can rest before dinner. "*Coronation* Drive?" Emerald winces. "Eww. Is this some sort of postcolonial masturbation?"

Tik hasn't thought about this before. It's true that around the rarefied Bukit Timah area, street signs are full of British royal references: Princess of Wales Park, Duchess Avenue, Victoria Park Grove, Queen's Road, and such. Tik watches as Emerald peers at Mr. and Mrs. Ong's big bungalow and yard from the window, unimpressed. Emerald doesn't know that the vast majority of the Singaporean population lives in public housing flats, cookie-cutter blocks with limited square footage, which seem to be getting smaller yet pricier every year. Tik was stunned by the palatial homes with the exclusive District Ten postal codes when she first started on the job; some driveways in Bukit Timah are so long you can't even see the front doors.

Emerald watches Tik as she pulls up the brake. Long fingers, neat nails. Silver thumb ring. Faint scar on the end of her left eyebrow; she once had a piercing there. The engine idles. "I'm sorry you had to babysit me." Emerald makes a face at Tik, half contrite, half gauging where things stand.

"You don't have to apologize."

"For what it's worth," Emerald admits, "my day started out in the shit pits. I was one hundred percent prepared to go full death metal on this tropical toy town in the middle of nowhere." Tik looks nervous about where this is headed. "But as it turns out," Emerald goes on, "I had an amazing day in a gorgeous city. So I just wanna thank you, for turning this whole ship around." *Turning this whole ship around?* Emerald wants to kick herself. *Are you in the navy?*

"It's my job." Tik inclines her head in a slight bow.

Tik's formality makes Emerald bashful—a feeling she hasn't felt in decades, maybe even centuries. And funnily enough, this unusual bashfulness makes her a bit more polite and grateful, unlike the blunt, entitled person she knows she often can be. Fuck, Emerald thinks with a sinky dreamy feeling, is this what they mean when they say you'll meet someone who makes you a better person? She can't wait to update Bartek on Tik, but that heartless bish hasn't even read her last texts. It's late in New York; he's probably making out with a random ex at Mood Ring in Bushwick.

Emerald looks at Tik. "And if it wasn't your job?"

Tik meets Emerald's gaze properly for the first time all day.

"If it wasn't my job? Then it would be my pleasure."

This time, it is Emerald who blushes. And it is Emerald, for once, who has no repartee. "Well," she stammers, shaking her phone stupidly, "I'd ask for your number, but I've already got it."

Tik nods as she presses the remote button for the bungalow's auto gate. It swings open. "And this one is for the main door." Tik passes Emerald a key. She unfastens her seat belt and is about to go around to open the car door, but Emerald gets out by herself, picks her bag up.

She waves at Tik from the pavement, trying to keep it cool as she calls out: "I'll text you or something!"

Wake up B, Emerald texts Bartek as the Porsche drives off, as she waits for it to disappear around the corner before she bursts into song, leaving her bestie a spirited, high-pitched, off-key voice note of her favorite Rihanna karaoke lyric: "*We found love in a hopeless place!*"

9

Pot-Bellied Deities Who Can Do No Wrong

To keep the waiting room from spinning, Su tries to focus on the wall art, but it is awful: a laminated Anne Geddes photograph of a baby, eyes closed and mouth slightly open, trussed up like a cabbage, with a big leaf on its head.

Like zoos, hospitals make Su nervous.

She has never been in a gynecological clinic or a maternity ward before—the milky odor of cheerful expectation makes her queasier than she already is. She tried asking if she could be seen first, but the receptionist was blasé: "Ma'am, miscarriage is not an emergency. And if this is really a miscarriage, there is nothing the doctor can do to stop it from happening. Please sit down and wait for your turn, OK?"

She passes Su a form to fill in. Su's heart is pounding, but protocol is protocol. Su leaves her emergency contact blank. The receptionist asks if there is anyone to call.

If she'd told Emerald on the plane, surely Emerald would be here with her now. But it wasn't just their silly row that stopped her. Something else pulled her back. Su is so used to the privacy of her feelings, she is unsure about sharing them, even with her sister. Having someone bear witness to your pain is risky: it takes the experience out of your hands, makes things real in a way you cannot unmake. Alone, you're free to rearrange the pieces till they sit right in your head. If no one else saw the way you cried, you can tell yourself it didn't matter that much, did it?

Support is superfluous. She prefers having control to having her hand held. No, she says, there is no one to call. The receptionist, a birdy lady in a sweater, prods: "How about the baby's daddy?" Her voice goes up in a presumptuous, nasal lilt at the word *daddy*.

"He doesn't know I'm pregnant," Su blurts out to end the conversation. It works: the birdy lady's friendly, pushy smile wipes itself off her face. She withdraws into her paperwork, but Su senses the laser pinprick of judgment from the others in the waiting room.

In a pronatalist society, pregnant women carry themselves like potbellied deities who can do no wrong. There are two specimens here in this waiting room. One resembles a beach ball in a pastel dress, water-retentive ankles strapped into Scholl sandals. The other has her second-trimester bump tucked into Lululemon joggers. Overhearing Su's conversation with the receptionist, both women instinctively flick their eyes to Su's ring finger, checking for a wedding band.

Suddenly self-conscious—she wouldn't want to be recognized here—Su shifts her hand to hide the three-carat Tiffany ring, princess cut. Paul went back and forth between 3 and 2.4, worried that as a standing politician, his wife should not be wielding such a sizable jewel. It might be used as evidence of the widening income gap between his voters and himself. But finally he said it was his duty to make sure that a woman as perfect as Su got what she deserved, and so: the larger diamond. "It's beautiful," she remembers telling him, holding it up to the light.

In the wild, diamonds are just carbon, utterly useless for survival. Even a feather or a soft-shell crab is a more valuable token of affection. But Su understands how women are supposed to feel about a man blowing a hundred thousand dollars on a polished bit of rock he can strap on metal to your finger, to tell every other potential suitor to back off, to accord you with the dignity of being spoken for. Emerald once asked why Su was obsessed with marriage, and Su told her that she liked being spoken for. To which Emerald snorted: "Why not speak for yourself?"

Su spaces out at the unlovely wall art. She isn't sure how long she has waited when she hears the birdy lady's voice: "Miss Bai? Doctor Ng will see you now. Is your bladder full enough for ultrasound?"

Su has been way too stressed to think about drinking water, and why didn't the receptionist mention it before? "I'm not sure," she says. The receptionist enunciates like she's a child: "Do you have the urge to urinate?" Su shakes her head. The receptionist points to the water dispenser in the corner with her thumb. "Please sit down, drink water, and let me know when you are ready." The receptionist calls in another patient, skipping Su. Su drinks cone after cone of water.

. . .

The gynecologist's teeth are white, but his breath is rancid. He breathes over Su while she adjusts herself on the examination bed. His qi reeks of cruciferous vegetables—an unholy trinity of stale cabbage, broccoli, cauliflower. He is a middle-aged man with a T-Rex posture, large head poking out of his shirt, skinny forearms hanging off his elbows. A female nurse stands by to assist. She covers Su with a paper sheet, clinically removes the blood-spotted pad, hands Dr. Ng a pair of gloves.

"You suspect a miscarriage, ma'am?" He pats her knees, prompting her to open up.

Su is finding it hard to keep her knees apart. "There was spotting, but I don't know—"

"How many weeks?"

"I don't know. This is my first scan."

"When was your last period?"

"I'm not sure. It's always been irregular."

Dr. Ng sighs audibly, as if to say: *Do you know anything at all, lady?* The ultrasound machine emits a low hum. The nurse applies a cold, clear gel to Su's abdomen. Su winces slightly as the gynecologist runs the transducer over her abdomen, going back and forth before he focuses on a specific spot, pushing in for a clearer view—"Congratulations." Dr. Ng points to the screen. "I can see the heart, beating."

A choppy image stabilizes on the machine's screen. Black, white, and fuzzy, like those silent shorts she'd stood in line to see at the turn of the twentieth century in London. Dr. Ng asks the nurse to turn on the Doppler to confirm the heartbeat. Hearing the rhythmically spaced *chug-chug-chug*, Su feels the blood catching in her own chest. This is the sound of her baby's heart, smaller than a snow pea seed, racing so hard. "One hundred sixty bpm," the nurse reports. A healthy rate.

Su is mesmerized by the tiny cardiac flicker on the screen.

Dr. Ng moves the transducer around. "Maybe about ten weeks."

Su is lightheaded. She wants to clamber out of here to call Paul. A baby. They're having a baby. It's a miracle. This is proof that she doesn't just *identify* as human, she *is* human—her body has made a baby. Tears of joy warm the corners of her eyes. Dr. Ng slathers more gel over her womb, moving the transducer for a closer look, pressing her flesh.

He purses his lips. "Ah . . ."

"What is it?" She tries to see what he's seeing on the screen. It looks like an early galaxy.

"I'm sorry, ma'am." He points it out to her. "The spine and torso appear to be elongated."

A hard pit of dread tightens in Su's diaphragm. "What does that mean?" Her voice is shaky.

"Birth defect," Dr. Ng explains. "I don't see any limbs, but there's a lot of vertebrae . . ."

Hot panic rises in the back of Su's throat as he traces the limbless crescent-moon shape of the life in her womb on the screen. The baby inside her is not congenitally defective. It's a snake.

. . .

The stiff leather straps of Su's brand-new Valentino pumps dig into her skin as she walks through the Flower Dome at Gardens by the Bay. The Flower Dome—the largest columnless glass greenhouse in the world—is a world of perpetual spring. The temperature and humidity in here are completely unlike Singapore's 24/7 hot-wet weather, enabling exotic species from all around the world to thrive right here, on an equatorial island in the tropics. Su admires this level of controlled sophistry. Under the right set of conditions, you can remake things about yourself that aren't possible.

Su looks at the flora around her. Of course, there is no accompanying fauna. This is not a habitat for animals, but a display built for humans by humans, to be Instagrammed to death.

Today, the seasonal bloom on central display is the tulip. Row after row of potted tulips in rainbow hues gussy up the concourse, but that's not enough. Photographic dioramas of the Netherlands—windmills, milkmaids—are strategically arranged amid tulips for a photo-friendly moment. Su watches as a girl in a frilly dress tugs on her boyfriend's hand, turning back to look at him demurely over her shoulder. He leans back at an awkward angle to make sure he captures their intertwined hands without cutting off her head. Beside them, a child reaching out toward the tulips is scooped up by his mother. "Cannot touch!"

Su looks away. Her abortion has been scheduled for the following morning. It was the earliest appointment she could make. There is a mandatory forty-eight-hour cooling-off period, and before she was allowed to schedule it, Su was led into a windowless room that smelled like mothballs. The nurse pressed play on a DVD player, and she was made to sit through a low-res video of a toddler running after a colorful ball. An unconvincing actress droned on about how this is the age her unborn child would have been if she hadn't chosen abortion. Su wasn't sure why she was crying, when her baby wasn't even human. She took a packet of three-ply tissue out of her Birkin and wiped her tears away, then touched up her eye makeup. She should be glad to have caught this early, to be rid of it. She didn't want to bring something like that into the world.

Even though shopping was the last thing that Su wanted to do, she went from the private hospital to the Shoppes at Marina Bay Sands. The colorful ads and frivolous fashions and window displays calmed her down. It was a simulacrum of possibility. She could exercise her decision-making here, and there would be neither mistakes nor consequences for these sorts of choices: Gucci heels, Miu Miu loafers, or Valentino pumps? All right then, Valentino pumps.

"Reservation for three under Bai Suzhen," Su says as she reaches Marguerite, the serene fine-dining restaurant housed in the Flower Dome. The waiter shows Su to a table with a view of the Marina Bay skyline. She's early. Emerald isn't here yet, neither is Paul.

Su is the one who was at the hospital, but she's still the person who made the reservation and texted Paul details, checked with Tik if Emerald was home, booked a cab for Emerald to Gardens by the Bay—all Emerald had to do was step into it. Su orders a sparkling water, trying to forget the sound of her baby's heartbeat. She checks the diamonds of her Rolex. A few minutes to 6:30 p.m.

Right on time, Paul walks in. The waiter pulls a chair out for Paul.

"Hi dear." Paul pecks her on the cheek. "How was your trip? Where is your sister? Everything OK?"

Before Su can answer, she spots Emerald. "Yo." Emerald saunters over, running a hand over her green buzz cut. She is the only person in this upscale restaurant in a T-shirt, a faded and fraying T-shirt that has seen better days. Paul's eyebrows rise up without going down for a full five seconds. The difference between the two sisters is stark. While Su presents as a buttoned-up taitai, Emerald has a provocative look about her, and when Paul stands up to draw her chair, she casually waves him down with a smile and does it herself. "I'm good, thanks."

"You must be Emerald?" Unsure if he should go in for a hug or handshake, Paul settles for a jocular fist bump. Su sees Emerald hesitate before returning it. "I've heard so much about you."

"Only good stuff, I hope." Emerald sticks her tongue out at Su.

"Of course," he says stiffly, "nothing but good stuff . . ."

"C'mon, dude." Emerald laughs. Transplanted into Singapore's rigid hierarchies, Emerald's shoot-your-mouth-off banter seems combative, even rude. Paul has no idea how to relate to her.

"So . . ." He forces a smile. "New York! How's the weather?"

The weather? Emerald sneaks a glance at Su, and just about manages to hold back an eye roll. "Right now, not so different from Singapore," Emerald tells him. "But summer in New York stinks to high heavens. Trash bakes out on the sidewalk, and subway piss is like a hot smog."

"Didn't you spend some time on the East Coast, Paul?" Su tries to ease him in.

"Yes," he says. "I was on a scholarship at UPenn. Visited New York a couple of times, but I never quite felt the draw of the big city . . . I guess you could say I'm more about the small-town feel."

"Do you think of Singapore as a small town or a big city?" Emerald wants to know.

"It's big-city infrastructure with a small-town mentality," Paul says. "That's what's so special about it." They've opted for the tasting menu; there's a vegan one for Su. The appetizers arrive, shaped like cigars. Charcoal-activated celeriac puree molded into crisp tuilles, filled with wild black trumpet mushroom duxelles. Su watches in dismay as Emerald picks hers up nonchalantly with her fingers, pretending to smoke it before chomping it down. Paul says nothing as he slices his food up into neat pieces. "So—" That opener from Paul again. "How do you find Singapore so far, Emerald?"

To Su's surprise, Emerald lights up. "Tik took me to this really cool place, Golden Mile?"

"Golden Mile Complex?" For Paul, it's a dilapidated giant gone to seed, an undesirable concentration of working-class Thai and Vietnamese guest workers on prime land, a dead weight the Party was hoping would be torn down and redeveloped into a more profitable prototype, but a new breed of urban activists has been making a racket about architectural heritage and all sorts of mawkish claptrap.

"Ah, I'm sorry"—Paul grimaces—"she should have taken you to Orchard Road or Haji Lane."

"Emerald isn't a typical tourist," Su tells Paul.

Paul frowns. "Haji Lane very edgy what. URA gets artists to spray paint on shophouses . . ."

The Urban Redevelopment Authority paid local street artists to tag specific walls with preapproved designs, usually in demarcated high-tourist-volume areas. Paul thinks this is exactly how it should be. Traveling to the US and Europe for work, whenever he passes by the devitalizing eyesore of heavily tagged building facades and highway bridges, whenever he has to extract a revolting wad of spat-out gum from the sole of his shoes, whenever he reads about a subway delay caused by a train door jammed once again by chewing gum, Paul is glad that the Chief Minister bothered to sweat the small stuff early on, by coming down hard on graffiti (jail term, with a few strokes of the cane to boot) and gum (hefty fines) in Singapore. Let the *New York Times* rehash its screeds on "soulless" Singapore's graffiti and gum laws every few years; he would take a smart-looking, highly livable city with polished walls, clean streets, and on-time trains anytime.

"Don't get me wrong," Paul backtracks a little to concede, "I know that a place like Golden Mile has its charms. It has a certain"—he makes air quotes—"*realness*, but we're a small island with a high population density. We have to value tangible pragmatism over putative authenticity."

"Huh," Emerald says. "That's not super fair."

Paul raises an eyebrow. "I beg your pardon?"

"Why do you put 'tangible' in front of 'pragmatism' and 'putative' in front of 'authenticity'?"

"Every deck needs to be stacked a little." Paul steeples his fingers. "Not for personal gain, but to achieve overall advantages for the common good." He smiles at Emerald. "Singapore is like a mini trick puzzle that must be solved in ten moves. No missteps, or everything falls to pieces."

Dramatic, Emerald thinks, but she's used to men in high places talking like mystic saviors. She pops the deconstructed fish dish into her mouth—a smoky piece of eel set atop tart green apple matchsticks, an oyster leaf, and horseradish gelato. She sneezes out loud as the wasabi hits her nose, then pivots the conversation for Su's sake. "Jie says you're the Minister for Education?"

"That's correct." Paul runs a hand through his hair, but it is too firmly Brylcreemed for this to have the relaxed effect he's hoping for. "I enjoy my portfolio, I feel a real passion for education, but it's been a difficult week. Remember the uniform thing?" He turns to Su. "It blew up on social media, and now we have a real problem—his classmates want to sue *us*."

"Us," Su clarifies, "as in the Ministry of Education?"

"Yah!" Paul says, throwing his hands up in disbelief.

He takes off his glasses, rubs his eyes, and puts them back on. "So in summary," he brings Emerald up to speed, "there's a male student who started wearing the girls' uniform to school, asked everyone to call him 'she,' showed the principal a doctor's memo saying he has gender dysphoria. One of my deputy directors investigated this doctor, and realized he's given out a number of these diagnoses to other teenage students . . . She called for a meeting with the doctor, explained that this is a slippery slope with generational repercussions, we don't want to have a transgender epidemic on our hands. When the student went back, the doctor said he couldn't give him a referral for the hormones anymore. Kids these days . . . I don't know what possessed him to make the situation public on TikTok, or why it went viral. Now a bunch of transgenders and gays are coming together to fundraise. They want to sue the school for harassment, and my ministry for negligence!"

"What?" Emerald's voice trembles.

"Yah, ridiculous." Paul assumes she's commiserating on the audacity. "Even if they raise enough funds and hire some third-rate freelance lawyer, do they think they have a chance?" A smug expression settles on Paul's handsome face, making it look flat and piggish.

Emerald regards him with complete distaste. She turns to Su. "You're OK with"—she waves her hand at Paul—"all of *this*?" Su's face has been reddening. She doesn't know what to say.

Only now does it dawn on Paul that Emerald is not on his side at all. "Just to clarify," Paul proclaims, "I'm not anti-trans, I'm pro-youth. That student isn't an adult, and I think that before he decides to contradict the natural order of creation, his body—"

Emerald loses it. She roars: "*Her* body!"

People turn in their direction as Emerald stands up, knocking into the table. She stalks off to the bathroom. When the diners stop glancing in their direction, Paul shoots Su a supercilious look. "Your sister can refer to the student as she pleases, but I for one am not going to be bullied into giving credence to alternative lifestyles by adopting pronouns that do not refer to a person's biological makeup." He clucks his tongue, *tsk tsk tsk*. "How long has she been in New York? This is exactly what we worry about when we send our scholars to the US, to the UK. We lose them to all these Western values."

"I don't think it's about that," Su says quietly.

Paul is surprised by this. "Do *you* have to contradict me as well, Suzhen?" The wayward sister is one thing—he could let that slide, she wasn't his problem—but his own wife is another thing altogether. She is directly under his jurisdiction. It's been a long day, and work was stressful enough—the very least he deserves is a woman who doesn't answer back to him.

Su doesn't say anything more. She doesn't want to escalate this in the middle of a restaurant.

When the maître'd brings out dessert, a coconut-flecked meringue with a mango-passionfruit sorbet shaped like a pretty daisy, Paul refuses his portion. "I'm no longer in the mood for something sweet." He looks briefly but pointedly in Su's direction, as if it's her fault that he won't get dessert.

. . .

Back at Coronation Drive after an excruciatingly tense and quiet car ride home, Emerald marches off to the guest room with her boots on.

"Hey." Su goes after her. "We're a shoes-off household."

Emerald kicks her Doc Marts off without looking at Su.

"Xiaoqing." Su sighs. "I hope you won't make things difficult between Paul and me. At the end of the day, he's still my husband."

"Congrats on being married to a transphobic asshole."

Su sits on the edge of the bed. "Can you have some respect? You're a guest in our house."

"Oh please." Emerald glowers at her. "Don't give me this hierarchy bullshit. How old is he, say, forty-five? I'm like ten times his senior—he should be the one serving me tea!" She eyes Su. "And let's be clear, I don't even want to be here! You made me come over. As usual."

Su blinks. "I did not *make* you do anything."

"Look. My life has been great without you. Everything was awesome until you came along."

For a moment Su is silent, but Emerald sees a dark look behind her eyes. "Really?" Su reaches out deftly and peels up Emerald's top to reveal her bullet graze wound. "Then what's this?"

Emerald pushes her hand away. Pulls her top down. "You knew?"

"I got on the first flight out," Su says softly.

When Emerald reaches out, Su thinks she's about to fold her into a hug—but Emerald clutches her by the shoulders, shaking her hard. "What the hell are you playing at? Are you spying on me? I'm not a child!" Su stays still, willing herself not to retaliate. She's much stronger than Emerald; Emerald knows it too. "God, you're such a creep!" Emerald lets go of Su. She lowers her voice. "He has no idea about you, does he?"

Su does not want to go there. "You know it's my policy—"

"You know what your policy is?" Emerald spits the words. "You pick powerful men who'll never see you for who you are, even if you were slithering naked in front of them, only what they project, because you have zero self-worth without them. What you present is just their idea of you."

"That's rich"—Su doesn't even raise her voice—"coming from someone who wears a push-up bra on an app called Sugarbowl."

Emerald is caught off guard by this. A thin, hot thrill goes through Su, like pushing a needle slowly into the flesh of her palm. "What was it again?" Su goes in for the kill now. " 'The only hair between my legs should be your beard?' "

"Even for a white krait," Emerald hisses, "that's fucking low."

She pushes past Su, out of the guest room.

In a moment, Su hears the heavy teak front door slam.

10

Do You Want Life to Have Its Way with You,
or Do You Want to Have Your Way with Life?

Emerald calls Bartek, but he doesn't pick up. It is almost noon in New York—he should be awake by now. She leaves him a ranty voice message, then rage-texts Tik: *Come. Save. Me. Now.* After a moment she adds: *Pretty please?*

It's close to midnight. She isn't sure if Tik will see her texts.

Barely five minutes later, Tik's reply brings a smile to her face: *Where do I get you?*

She sneaks out of the house and waits for Tik on the corner of the street, chewing down a fingernail in anticipation. When Tik shows up on a silver Vespa and asks if Emerald is comfortable with riding pillion, she finds herself blurting out that she's never done it before: a big fat lie. Not only has Emerald ridden pillion, she herself can ride a motorcycle—and not just a scooter on brightly lit Singaporean highways, but a cruiser through dark and uneven Castilian alleys. She doesn't even know what she is fibbing for—to make it feel (not just for Tik, but for herself) like it's her first time? *Ugh!* Emerald is disgusted with herself, but also enjoying the fluttery feeling as she holds on to Tik more tightly at the slightest bump—which hardly ever happens on Singapore's smooth, well-maintained roads.

They settle at a plastic table in a back alley at Swee Choon, a twenty-four-hour dim sum establishment along Jalan Besar. Tik used to come here with Ploy, who loves Cantonese food and has convinced Tik that it doesn't make sense to observe halal for food as long as she is dating someone as haram as her. Tik hasn't been back to Swee Choon since they broke up.

She sees Emerald brighten up as she pores over the extensive menu. "Any recs?" Tik points out Ploy's favorites: cold cucumber black fungus salad dressed in vinegar and spice, sliced duck in spring onion pastry, deep-fried battered eggplant—crispy on the outside and soft on the inside, topped with feathery pork floss—salt-and-pepper shimeiji mushroom, shrimp-paste-coated chicken wings, smoky hor fun flat rice noodles with sliced fish in a silky egg sauce.

"Oh," Tik adds, "and honey sea coconut with longan for dessert."

"Marvelous." Emerald puts in orders for everything. "Do you come here often?"

"It's been a while," Tik says. A pot of tieguanyin tea is served alongside two porcelain teacups in a metal bowl of boiling water. Tik sterilizes and warms the cup for Emerald, swirling it in the hot water before pouring tea for her. "You know, I didn't think you'd text me . . ."

"Why?"

Tik thinks about how to put it. "We run in different circles."

"I'm not like my sister and her husband," Emerald says airily. Tik is impressed by how direct she is. "I'm more like you and Ploy," Emerald goes on. "Umm, are you seeing each other?"

Out of habit, Tik freezes up. At work, because of how she looks, she assumes that her colleagues and bosses know, though no one ever brings it up. On the gender front, she had a mortifying exchange with an older female inspector with a thinning perm who screeched and chased Tik out of the female bathroom, mistaking her for a male officer, but with regards to her sexuality, there has been nothing but a steadfast radio silence. Someone else may have found it uncomfortable, but Tik is, in fact, comfortable with it. It's status quo, and status quo is gold. Untouchable. Tik isn't about to question it when she's grateful that she's been allowed to serve, when she's proud she's been recognized for doing well in her cohort.

Tik doesn't know if it's because Emerald doesn't know anything about her, because Emerald's just stepped off a plane from New York, because she has a funny feeling Emerald may actually have eaten the butterfly at the airport, or because Emerald's been wearing her heart on her sleeve all day, but Tik wants to be honest. With her, it's possible to say what you mean without adornment.

"We were," Tik answers Emerald, "but not anymore." Suddenly it's this easy, to not have to pretend. It feels good, but it hurts more than she expects. Hardly anyone from her own life knew about Ploy, so she hasn't talked about the fact that it's over.

"Aw," Emerald says. "I'm sorry to hear. What happened?"

At home, it was just Tik and her mom. Tik's younger brother had married and moved out a few years earlier. Mak liked to tell relatives that Tik was so filial, she'd remained a spinster to be by her side.

Tik goes to Hotel 81 motels for hookups—Bugis has fake Degas ballerina paintings, Joo Chiat has lucky cat noren curtains—but she brings serious girlfriends back home to Tampines. It's impossible to explain to someone from the outside, but she brings them home for what she thinks of as Mak's tacit approval. Tik cherishes how her mom cooks for her girlfriends, asks them to call her Mak, and even refers to them as her anak angkak, her adopted children. Tik considered this Mak's way of acceptance, until one of her exes, a linguistics undergrad, posited that it was not an act of affirmation. "Your mom is trying to desexualize your relationships," she said. And it was true. Tik had heard Mak tell her friends, "My Atika is so pure, she's never had any of *those* relations. Atika's not interested in love lah, she's more interested in her job." But Tik's glad enough that Mak is kind to her ladies, even if Mak refuses to see them as her lovers.

With Ploy, however, it's different. After surmising that she wasn't local, after seeing what she was wearing—a low-cut dress, fishnet stockings—after hearing how she spoke English with a Thai accent, Mak said to Tik, "This sort of woman cheat men's money." The worst part of it, Tik thinks, is that Mak couldn't even bring herself to say "This sort of woman cheat your money."

After almost three years—Tik's longest relationship—her mom had never cooked for Ploy when she came over, had never talked to her, and certainly had never asked Ploy to call her Mak. A few months ago, Tik and Ploy forgot to lock the door on a late weekend afternoon.

Mak came into Tik's room with the TV remote. "Atika, you got the AA battery?"

Tik and Ploy had sprung apart the moment Mak stepped in, but it was too late. Mak walked out of the room, crying. Later that evening, she said to Tik: "I won't have that sort of thing happening in my house. What has that Thai woman done, put a spell on you?" Mak had never been strict about prayers, but for the rest of the month she made it a point of unfurling a dusty prayer mat in the living room. She gave Tik the cold shoulder, refusing even to accept the monthly sum that Tik had been giving her ever since she started on her job.

Their four-year anniversary was coming up. Tik waited as usual in a corner of the Golden Mile car park, leaning against her Vespa. She heard the sound of Ploy's heels against concrete, looked up to see her glitter eyeliner, her cute smile. "Tiki-tik! Wait long?" Tik blindsided Ploy with the breakup. She couldn't bring herself to tell Ploy the real reason, so she lied that there was a new girl.

Their hot dishes are served. Duck, mushroom, chicken wings, noodles, and crispy eggplant. Tik picks up a piece of eggplant. "Letting her go was the biggest mistake of my life."

Suddenly Emerald feels very old as she looks at this young, adorable bag of human skin before her, barely thirty probably, proclaiming that an easily reversible thing was the biggest mistake of her life. "Don't be a dumb-ass. Why can't you get back together? She still likes you, I can tell."

"She's better off without me anyway."

"Why's that?"

Tik shrugs. "Cos I'm not a guy."

"What?" Emerald puts down her chopsticks. "Are you serious?"

"Maybe it's no big deal in New York. But it's not normal here, for most people."

"What does this place do to you?" Emerald is retriggered by Paul's comments over dinner. "If straight folks are homophobic, that sucks, but I get it. But you? Why are you putting yourself down?"

She tells Tik what Paul said about the trans kid uniform case. "Can you fucking believe it?"

Tik is quiet. That sinking feeling is back in her chest. "It's not easy being"—she hasn't used words like *gay, lesbian,* or *queer* in her conversations, so it's too hard to say it now—"someone like me in the police force, but Mr. Ong has always been fair to me. Not everyone is so nice, you know?"

"Why do you think him being fair to you is *so nice*?" Emerald challenges her. "Being fair to you is what you deserve."

What I deserve? Tik has never felt entitled to think that.

"You're not asking for anything more than anyone else," Emerald points out. "But you shouldn't settle for anything less either."

"Mr. Ong needs to think for the whole country," Tik says.

Emerald looks at her. "Aren't you part of this country too?"

. . .

After supper it is close to two, but Emerald still doesn't want to go home. They amble around the near-empty streets of Little India, lit by the amber shift of streetlamps. Unlike much of wide-paved, high-rise Singapore, the roads here are narrow, lined by two-story shophouses, some faced in pastel floral Peranakan tiles, others with stucco carvings of animals or plants on the exterior wall. Emerald stops to take pictures of an intricately painted white crane and red hibiscus, sends them to Bartek. As they cross a mosaic-tiled five-foot way, Emerald's shoulder brushes against Tik's. Impulsively, she slides her hand into the crook of Tik's elbow.

"Your hand is so cold," Tik murmurs, tucking Emerald's hand closer to her own body.

Emerald feels the heat of Tik's skin through her thin cotton T-shirt, her knuckles brushing against Tik's rib cage. She is struck by a discomfiting sense of how fragile humans are, something she hasn't thought about in a while. It used to pain her terribly to see lovers aging and ailing when none of it touched her. How unbearable to be adrift, floating above the passage of time, as she watches others drown in its implacable current. She must've broken up and gotten back with the Francophone Haitian poet, he who wrote like Rimbaud and drove like Rajo Jack, a hundred times. She stayed with him in Harlem for decades, at first as his lover and at the end posing as his adopted daughter, caring for him through his polio. The limp leg of his paralysis, his initial refusal to use a crutch, the muscles withering away till he was a floppy sack. When Jean-Baptiste couldn't breathe on his own anymore and had to rely on an iron lung, sealed around neck and waist, he begged her to give him an easier way out. But she could not bear to intervene. She sat unmoving by his side until his breath grew short and at last he sighed his final wet exhale. And Emerald told herself, never again.

She has all the time in the world to figure out her coping mechanisms. It's easier to hurtle like a temperamental breeze through cities, not staying long enough for anything to coalesce around the slipperiness of her immortality. It's simpler to initiate temporary and transactional exchanges with people, not risking the stickiness of real feeling.

Flirting is fun, as long as she doesn't mean it. Emerald has only been in Singapore for a day, has only known Tik over the course of several hours, but she is beginning to be afraid to lose her.

Abruptly, she lets go of Tik's elbow. But her palm has already been warmed by Tik's skin.

It's almost three in the morning by the time they get back to Coronation Drive. "Thanks for coming to get me," Emerald says as she hops off Tik's scooter.

"I would like to thank you too," Tik says with a sincere solemnity.

Emerald has lit a spark in Tik. All her life, she's used to keeping her head low and staying in line. If anyone shows her acceptance, she feels as if they are going hugely out of their way to accommodate her. She's good at taking orders, but not at making decisions. It comes up in her evaluation reports—she *understands the chain of command*, she's *a good team player*. But when it comes to taking the initiative, she finds it difficult to make a move.

"Sorry if I sounded too intense," Emerald says. "I just got here, and I just met you. I'm sure there's a lot I don't understand. I don't want to be shooting my mouth off when I don't know—"

"No," Tik says. "Thank you, Emerald." She's dropped the "Miss," and it feels right. Emerald unbuckles her helmet and passes it back to Tik, who stows it back in the helmet box; it hasn't been used in a while.

"Also." Tik runs a hand through her hair a bit ruefully. "Can I give you my number?"

"Huh?" Emerald looks confused. "Haven't we been texting?"

"Yes, but that's my work phone. I'd like to give you my personal number."

"Ah." Emerald hands her phone over immediately, then wishes she'd moved a little slower. And it's the most basic, most precursory thing, but her heart is hammering in her chest as Tik inputs her digits. She's giving you her phone number, for god's sake, Emerald tells herself, not a tantric massage.

When Tik hands the phone back, Emerald takes one step closer, cherry drop earrings swinging on her earlobes. The air particles in the sliver of space between them are charged with a live voltage. Emerald is so close, Tik can see the freckles on her cheeks, the curl of her eyelashes—and then it is Emerald who leans in. Their lips touch. Emerald is an incredible kisser. The soft intensity of her mouth, the nimble dexterity of her tongue, it sends crystalline glimmers through Tik, and then there's something else she has never felt before—like the wind's being knocked out of her. Like her breath is being taken away. Tik feels lightheaded, but it's so pleasurable—

It is Emerald who suddenly pulls away. "Fuck," she cusses under her breath. "I should go."

Wordlessly, Tik watches as Emerald makes her way back into the house without turning around or saying goodbye. Riding down the empty East Coast Parkway, wind whipping around her, Adidas jacket slapping against her back, Tik is worried she's crossed a line.

. . .

At home, Tik takes a shower and climbs into bed. She's barely gotten a few hours of sleep when she receives a text message from Cheng—Mr. Ong wants her to take over his shift for today.

Back at Coronation Drive again at 7:30 a.m., Tik slugs down a Red Bull energy drink, tapping ash from her Sampoerna into the empty can. She leans on her Vespa as she finishes the cig. Tik looks up nervously at the bungalow's imposing facade, wondering which room Emerald is sleeping in. Tik has the keys to the house, but she's never stepped inside before.

Like clockwork, Mr. Ong emerges at a quarter to eight.

"Good morning, Mr. Ong," Tik greets him as he settles into the back seat. They drive off.

Mr. Ong nods at her. "I heard you took Emerald to Golden Mile yesterday afternoon."

"Yes, sir," Tik says carefully. Surely Emerald hasn't told him about last night? He is looking at her in the rearview mirror.

"What do you think of her?"

"She's, umm . . ." Tik stalls, trying to figure where this is going, trying to be discreet in front of the poker-faced chauffeur. "She's very different from Mrs. Ong."

"I concur with that." A pause. "How long have you been working for me, Tik?"

Tik counts in her head. "About half a year now."

"And you like being part of my personal security team?" His tone is light, even friendly.

"Yes, sir." Is there anything else she can say?

"Good." He leans back. There's more coming—she can feel it in the air between them. "I want you to keep an eye on Emerald," he says. "See what she gets up to. Do you think you can do that?"

Their eyes meet in the mirror. It occurs to Tik that she has never said no to him before. He nods, already assuming her allegiance.

"And, Tik? You report to me. Not to Suzhen."

. . .

Emerald wakes up with the faintest taste of Tik's qi still on her tongue. Cherry cola, with an afternote of cloves. Delicious. She bites down on her own tongue hard enough to draw blood as a punishment. How could she have sipped on Tik? She just wanted to know what she tasted like—and, to be honest, she's glad she found out. Some people look cute but taste ghastly.

Make sure it's a one-off thing, she scolds herself.

She sighs, checks her phone. It's 9:00 a.m. in Singapore, 9:00 p.m. in New York. Still no new messages from Bartek. Maybe he's in a hypomanic painting spurt. She sends an update anyway: *Help, I think I might be falling for real.* Emerald closes iMessage, peeps at Bartek's Instagram. No new updates, no new stories. She taps on his last post: a photo she took of him in his apartment. Just the right amount of sunlight is shining on the Neapolitan ice cream–colored grandma couch they filched off the street. Bartek is lounging on it in his boxers, drinking his first coffee of the day. She held up her phone, and he immediately started posing. She got him to unbutton his shirt as she arranged a lush pot of monstera in front of his crotch. "Give me love eyes," she directed. He put it on main, captioning it "bloomers," followed by a green leaf emoji and the eggplant emoji. She missed his silly, lopsided grin. She leaves a slew of green heart emojis in the comments so he'll know she misses him.

She steps into the freestanding shower. The night out with Tik has left her in a more contemplative mood than usual, which always happens when she's falling in love. It's so easy to blaze through a day picking a bone with people, the weather, yourself, the news, but even after all this time, in the first flush of a crush she is reduced to a thing that wants to make a killer playlist, that stares at dust particles catching the sunlight like they're distant stars. How gross and cute it is to be human. Once in a while, she misses the cutting truth of the wild: *eat fuck kill*.

Emerald shakes Tik out of her mind by switching the water to cold, letting out a tiny shriek as she avoids the wound. It's healing nicely, after Bartek's handiwork. So Su knew about it. The immediate sense of violation she experienced the day before has cooled by now. She tries to weigh it out—whether there's something good, something sweet, in this. Su is always there for her when she gets herself into trouble. It's something Emerald is grateful for, yet she's never thanked Su for it.

Emerald towels off, changes into a vintage chartreuse silk slip, and opens the door cautiously. Outside the guest room door, on a small walnut tray, is a wabi-sabi ceramic bowl of sweet soybean pudding, with a walnut spoon beside it. A humble dessert, but douhua means something between them. It was one of the first foods they were able to eat in their human skins back in Hangzhou—it was easy on the stomach, just a warm silkiness that slid down the throat.

Emerald is already in the mood to make up. Now she lets herself segue into full-on nostalgia as she tastes the delicate flavor of the soybean pudding. She patters out of the room, feeling soft as a kitten that's just lapped up some milk and is waiting to be picked up.

Su is at the kitchen sink, washing cooking utensils, a cotton apron loose around her slender waist, her hair gathered neatly in a low chignon. She moves around the kitchen with such familiarity, grace, and comfort—

humming Chopin, bumping her hip against a soft-close drawer to shut it, carefully placing a jar of paprika back in its proper position on the spice rack. Su's attention to detail, which sometimes drives Emerald crazy, now makes her heart melt. There is something so unspeakably vulnerable in her need for order as she shifts the rosemary and cinnamon so that the jars are evenly spaced. Emerald watches as Su returns a slab of butter to the fridge. The fridge is bursting at its seams with fresh produce—stalks of celery, a bushel of ripe red tomatoes.

Emerald has never seen the draw of a well-stocked pantry. On the few occasions when she had her own place, her own fridge, the only stuff she chucked in it was Coke Zero and free-range raw eggs. Anything else seemed too daunting, too permanent, too pinned-down.

On the marble tabletop is a breakfast spread for one. Two perfectly roasted spears of white asparagus, a poached egg, and hollandaise sauce. A bowl of consommé. Pour-over coffee—Emerald spots the precision scales—and a jug of oat milk beside it. "Damn," Emerald says as she approaches Su. "Is this what Paul wakes up to every morning?"

"I try to rotate the menu for variety," Su says earnestly as Emerald slips into a chair. "I wasn't sure what time you'd be up. Food's gone a little cold now, maybe I should pop it in the microwave?"

Emerald shrugs. "I'm easy."

Su takes the plate, then hesitates. "But if I microwave it, the poached egg will overcook . . ."

"Oh my god, Jie, chill. It's nice enough that you cooked, it doesn't have to be Top Chef." She digs in, it's delicious. "Oof, I love a good consommé. You just keep leveling up."

Having Emerald in her home, drinking soup she's been up clarifying with egg whites since seven, makes Su happy in a way that she hasn't been in a long time. I've really missed you, she thinks.

"I, uhh, said some stuff I shouldn't have last night," Emerald mumbles, her mouth full.

"Likewise." Su is glad that Emerald has brought it up. "I'm just glad you're safe." Once every couple of decades, Emerald is bound to pull something like that on herself, a brush with death that was the result of an idiotic, banal decision, and in Su's eyes, completely avoidable. Given Emerald's reckless ways, Su is surprised she's made it through the centuries in one piece.

"By the way," Emerald asks, "how did you find out?"

Su reddens, shakes her head.

"Tell me," Emerald presses. "I promise I won't get mad."

Reluctantly, Su shows Emerald her Google Alerts. "I didn't know what else to do . . ."

As Emerald scrolls through myriad pings for "green+snake," she doesn't know whether to laugh or to cry. Picturing Su screening these alerts on a daily basis, looking for any glimpse of her in them, makes her feel sick and sweet. "Jie, I don't know. Can't you just, like, text and ask what's up?" They're both quiet for a bit. They know it's not as easy as that.

"More coffee?" Su asks to break the increasingly pensive silence. Emerald shakes her head. "I booked us a spa," Su goes on. "Thought we could use some pampering after the long flight."

"Oh," Emerald says, "OK." She misses the old days where they would sprawl in their snake skin on the bank of West Lake, doing nothing, lying so close she could feel Su's breathing.

In their human skin now, everything comes with a fancy framework: putting tiny pieces of food in their mouths in pricey restaurants, getting their skin kneaded at luxury spas. The bells and whistles of consumption save them from having to really connect. They can while away hours engaged in some form of opulent activity, seemingly together, yet without exactly being with each other. Su catches the surface of her doubt. "Or we could do something else?"

"No, no," Emerald says, not wanting to spoil Su's plans. "Sounds good."

. . .

Sentosa Island is a strip of mostly reclaimed land on the southernmost tip of Singapore, positioned as a beach resort, a gated enclave for the global rich with yachts docked in their backyard waterways.

The beachfront, with its glittering powdery white sand, is manmade. The exclusive spa that Su has booked is nestled in the western tip of the island, housed in a refurbished barracks flanked by palm trees. Several Europeans make up the hospitality staff, each displaying an attentive smile and a frangipani flower tucked behind an ear. A Swedish lady leads them into their private treatment room: two teakwood massage tables on a veranda that opens into unspoiled tropical jungle. Balinese strings play from enclosed speakers, intermingling with the rhythmic chorus of cicadas, harmonies rising and ebbing like polyphonic tides.

The masseuse warms an aromatic oil, applying it to Emerald's back in flowing strokes, easing into an Ayurvedic massage style. Whatever windy notions Emerald had about the superficiality of consumption and capitalism have floated very far away right now—this feels amazing, just what she needs. Emerald is falling asleep as they near the end of the session. She hears Su's masseuse say to her in a thoughtful tone: "Would you like to try our Dead Sea exfoliation treatment, Miss Bai? Your skin is a little on the dry side."

Emerald turns to peek at Su. The skin on her face, neck, and arms is well moisturized, but the skin on her back looks dull, even a touch gray. "That won't be necessary." Su pulls on a linen robe to cover herself. The masseuses serve mint tea before leaving the room to let them rest. The moment they are alone, Emerald turns to Su.

"How long has it been?"

"Since?"

"Don't be an ass. You know what I'm asking."

Su can fool anyone else, but not Emerald.

"Eight years," she says, relenting.

"*Eight years?*"

At first Su's skin itched terribly when molting season came around. Spending torturous hours in the tub, she exfoliated with a loofah till her skin tore. Molting is necessary for the healthy functioning of her body, but she finds it shameful. Not everyone is a natural at passing.

Even if Su makes sure she looks just as she wants to look, moves how she's coached herself to move, and relates to people in accordance with the scripts she's observed other humans using, it's still impossible for her, on most days, to go about her life without worrying that the meticulously painted stage backdrop will slip and she'll be caught with her tail up.

"That can't be healthy. Don't you break out?"

Su doesn't want to tell Emerald about steroids and peels. Torn skin and midnight sweats.

"You can learn how to manage an itch," Su tells her. "Eventually it goes away."

Su lives defensively. Anxious to blend in as much as she can, so no one will see that she isn't one of them. Emerald lives audaciously. Do you want life to have its way with you, or do you want to have your way with life? She doesn't seek to be visible, but the ease with which she moves through the world makes her stand out. Assured in her duality, she doesn't place passing on a pedestal. Emerald coos at reptiles. Winks at people who find her sinuous walk sexy. A few times, caught with her forked tongue, she's passed it off as goth-girl body mod with a roguish grin.

"Sure," Emerald says, "but the more you try to control it, the more pleasurable it becomes to scratch it, when you finally cave in."

In Victorian London, after Emerald left, Su saw the Oscar Wilde play *Lady Windermere's Fan* with her husband. When a character declared in act 1, "I can resist everything except temptation," Duncan patted her knee. "Sounds just like your sister."

A koel bird cries its distinctive *ooh-woo, ooh-woo*, breaking Su out of her guilt-laced recollection. She watches as Emerald climbs off the massage table. Puts on a linen robe. Drifts toward the timber deck, looking out at the jungle below. The single-story veranda is some fifteen feet from the ground. Su catches the loamy scent of decaying foliage mixed with the musk of unseen creatures—she doesn't want to admit it, but it smells so *good*.

Emerald's smile is beguiling. "C'mon, Jie. Old times' sake?"

Emerald reaches out to her. Su feels unusually alert as she takes her sister's hand. Being with Emerald is like taking in an exquisite stream of qi. It makes you feel ready for just about anything. They're standing together on the edge of the veranda, hand in hand.

"Let's go," Emerald whispers. Before Su has time to think, Emerald jumps off the veranda, pulling Su with her—

Su's stomach lurches, but Emerald squeezes her hand as they glide past mossy trunks and wild orchids, wrapped in the fecund aroma of moist soil and overripe fruit. Su lets her palms touch the waxy leaves and soft flowers. Looks up at the towering trees reaching toward the sky, branches heavy with fern and liana. Shafts of dappled sunlight pierce the thick canopy, casting feathery shadows on the forest floor.

Ooh-woo. Emerald whips around, distracted by the sound.

Silently, Emerald cracks the bones in her neck from side to side.

She takes a sniff of the air, and spots the koel bird in a rain tree. The whites of her eyes have turned a coruscating amber gold. Su watches, transfixed—it's been so long since they've hunted together.

Emerald stares at the bird. At first it continues to groom itself on the branch. But as Emerald trains her gaze on it, the bird begins to skitter. Spreading its wings, it tries to take flight but falters, as if weighed down. As if it's being reeled in, faster and faster, by an invisible line toward Emerald, who catches it in her hand. The bird is a desperate flurry of feathers—

For a moment, Su is back in the drawing room in London. Standing on a chair, opening the gilded cage. She can feel the canary's struggling warmth between her fingers as she brings it to her mouth—

Emerald takes a bit of the koel's qi, then releases it, without making a mess. It shoots off into the treetops. "Tastes like corn chips. What does Paul taste like? Soup without stock?"

Animal spirits who partner up tend to leach qi off their other halves. As a one-off snack, it isn't harmful, but if done regularly, qi depletion takes a toll. The spouses of animal spirits often die young, of unspecified causes. It can't be pinpointed in a medical examination or postmortem, and tends to be attributed to undetectable respiratory issues. The temptation—the ease of its supply—is always there, but Su has never liked to take her husband's qi.

"I only do it once a month," Su says, trying not to recall the gamy scent of the goat farm.

"No details please." Emerald assumes she is talking about Paul. "I don't wanna know about your sex life!"

The jungle's dense foliage gives way to a sandy dune. They reach a rocky slope that descends to a small hidden beach. Su can feel the powdery grains of sand molding beneath her feet. Under the rugged overhanging precipice of the cliff is a narrow fissure, not much wider than an outstretched arm. Emerald squishes herself sideways into the gap, but she can go no farther. She sticks her hand in as far as it will go. "Huh." She sniffs her fingers. Holds her hand out to Su. Su inhales. She too catches the unmistakable mineral vapor of underground water.

"Ready?" Emerald slips the robe off her shoulders suggestively, turning to look at Su.

Su's eyes widen. "Wait wait wait, this is Singapore—"

"Why do you say that like it's a warning?" Emerald scoffs. "Look at this gorgeous place!" She sweeps her hand vaguely at the broad fronds of the palm trees along the shore, the verdant canopy of the jungle behind them. With a lilting, tempting inflection she repeats Su's words, only now it sounds different, like an open invitation, full of possibilities: "This. Is. Singapore!"

Su spins around to be sure there's no one. The beach is secluded.

When she turns back, Emerald isn't there anymore. Her robe is on the gravelly ground. Su shimmies into the gap.

"Xiaoqing?" she calls into the darkness. Her voice echoes.

. . .

The massage appointment was for an hour. Tik has been waiting around the motorcycle area of the car park for close to two hours, but she hasn't seen Mrs. Ong or Emerald leaving the spa. She's scoped it out. There's only one point of entry and exit, through the glass front doors of the refurbished barracks. Cautiously Tik enters and heads for the reception counter, where she receives a tepid welcome—none of the solicitous hospitality so readily extended to other guests.

"Grab driver?" the receptionist asks in lieu of hello. "Please wait outside."

Tik's prideful part wants to say no, she isn't just some ride-share-app driver, but her coolheadedness kicks in, and she tries to make the casual racism work for her. "Sorry to bother you. The passenger isn't picking up my calls, so I'm wondering if she's still here—Suzhen?"

"Her session ended an hour ago."

"Did you see her leave?" Tik presses.

"I don't think your passenger is here anymore if it's been an hour . . ."

Tik smokes a Sampoerna in the carpark, then goes around the back of the spa center. It opens up to the jungle: she can see a few treatment beds on patios shaded by bamboo curtains and ficus trees. Tik walks around the fringe of the jungle, venturing a little deeper, but the underbrush is thick—it's not easy to get through—and the carpet of fallen leaves doesn't leave any traces of footprints. The jungle pulses with the rhythmic drone of cicadas, the high-pitched hum of beetles. A macaw screeches, breaking the buzzing crescendo. When the wind stills, the leaves and branches stop rustling for a beat, before a breeze starts them up again.

Tik is making her way back out when she sees it on a patch of soft moss. A single cherry drop earring, thin gold stem and polished wine-red resin gleaming in the sunlight.

11

To Toe the Line She Swallowed the Hook

Al Su can hear is the soft rasp of her own scales brushing against the rocky surface, like dry leaves ready to catch fire at the slightest spark. At first she dissociates from seeing the world in dichromatic vision. It's been such a long time. But as her eyes get used to the blues and greens, she calms down and uncoils herself.

The white snake can't see the green snake in front of her, but she grows aware of scents and vibrations farther ahead. There is only one way forward: darker and damper as the surface cave opening narrows into a tunnel that winds deeper into the earth.

Her muscles, lean and contiguous, beg to undulate, but she has forgotten how. The white snake moves with great caution, inching forward like a woman in heels taking small, careful steps. As she pushes forward into these enclosed confines, farther and farther away from the hyperpresence of prying eyes, traffic noise, advertisement billboards, banner notifications, professional meetings, and social obligations, the corseted cinch of anxiety begins to unclench from her mind.

She starts to shake her long, hipless body from side to side, at first shyly, then with vigor, and finally, pure abandonment. She writhes through the twists and bends of the rocky passage, a silvery sash hypnotized by her own coiling motion, the earthy pleasure of rubbing the entire length of her underbelly against textured stone, the sensorial grounding of having her chin so close to the ground, of flicking her tongue through the air to collect dispatches of information.

The air is tinged with moisture—there's water up ahead. A musty, fungal odor—likely bats. And above it all: the brisk, summery notes of the green snake's citrusy scent.

The percussive rustling of the white snake's scales whispers through the tunnel as she picks up speed—

Around a tight bend, the narrow corridor dips and opens up into a cavern with a sinkhole. The white snake raises her head in wonderment. An underground lake, unevenly shaped but close to fifty feet wide in some places. Dim light filters through a few cracks, faintly illuminating the cavern. Stalactites protrude from its rocky ceiling, wavy reflections mottled in the lake's currents.

In the middle of the lake, the water shimmers, rippling gently.

Xiaoqing. The white snake plunges into the water, hurtling toward the viridescent jewel-green glow. Underwater, the two snakes meet face-to-face and intertwine their bodies, green over white, white over green. It's been so long since they've been side by side, scale to scale.

They race around the lake in concentric circles, bolts of light slicing through subterranean darkness.

As snakes, they went years without the company of anyone else, and they were more than enough for each other. Happiness was astonishingly easy. Chins and bellies on sun-warmed rocks. A new hide. The taste of a wild mushroom, and someone to share it with. How seamlessly they had foraged, hunted, and nested in Hangzhou. The white snake looks over at the green snake.

It is glorious to be by her side. To be without language, without distraction, with someone you love. Language has given them ways of hiding from each other. She used to know Emerald so well. How she stretched her mouth back to read the wind, the kink in her tail whenever she was stressed. Now she is used to the lonely malleability of her own human face, this skin's repertoire of disguises. The grins and grimaces she puts on for the mood, for the occasion. The currency of spoken language forces everything to be too precise, yet not enough. Each time they went out to hunt together as snakes, everything was unsaid, but they knew they would have died for each other in a heartbeat. She didn't realize how much she has missed this primal immediacy.

The white snake's skin tingles from head to tail. Vortices of dark water swirl around her.

Su breaks the lake's surface first, whipping her long, dark hair behind her, catching her breath. As the air fills her human lungs again, she is pulled back to that first night in Hangzhou, under the midautumn moon at West Lake, where the azaleas were still in bloom.

Then Emerald appears behind her, laughing and splashing, disturbing the placid surface of the water and the quiet stillness of the cave.

"Jie," her voice echoes, "it's been so long!"

Bats fly out of eaves in the rocky ceiling, flapping their wings across the lake. With a flick of her tail, Emerald sends a wave of water to disturb the bats. They screech, circling around the cave before flapping back to the corners of the stalactites. Emerald laughs and sends an even larger wave this time. The displacement of the tide momentarily exposes the creatures in the shallows of the cave's shore: a bunch of small button snails, a big crab, a knobbly sea cucumber.

Su uses her own tail to calm the water. "Don't make a scene."

Waist up, they are their gorgeous human selves. Belly button down, their skins meld into a tapestry of iridescent scales—Su's white and Emerald's green—tapering seamlessly into snake tails. Neither human nor animal, it is the form truest to what they are, but one they rarely take. It combines their best strengths, but it gives them away immediately as otherworldly beings.

"It's not a scene if there's no one here to see it." Emerald backstrokes leisurely. Then she paddles up to Su and looks into her eyes. "Come on," she offers, "let me help you with it . . ."

Su shakes her head. "I told you, I don't need to molt anymore."

"Maybe you don't *need* to. But maybe you *want* to."

Emerald swirls behind Su. When Su doesn't protest, she uses the end of her fingernail to draw a fine slit from the back of Su's neck down the length of her spine, stopping just above her tail. Carefully Emerald peels back the thin layer of Su's old skin on each side. It comes off in an unbroken, filmy piece, as if she's unzipping Su out of a body-con dress—shoulders, arms, waist, tail. The old skin slips off Su like a used stocking, down into the water, as they swim across the lake. Her new skin beneath is dewy, her scales bright. There isn't a bump to give her pregnancy away yet, but just about where her skin meets her scales, she feels a warm flutter from deep within.

"You're so pretty this way." Emerald trails behind Su so she can watch her swishing.

Does Emerald really think so? As far as Su knows, Emerald does not experience her dysphoria. Hours in front of the mirror, knotting silk scarves around her long, slender neck to make it look shorter before she can bear to step out of the house, checking her eyes repeatedly in a pocket mirror to make sure her true pupils are not visible. Practicing her walk, back and forth endlessly down the corridor, when Paul isn't home. Hiring a voice coach to make sure her tongue doesn't betray any sibilance, not believing him when he says her enunciation is perfect.

"Xiaoqing," Su asks as they swim toward the shore. "Why is it so easy for you?"

"Why is what so easy for me?"

"Being this . . . and that. It's like there's no difference to you."

"I like myself as a snake as much as I like myself as a woman."

Su can't understand why Emerald doesn't delineate between *snake* and *woman*. Isn't the point of transitioning to stay above the fold? To relinquish what's underneath, where they've come from? Su tries to place as much distance as she can between what she thinks of as her higher self, the beautiful woman everyone wants to be around, and her base instincts, the white snake they would exterminate without hesitation. Su asks: "But aren't you afraid of being found out?"

"What makes you think I'm not afraid?" Emerald says as they pull themselves up onshore, bellies down, tails in the shallows and elbows in the sand.

"The way you move about the world . . ." Su shrugs. "It's like you think you're invincible."

"I'm afraid of getting caught," Emerald says, "but I'm even more afraid of forgetting who I am to survive. And let's be real, what does survival mean these days anyway? It's not just food and shelter. Humans have gotten themselves stuck shitless by trying to jump through stupid hoops."

Su doesn't think the hoops are stupid—they give life some structure.

"Jie—" Emerald inches closer. "Do you ever think about that tree?"

"Which tree?" Su asks, but she knows which one. The weeping willow on West Lake.

"Never mind."

Su turns to her. Their foreheads are almost touching. "Of course I remember that tree," she says softly. "How could I ever forget?" She pauses. "Have you been back to West Lake?"

Emerald is shaking her head.

"No?" Su is surprised.

"I've thought about it." Emerald beats about the bush as she avoids Su's gaze. But when their eyes meet, she says it straight: "Don't you know? Hangzhou wouldn't be Hangzhou without you."

"I've never been back either." Su presses her cool forehead against Emerald's cheek.

A gentle wave rocks their bodies back and forth. Then Emerald flips around, jolting the current with her tail. Su dips her tail into the sand so she doesn't get washed away. "Fuck all this human bullshit," Emerald declares. Su sees the light dancing in her eyes. "It's overrated. Aren't you sick of it?" She cocks her head at Su, and switches to Mandarin: "Let's go back. We can live as snakes at West Lake again . . ."

Su's heart catches at the familiar cadence, but she doesn't know if Emerald is serious. The butterfly sensation presses her abdomen, a buoyant feeling swirling within. Su stares at the tip of a stalactite and replies in English: "I don't know if I could live like that again."

"Why do you say *like that* as if it's such a bad thing?"

"I have a husband," Su reminds her, reminds herself. "And the house—we just renovated it."

Emerald groans. "Jie, seriously?"

Su doesn't like the way Emerald talks and makes her feel. Isn't there a certain tyranny in her easy presumption that her bohemian way is better than everyone else's bourgeois tendencies?

"I like it here in Singapore," Su says. "I really do."

"Tell me exactly what you like about it."

"Many things." Su generalizes. "It's clean. It's comfortable. It's convenient . . ."

"It's gotta be more than that. Tell me, for real. I want to know."

"It's a place where . . ." Su tries to pinpoint it. "As long as people follow the script, they're safe."

"*Safe?*" Emerald scoffs. "There's so much more to life than being safe."

But at the end of the day, is there really? People need safety as a bedrock. There is nothing embarrassing about that, it's how most humans function. Let Emerald think it's prosaic if she wants. Su knows better. Safety is grounding. Stability is strength.

"What about the people who go off-script?" Emerald is asking. "Those who have no script?"

"Well—" Su considers this briefly. Her tone turns cold. "I'm not one of those people, I guess."

Emerald falls silent. Su registers the disappointment in her eyes. They are lying on the same sand, but a gulf opens up between them. The hope in Su's stomach chills into a hard, rubbery thing. The stalactites are no longer pretty. They're sharp and ominous, ready to fall at any moment, to pierce through them. She is suddenly conscious of their stark nakedness. Her nipples prickle, and a shrinking, sobering shudder runs through her from head to tail.

Her *tail*. What is she doing?

They must get out of here. She's lost track of time. Emerald led them to this underground lake, but Su won't be seduced by her feral liabilities. She needs to get back on schedule. The abortion is set for tomorrow morning. She planned to make roast beef for dinner, Paul's favorite, but now she won't have time to thaw the frozen cuts of prime Wagyu. When she went vegan, he told her it's sissy for a man to subsist on vegetables, and he needs his red meat to function, so she makes it a point to cook accordingly.

"It's late," she says abruptly. "Paul will worry if we're not home."

"Why do you let him enslave you like this?"

"No one's enslaving me." Su is annoyed. "Must you use words like that?"

"Then it's you." Emerald's eyes flash darkly. "You're keeping yourself down."

. . .

Paul opens a bottle of chardonnay as he waits for Su and Emerald to get home. Su is a teetotaller, but let's see about that sister. On a typical day, it ticks him off when Su isn't home before him. Her activities are leisurely, her meetings ad hoc; surely they could be arranged around his schedule? The stress of the workday starts to melt away once he opens the door and can see all the way through into the kitchen, where Su will be fussing over whatever she is preparing for dinner.

Today, however, he's got other things on his mind. Tik rode over on her motorcycle to the Ministry of Education, waited around until he knocked off. "So?" he asked expectantly. She started sputtering about Sentosa, how Su and Emerald didn't leave the spa through the front.

"Through the front?" He tried to understand what she was saying.

Tik explained that there isn't a back door to the spa center, that she waited for two hours with her eyes on the glass doors in the front, the only point of entry and exit. When she walked around the jungle in the back, though, she found this—she showed him the cherry drop earring.

Paul took it from Tik and turned it over in his hand. He'd noticed the cherry earrings in Emerald's ears the night before at dinner, and tried not to look at them. They felt vaguely sexually suggestive.

"I think they went into the jungle," Tik said.

She showed him a picture she'd taken on her phone. It was real jungle, not a paved path. He could not imagine Su going off into the wild like that. She liked to remain in air-conditioned spaces, didn't like to perspire, and didn't even own a pair of sports shoes, only heels and ballet flats.

Paul might have doubted Tik if not for the goats.

A man had come up to him at a Meet-the-People session some time ago, very nervous, asking to speak with him privately. "Mr. Ong. I don't know how to say this. But every now and then ah, your wife comes to my farm to kill goats." Paul was about to dismiss him with a warning about slander, when the man said he didn't know exactly what she did in the shed, but whenever she left, the goats had been suffocated to death, and there was a strong jasmine smell.

Paul froze at the last part. "Jasmine?"

The man nodded. "Yah, like the flower . . ."

Paul wanted to pay the man to keep all of this to himself, but he declined. Su already paid him good money, he said, and swear to god, he wasn't going to tell anyone else—but he thought that as her husband, Paul should know.

Paul returned home that day and observed Su.

She was just as beautiful, just as dutiful. She put gourmet meals on the table, picked up after him, lay down in missionary for him. She was his trophy wife. She looked the part. She played the part. So what if she had an unusual coping mechanism? Everyone was stressed out of their skulls and needed somewhere to act out. Some people took spin classes. Others floated around in sensory deprivation tanks. Su strangled goats. He could live with it. Don't ask, don't tell. Then it sprang to his mind: perhaps asphyxiation turned her on! And so he tried to choke her lightly the next time they had sex, but Su merely looked amused at how unconvincingly he did it. That spoiled the whole mood. He deflated instantly. Turning away, lying beside her, he was struck by a soul-crushing visual: she might have done this somewhere else, with someone else, and it could have been a good time.

He tried to focus on what Tik was saying. "You think they went into the jungle."

Tik nodded. He took his phone out and called Su. Several rings later, she picked up.

"Hi my dear." He kept his voice even. "Where are you?" She said that they were on their way home, and dinner would be late. "No problem," he told her. "I'll see you back at home." He hung up.

Tik looked worried, as if he might think she was lying or, perhaps worse, incompetent.

"Mr. Ong, I swear—"

He cut in. "Next time, I want you to go after them, or stay there until they appear again."

On the ride home, Paul seethed in silence. He'd known Emerald was bad news from the start. And it wasn't just the weird hair and sharp tongue. She was the sort of self-centering, self-regarding woman he despised. She didn't see how selfish it was to put her freedom ahead of all else, at the expense of social conventions and familial imperatives. If everyone was like that, birth rates would plummet, the economy would stagnate, and morals would degenerate. He wasn't even exaggerating.

Paul is still swirling his red wine sullenly when he hears the key turn in the lock. The two women spill into the house, linked elbows and enigmatic smiles. Quite the pair, he has to admit, but why can't Emerald dress more decently? Today she's in what looks like a nightie.

"Hi girls." He waves at them stiffly, makes a point to look at the wall clock. "Hello."

"Paulie." Su comes over. "Sorry we're late, are you hungry? I wanted to make roast beef—"

"Something simple will do." He pats Su's hand primly, hoping his dissatisfaction registers.

Just as he expects, Emerald does not join Su in the kitchen. She sprawls on the Eames recliner in the living room. He sits on the opposite sofa. "Would you like a drink while we wait?"

"No thanks. Jie doesn't like me to drink. She thinks it makes me lose my—temper."

He raises a brow. "What happens when you lose your temper?"

"Ha." She makes a scoffing sound. "Let's not go there, Paul."

There's an unflappable confidence about Emerald that rankles him. How can this nobody disregard the respect his stature accords him? At work, it's a no-brainer. Everyone junior to him—whether in status or age—is so deferential. No one dares to call him by his name, even when he tells them explicitly that they can, in an attempt to make himself seem more approachable.

"So," he asks, would-be casually, "what did you ladies get up to today?"

Emerald shrugs. "Hung out a bunch."

"It's a pity we didn't start off on the right foot," Paul tries to connect with her in another way, to find common ground with her. "You know, you made me think about my UPenn days . . ."

It's been so long since Paul's talked about that time of his life. The first thing that struck him was how blue the Philly sky was, he tells Emerald. It was the farthest from home he'd been; the only other country he'd previously been to was Malaysia, just across the border. As a scholar, he lived in a single college-house dorm, and he could not get over how quiet everything was, how much control he had over his environment for the first time. His mother had absconded when he was a child; his father was an alcoholic security guard who lashed him with a thick leather belt for kicks. Just being on campus was magical—like when he discovered the Henry Charles Lea Library tucked away on the sixth floor of Van Pelt Center, with its handsome dark wood shelves, ornate busts, rare books and manuscripts.

This was where Paul discovered Walt Whitman's patriotic, rhapsodic free verse. *I will make inseparable cities with their arms about each other's necks / By the love of comrades.*

It lit a fire in him. He wished he was studying literature instead of philosophy, politics, and economics, but that wasn't something he had a choice in. It had been decided in advance for him. Any deviation from the plan was out of the question. In his second year, Paul saved up enough money for a secondhand motorcycle and got a license. His very first trip out of Philadelphia, he took Route 611 all the way to the Pocono Mountains. When the roads curved, he surprised himself.

Speeding up instead of slowing down, pushing past eighty miles per hour, feeling like he could throw everything—the 4.0 GPA, the deep validation that came with the distinction of being a President's Scholar, the solid promise of an iron rice bowl and a fast-tracked career once he entered the Party as a junior cadre—away just for this fleeting, hot exhilaration. Hurtling by ghost towns without stopping, Paul felt possessed by the freedom of the road and the majesty of the landscape as it grew more and more dramatic before his eyes, till he reached Mount Pocono. This was the closest he'd ever come to a spiritual awakening: the world was so big, and he was so small. It was the opposite of how he would end up feeling in Singapore. The world was so small, and he was so big.

The wine must have loosened his tongue. He has been babbling for a while now.

Emerald's eyes have softened. "What do you miss most?"

"Just responding to the call of the open road . . ."

Emerald smiles a little. "Why don't you do that here?"

"I'm a minister now. I have to act like a minister."

"Ministers can't ride motorcycles and read Walt Whitman?" Emerald looks genuinely sorry for him. Paul realizes with an abrupt, unfamiliar jolt that he may have overshared.

Su arrives with somen in tsuyu sauce, blanched vegetables, delicately crisped agedashi tofu. She could hear the to-and-fro of their voices from the kitchen, and at first she was pleased that they seemed to be conversing without arguing, but as it went on, she grew worried that Emerald might be flirting with Paul, and Paul might be enjoying it. She hates this suspicion, and knows full well that it stems from the Hangzhou scholar poet baggage rather than from any of Emerald's current actions, but that self-awareness doesn't make her distrust go away.

She produces a smile as she sets the dishes down. "What were you two talking about?"

"Paul was just telling me about his time as a student in Philly."

"Oh?" Now Su is genuinely surprised. He's rarely talked about that, even with her.

"He said the thing he misses most—"

"It was a very long time ago," Paul cuts in. He surveys the dishes. "Is this all there is to eat?"

"I thought you said something simple would do," Su falters. "I can heat up some pork belly?"

"There's no need for that." Paul says passive-aggressively. Every time he drips a tiny fleck of sauce on the table, he picks up his tissue, folding it into ever-smaller squares to wipe up. When he finishes, he excuses himself to the master bedroom curtly: "Some of us have to work tomorrow."

Tossing and turning in bed, Paul reflects that it is the romanticized persona of America—the road, the wind, the speed, and his bike melding to create an illusion of freedom—that he is nostalgic for. But even as a student back then, he could already see that this ideal was neither concrete nor real.

Sure, detractors would call the Party's approach heavy-handed. Naifs might bleat on about how Singapore isn't a true-blue democracy.

But any pragmatist who wants to get things done, and who has a real heart for the people on the ground, will understand that it is an absolute hard-fought boon that Singapore's effective governance does not operate like DC's political circus.

A spoiled, individualistic party girl like Emerald would never understand the social cohesion and greater good the Party tries its best to support, so that Singapore can move forward together.

New York suits her well, Paul thinks. She should head back there sooner rather than later. He closes his eyes and pretends to be asleep when he hears Su enter the master bedroom.

She slips into the adjoining bathroom. As Paul listens to the soft whir of her electric toothbrush, he thinks about how much he loves her. He thinks about how she never expresses any political thoughts of her own, and how this is part of what makes her a perfect woman. A woman who is glad, even grateful, to follow his lead on all matters, who acknowledges that he knows better, who understands that his micromanaging comes from a place of deep care. She trusts him to act in her best interests, and he takes his responsibility toward her sincerely and seriously. He realizes, with a warm feeling, that this mirrors the relationship between Singaporeans and the Party, too.

. . .

Pink lotus fronds are in full bloom at the crooked courtyard on the southern end of West Lake. Su has forgotten what they smell like—a touch of sultry spice in the faint scent of sweet mud. Goldfish swim up to the sides of the pond. People around her are feeding them little brown pellets. The goldfish overlap each other to get to the food, mouths gaping greedily, bright orange bellies protruding, dappled tails swishing from side to side. Su can't take her eyes off them. They are so shiny, and they won't stop wiggling. Her eyes trail a particularly fat one, close to the edge. If I move fast enough, she tells herself, no one will notice. She is about to dart at it when someone taps on her shoulder. Startled, Su freezes. When she opens her eyes, she sees Paul peering down at her.

"Suzhen." He is visibly irritated. "Where's my shirt and tie?"

The helper presses each of Paul's shirts and ties before they go into the wardrobe. Of course he knows where all of them are kept and could have done it himself, but Su has always picked out a shirt and tie for him the night before, hanging the ensemble neatly on the powder room rack.

"Oh." She sits up, getting her bearings. It's a few minutes to seven. Her daily wake-up time is typically around six thirty, so she doesn't need to set an alarm, but today she's slept right through.

"What is going on with you?" Paul demands. Answering back, staying out late, derelicting her duties—this was not the Suzhen he knew. "It's Emerald, isn't it? I don't know what the two of you have been up to, but I'm not comfortable with having her as a guest in our house for much longer . . ."

"She's my sister—"

"And I'm your *husband*!" Paul says in an angry whisper, as if that's the final word in the world.

She slips away to pick out a pale-blue shirt and a navy tie for him, then goes down to make soft-boiled eggs, bacon, and toast for breakfast. When Su hears Paul coming down the stairs, she notices that he is in a white shirt and a maroon tie instead. Paul goes straight to the dining table without looking at her. She puts breakfast before him.

He stops eating when he finds a tiny bit of eggshell, picking it out of the corners of his teeth and flicking it on the table in front of her as if he expects an apology. When none is forthcoming, he drags his chair legs across the marble flooring with a nasty screech. Slams the door as he leaves. In a moment, Su hears the car leaving the porch.

Money lubricates. It would have taken Su up to a month to schedule an abortion at a public hospital, but she is back in the private ob-gyn clinic forty-eight hours later. She wishes she were alone in the reception area, but across from her is a mousy-looking woman, her husband, and an older lady, ostensibly her mother-in-law. When the mousy woman goes to the bathroom, the older lady says to the husband in Mandarin: "If it's not a boy this time, just divorce her and marry your mistress . . ."

Su distracts herself on her phone, opening up the Spice Girls group chat, where they are comparing collagen treatments and trading screenshots of Divya, with comments that her droopy eyelids and heavy eyebags are getting from bad to worse—don't blame her husband, a tech CEO, if he kena affair with an intern! And what's wrong with young girls these days, it's like no one wants to wear a bra or shave their armpits anymore, why don't they have any sense of shame?

Su ignores them and checks her emails instead—*Vanity Fair Asia* recommends the hottest tables in town with omakase dinners. Her banker wants to fly her to the World Economic Forum at Davos. Various organizations are hoping for her to sign on the dotted line for cancer research; disaster relief; female empowerment. Her tax adviser needs her to fill in some residual forms. Her florist is asking for keywords so they can customize next month's "lifestyle blooms" for her.

"Miss Bai?" Su startles when she hears her name. Goes up to the counter. It's the birdy lady again. "You sure ah, you don't want to inform the daddy before the—the procedure?"

En route to the examination room, Su passes the empty operating room. The stirrups look like a kind of gallows. In the examination room, the nurse places a paper toilet seat cover on the PVC bed before

Su gets on top of it. The day before, Su found it hard to keep her knees apart. Today, she doesn't even flinch when the speculum is inserted. The nurse probes around to get a clear view of her cervix. Another set of footsteps shuffle in. "Dr. Ng, you want to check?"

He peers into her as well, then reaches for the transducer. Su keeps her head resolutely turned away from the ultrasound machine. Cold gel is squirted unceremoniously on her abdomen.

"See there?" Transducer presses harder. "The spinal cord, so long. Like a tail like that."

From the corner of Su's eye, she sees the nurse's mouth dropping, as if she isn't around. After Su gets up, the nurse takes her to a resting room. She gives her a pink gown to change into, and a tablet. "Misoprostol, to soften your cervix. You can rest inside here after you take."

Then she hands Su a clipboard with a form, about how to deal with "sensitive remains."

"Actually right, Dr. Ng got a request. He wants to ask if you'll consider doing the medical procedure instead of the surgical procedure, so he can preserve the fetal abnormality." The nurse says it as if she's asking Su if she wouldn't mind her coffee black because they've run out of milk. She draws the curtain around the bed. "You take a moment to think, ma'am, I let you change first."

The nurse flits out of the room to assist Dr. Ng with the ultrasound for the next patient, the mousy woman. Her husband and her mother-in-law are standing by. Dr. Ng announces that it's a girl, and she bursts into sobs. The nurse helps to see her out. Next up, a woman requesting tubal ligation. The audacity! Dr. Ng doesn't even ask for her reasons, doesn't check if she is in danger of a high-risk pregnancy or has a genetic disorder. He tells her flat-out that he can't help her. She is still in her thirties, of childbearing age, and a university graduate. The Ministry of Social and Family Development keeps tabs on such matters. They previously rang up a colleague to chastise him for sterilizing potential mothers, especially those with higher education. Besides, ladies are obligated to pop one for Singapore. Men have to do National Service. Childbirth is the feminine equivalent. The woman slams the door when she leaves, and he is appalled by her rudeness. A girl in her twenties enters next. Dr. Ng casts a beady eye over her—unapologetically busty in a spaghetti strap—and immediately suspects what she is here for. And he's right: birth control pills. Nope, he tells her flatly, he can't write her a prescription. He won't be a stooge for promiscuity! And in the long run, he adds, let's just say her future husband will thank him for keeping her *pure*. Wink. Run along now.

He lets out a great sigh after she leaves. "What's next?" he asks the nurse. What, not who.

"The pretty lady with the weird fetus. Abortion."

Ah, yes. Don't judge a book by its cover. You could never have guessed that such a beautiful woman would produce such a defective specimen. A baby with a tail. A freak of nature. Did she agree to the medical procedure so he could have the alien-like fetus for his collection?

The nurse says she'll go check. She knocks on the resting room door.

"Ma'am?" The curtain is drawn around the bed. She peeps in— the beautiful woman is gone. The pink gown, tablet, and "sensitive remains" form are on the bed. Unused, unswallowed, unsigned.

. . .

An unseasonably cool breeze blows through the taxi stand, fluttering Su's white Dries Van Noten silk blouse away from her damp back. The sun seems less harsh. On the way back to Bukit Timah, every traffic light turns green as they approach. Su's shoulders are light as they turn out of the shopping district. The cabbie starts to whistle along as a shimmering oldie, The Shangri-Las' "I Can Never Go Home Anymore," plays on the radio: *I packed my clothes and left home that night—*

Su looks at the trees flying by the window. Hovering her hand gently over her womb, she can feel her heart expanding. *Hello*, she whispers to the baby snake, growing inside of her, *hello*.

For too long, she has gorged herself on convention and consumption, using them to feel more comfortable in her human skin. Credit cards and Louboutin heels. To toe the line, she swallowed the hook. Gourmet dinners and branded goods provide the illusion of choice, when so many other matters have been taken out of her hands.

But now things are different. These mortal trappings are starting to feel so hollow. There's another life in her, and it is making her feel full. Already she can feel her priorities shifting. She'll do whatever she must to keep this baby.

The cab pulls up to the house. She gives the driver a big bill, tells him to keep the change. It may not be possible to have this baby with Paul, here, as the consummate housewife ensconced in a good-class bungalow—but that does not mean it's impossible elsewhere, without him.

They could go back to Hangzhou, just like Emerald said. Live as snakes, in nature.

Birthing will be easy. She'll teach her baby how to slither, how to swim, how to suss out the best hides. Hunting for prey—the three of them. She'll probably be the disciplinarian, and Emerald will balance her out as the permissive one. There will be no more emails to reply to, no more shopping to fill the monotonous days, no more small talk to make with the Spice Girls, no more being at Paul's beck and call. No more rashes from not molting, no more suppressing that undulation. Replaying the hot rush of freedom and pleasure she felt in the cave, Su floats past the gate, down the driveway. She's going to go home and have this baby, with her sister by her side. Maybe as snakes they can finally build back the bonds they've broken in their human skins.

Unlocking the door and stepping into the house, she can hear the kettle whistling madly. Emerald must have put it on and forgotten about it. Su rushes toward the kitchen to turn it off—

Broken jars, overturned containers. Flour, spices, and rice all over the floor. Su gapes. Someone has sacked the sanctity of her kitchen. Copper pots and cast-iron pans knocked off their hooks, full set of matching Raynaud tableware smashed to pieces, Paul's wine bottles and crystal drinkware in smithereens, bits of glass pooling in red wine all over the floor.

With a trembling hand she turns off the stove so the kettle will stop screaming. The fridge beeps insistently. Its door is wide open. All the produce inside has been swiped off the shelves—splatted tomatoes, melted ice cream, broken eggs, the butter palely deliquescing.

An intruder has stormed her house. Su's senses switch to high alert as she runs up the stairs. If they've touched even a single hair on Emerald's head—she bursts into the guest room.

Emerald is sitting on the corner of the bed in a rumpled Siouxsie and the Banshees T-shirt.

She appears unhurt, but her eyes are glassy, dissociated. Su runs over to her. "Are you OK? What happened?" Emerald is blank, silent. She's in a state of shock, Su thinks.

Emerald holds out her phone. An *NY Daily News* article. Fatal Adult Asthma Death. Photo of a body bag outside Dunkin' Donuts on Fifty-Ninth Street. A smiling profile picture of Bartek from his socials.

Su stops breathing when she sees his face. A wave of unsyncopated dread rises in her chest.

"Bartek doesn't have asthma," Emerald whispers. "You took his qi, didn't you?"

"I can explain." Su's head is swimming. So there wasn't an intruder, so Emerald is the one who decimated her kitchen, so Emerald has found out. "If you'll just let me explain—"

"Explain?" Tears are falling from Emerald's eyes. "If I harmed Paul, would you let me explain?"

"That's different," Su stammers. "He's my husband . . ."

"I *trusted* you." Emerald starts to sob. It hurts Su to see her crying like this. Su reaches out, but Emerald recoils. "Don't fucking touch me!" She shoves Su's hand away. "You're right, it's completely different. Know what the difference is? Bartek knew what I was, and he still showed up for me."

"Paul loves me," Su finds herself saying, clinging to it like it's a safety blanket even though she was prepared to walk away from him, from this house, five minutes ago.

"If he loves you so much, why don't you tell him?"

"Well," Su says unconvincingly. "There's no need to."

"Bai Suzhen." Emerald leaps out of bed and advances on Su, who backs away. "You may look like a human, you may know how to act like a human, but you will never be one!" She is practically screaming now. "I might be a snake, but you—you're a fucking monster!"

"Keep your voice down, please," Su pleads. "The neighbors—"

"The *neighbors*?" Emerald hisses with spite and scorn, forked tongue flaring from her mouth.

Su feels it before she hears it. A tremble in the air. A high-pitched tinkle. The whites in Emerald's eyes disappear, replaced by coruscating yellow pupils that burn with hate. She looks up. The clear glass of the sky light splinters into a million pieces. Su bends over, shutting her eyes. Something metallic hits the wooden floor with a clink.

When Su opens her eyes, Emerald isn't in the room anymore.

In a stupor, she sinks to the floor, cutting her feet on broken glass. She doesn't feel any pain. Gazes up at the ruined skylight. Small square of blue sky. They were going to Hangzhou. They were going to go home together. They were going to—how did it turn out like this?

A flock of birds flies across, cutting the early-afternoon light.

Su wants to cry, but the tears won't even come. She is dry-eyed as she picks up the Bulgari Serpenti necklace that Emerald has left behind on the parquet. Su turns it over in her palm, letting the diamonds catch the light, staring into the bright glint of its jewel eyes as her blood runs cold.

12

A Pretty Girl Like You Shouldn't Be
Batting for the Other Team

Emerald throws back a stolen Bellini as a DJ in a fedora spins the Human League's "Don't You Want Me" followed by Bonnie Tyler's "Total Eclipse of the Heart" followed by Culture Club's "Karma Chameleon." The night wind is strong. She's more than fifty stories up in the sky. Her best friend is dead. Her sister sucked the living daylights out of him. She's striding through this luxe alfresco rooftop bar, grabbing every drink that is unattended.

Emerald puts down the empty glass and closes her eyes.

Bartek's smile blows through her mind like a blurry pinwheel: strolling over to the Meserole Avenue Café Grumpy for a morning coffee, Bartek updating the friendly barista on his latest lay. Sharing a changing room at the Guernsey Street Beacon's Closet, serving up look after look. Reading the last line of Maggie Nelson's *The Argonauts* out loud to each other in Books Are Magic: "I know we're still here, who knows for how long, ablaze with our care, its ongoing song." Picking out matchy red silk cord friendship bracelets threaded with jade beads and tiny wooden gourds at Wing On Wo. Cycling Citibikes up Williamsburg Bridge, blasting St. Vincent's "New York" from their shitty phone speakers, sing-shouting at the top of their lungs: "*Well you're the only motherfucker in the city who can handle me—*"

It's '80s Night at the sky bar on the panoramic fifty-seventh floor of Marina Bay Sands, a casino resort topped by the world's longest elevated swimming pool. Emerald blinks back tears as she wades into the infinity pool. She's a little out of place in her baggy T-shirt; most of the women are in tiny bikinis. There's just one side of Bartek's cherry earrings left—she removes it from her earlobe and shimmies to the pool's edge, overlooking the glittering expanse of the central business district.

She kisses the earring and looks for the stars in the sky, but there's too much light pollution. All she sees is an unblinking speck of white that must be a satellite. She fixes her gaze on it anyway. "I'm so sorry, B. It's all my fucking fault." Hand outstretched, she lets the earring fall away, down into the maw of the city below. The tears flow. How stupid she'd been to defend Su, to reassure Bartek, she should never have trusted her—

A hand grazes the small of her back. The pool is crowded. At first she thinks it's an accident. Then, a low Australian accent: "Tell me who made you cry, and I'll rough him up." Tall guy in his thirties, wiry chest hair in a corn circle formation. Emerald is about to tell him to go screw himself, but the malty smell of his breath trickles over her. She runs a tongue over her lips.

"Not a him," she informs the guy. "A her."

He sucks air through his teeth. "A pretty girl like you shouldn't be batting for the other team."

She turns to face him. "Who should I bring it home for then?"

He steps closer to her, lets his Speedo-clad member brush the side of her thigh as a vibe check. OK, she doesn't move away, that's consent right there. Emboldened, he puts his palms on either side of the edge of the infinity pool, hemming her in as he takes in this gorgeous sight: hot girl, city lights. Singapore is awesome! Back in Adelaide he was probably a 5, but in Asia he feels upgraded right away to an 8. He's only been here a month, but he's seen how his height and the mention of PricewaterhouseCoopers lit a spark in his dates' eyes. He's been using his "pretty girl" line on heavy rotation, and he's even started to exaggerate his Aussie accent. This girl, though—her buzz cut, her insouciance—is neat for a few nights' stand, but she's not the kind of biddable wifey material he eventually wants to whisk home to Bowden and start a family with.

Emerald sticks her forked tongue out at him. He blinks like it's his very own present. "Mmph." He tips her chin toward him. "How does it feel to kiss with that?"

Now the crowd is bopping to Soft Cell's "Tainted Love." *I give you all a boy could give you—*

Emerald kisses the hell out of him, and he does his best to keep up. It's almost like they're mouth wrestling. His qi tastes like Vegemite on toast, kinda disgusting and kinda comforting at the same time. She rolls with it. Even when he starts struggling, she doesn't let him come up for air. She clamps her mouth against his, looking for all the world like sordid PDA. A muffled moan and a few silvery strands of breath escape him, barely attracting the nonchalant distaste of nearby revelers: sarong party girls and expat finance bros are getting way out of hand. Finally she lets him go, flicking her tongue recklessly around the last bits of translucent qi in the air between them.

"What the fuck were you doing, you crazy bitch," he yells hoarsely. "I couldn't breathe!"

Emerald watches his scared face with sick satisfaction as he scurries out of the pool. That's when she spots someone familiar in the thick midsection of the predominantly expat crowd—Tik. Briefly, their eyes meet. Emerald registers the shock on Tik's face, mixed in with a sinister sense of recognition. Tik must have seen her tongue curling around the guy's qi. Did Tik realize it was what she'd done to her that night, too? Emerald's heart sinks as Tik turns away swiftly, disappearing into the crowd. "Tik!" Emerald calls out as she wades through the pool, trying to get to her.

Tik rarely loses her head in a work situation, but seeing Emerald making out with that sort of guy, really going for it like she wants him to take her right there in the pool, leaves an awful taste in her mouth. So Emerald is one of those girls who teases girls but fucks boys. The kiss they shared that night must have meant nothing. Tik knows she doesn't have a right to be upset, and, what's worse, she's here because she's tailing Emerald on Paul's orders, but it still hurts to watch. She's heading toward the adjacent open-air car park when she hears Emerald behind her.

"Tik!" Emerald catches up with her. "It's not what it looks like . . ."

"You can do whatever you want with him. Just leave me out of it."

"I would never hurt you."

"Then what was that?"

"It was different with you. I wasn't feeding, I just wanted to know what you tasted like—"

The skin on the back of Tik's neck prickles. *Feeding? What I tasted like? What does she mean?*

"Fuck." Too late, Emerald realizes from the look in Tik's eyes that this wasn't what she was talking about, not at all. Emerald's head is spinning. "Tik—" But Tik is backing away from her.

"Please." Emerald doesn't want to, but she's starting to cry. "I just found out my best friend is dead . . . My sister . . ." She's a complete mess, but she manages to hold herself back from telling Tik what Su has done. Then it strikes her that she may be endangering Tik by being close to her. If Su killed Bartek—Emerald turns abruptly toward the Marina Bay boardwalk.

Now she hears Tik's footsteps, following her. "Emerald—"

"Stay away from me, and stay away from my sister."

"Emerald, what is going on?" Tik sounds worried.

There is no one else on the boardwalk. With a surge of manic energy, Emerald breaks into a run. Tik instinctively goes after her. When Emerald reaches the railing, Tik slows down, thinking she'll stop now. Her jaw drops when Emerald vaults over and jumps into the water.

"Emerald!" Unnerved, Tik leans over the railing, trying to spot her.

There is no clumsy splash. No thrashing arms or kicking legs. Just a hush and a silken rippling. For a split second, Tik thinks she sees a dark, sinuous shadow coming up for air. Then it dives under with preternatural grace, and there is nothing else to see across the dark quiet waters except a lateral buoy marker, bobbing up and down in the middle of the marina.

. . .

The cold water of the marina is a massive relief to the green snake. It freezes the mad heat and bitter regret in her head for now. She pokes her head out and takes a long, deep breath before going back under, waving her tail rapidly from side to side to sluice through the water.

The current carries her; she doesn't know where she's going, but it doesn't matter, as long as she can get away from it all. The darkness underwater matches the murky silt overflowing from her heart into her chest as she focuses on the immediacy of her senses, not letting any feelings cut through.

The artificial waters of the marina spread into the sea. By instinct she stays close to the coast, forging right. The west coast narrows into a reservoir before easing into a canal that leads to a stream in the jungle. An owl's screech cuts through the night. She leans into her snake skin, letting it rip—

The green snake leaps out of the water to massacre a honky-tonk chorus of paddy frogs, crushing them with her body, tearing through them with her teeth as they scream in deep croaks and high-pitched trills, not even taking their qi—cold-blooded vanity kills, just because she can. The green snake smells their fresh blood on her scales. She licks her fangs clean, sticks her forked tongue out in the night air like a litmus test. Her muscles ripple. She is ready for more.

The bloodlust pounds in her veins, momentarily driving the sorrow from her head. She catches the musky scent of the black-crowned night heron before she spots it downstream, probing the water with its beak for fish. She is careful to trace small arcs with her tail so the vibrations won't carry through the water to alert the heron. When she is close enough, the green snake strikes out. The heron does its best to take flight, but she surges an extra inch to reach its neck, sinking her fangs deep into its warm, feathered flesh.

A good bite is orgasmic.

The heron lets out a great screech that scatters the other night birds, spreading its wings in a brief, berserk dance as the venom hits before careening into the water. The green snake pulls the heron to the side of the stream. Nudging its unmoving head, she expands her jaw, pushing herself forward, mandible by mandible, pulling her mouth over its still-warm neck, pausing before the plumed midsection. Wrapping her lower half around her prey, the green snake stretches her mouth wide to work through the meatiest part of the bird.

The heavy meal makes her drowsy. She settles into a mossy alcove.

Lying by this gurgling stream, she lets the night jungle calm her senses with its cool air and earthy fragrance. Suspended in a patchy sky, the half-moon shines down through a dark lattice of leaves and over-hanging branches. She watches the trees sway gently till she falls asleep.

. . .

The trio of hikers from the National University of Singapore's outdoor adventure club are kitted out in rainproof jackets, spandex pants, combat boots, torches, and a kitchen cleaver to clear the brush as they hike through the west end of the Ulu Pandan jungle. They're not doing too well with the cleaver.

"I told you," the bossy girl, an architecture major, says, "we should have gotten a machete. This chopper does shit for vines, it's for cutting chicken!"

"Baobei," her boyfriend, a business major, reminds her, "machetes are illegal."

"What we are doing is already illegal," the architecture major reasons. They'd looked it up before, and under the Parks and Trees Regulations Act, it appears to be an offense to go off a designated trail and to enter any closed public land area. But after successfully tracking down an old Shinto shrine in the Central Catchment Nature Reserve, they've caught the exploration bug.

"Are you sure we're not lost?" the other guy, her best friend, a law major, asks.

"Of course not," the architecture major says, although she has in fact just noticed that she may have taken them past the same rambutan tree they passed before. She raises the cleaver and hacks at the vines blocking their way, then trips on a log in front of her.

"Steady, steady—" Her boyfriend reaches out to support her.

The architecture major kicks the log away. There's a low groan.

All three of them look down—and see a naked woman. There are a few leeches crawling over her body. The biz major yelps in shock and jumps back. The archi and law majors kneel to help the woman.

"Cheebye," the archi major swears, "is she alive?"

"She's breathing, she's breathing," the law major says. The woman's chest is rising and falling.

"Wait wait wait," the biz major says cautiously, "what if she's a— what if she's a hantu?"

"Hantu?" the archi major retorts. "Do you think a ghost would have a green buzz cut?"

They wrap her up in a reflective thermal emergency blanket, feed her some isotonic water. They try to call 995, but there's no signal on their phones here, so they carry her through the brush together.

Dawn is breaking—they had planned to catch the sunrise at an abandoned quarry on the other side of the jungle. When the foliage thins out and they spot the footpath, the guys put her down to take a break, and the archi major goes ahead to try for reception. They hear snatches of her assertive voice—the call to emergency services has gone through.

"I should have shaved," the biz major says as he pisses against a tree. The law major looks at him like *huh?* "This sure come out in newspaper. 'Three Good Samaritans Save a Girl in the Jungle,' y'know?"

"Yeah, you can tell the reporter you wanted to leave her behind cos you thought she was a hantu."

"Aiya, bro." The biz major pats the law major's shoulder. "I was joking only lah—"

The archi major returns triumphantly. "They'll be here in about fifteen minutes. I hope I gave them the right coordinates, I was—" She peers behind them. "Umm, boys? Where the fuck is she?"

Emerald walks toward Coronation Drive with the thermal blanket tied like a toga
around her shoulders. After escaping from the well-meaning hikers,
she hid in a shaded thicket and slept till the late-afternoon sun shone
through, rousing her. She woke up empty and hungover. There was no
grief, just shock. She found the footpath and followed it till she got to
a gleaming MRT station.

She stopped to clean up in the bathroom. People shot her dirty
looks, but with her buzz cut and the artistically draped shiny blanket, they couldn't quite tell if she was a hobo or a fashion student. A
nice lady asked if she was OK, if she needed any help. Emerald asked
for directions to Coronation Drive. It was fifteen minutes by train,
or a forty-five-minute walk. The lady bought Emerald a train ticket
and told her to take care. Still in a daze, she alighted a few stops later
and walked down Duchess Road, passing Prince of Wales Road before
reaching Coronation Drive.

Now she draws herself up as she approaches the bungalow. Rings
the doorbell. Hears Su's crisp voice on the intercom: "Who is it?"

Emerald wishes she could get her passport and essentials out of the
house without seeing Su's face. She steels herself. "I'm here to get my
stuff."

The auto gate flies open. Su dashes out of the door, rushing Emerald into the house, a bundle of nerves upon seeing her disheveled state:
"Where did you go? I was so, so worried—"

Emerald does not want to deal with her. "I'm here to get my stuff,"
she repeats mechanically.

Su is trying to push a mug of water into her hands. Emerald drops
it deliberately. The ceramic breaks against the floor, water spreading
over the marble. Without looking back, she pads slowly to the guest
room.

"Emerald!" Su so seldom calls her by the English name she's given herself, it feels odd to hear her say it. Emerald ignores her and enters the guest room, opens her duffel bag. It's empty.

What the fuck has Su done, hidden her clothes? Cut them up? Thrown them away? Emerald feels the blood rushing to her head. "Is this your idea of a sick joke?"

Emerald hears Su coming up the stairs. She is carrying a rattan basket, in which are Emerald's clothes—clean and neatly folded. Laundry. She has laundered Emerald's clothes.

Emerald loses it. "*Are you a psychopath?*" she roars at Su, grabbing the rattan basket from her hands and flinging it against the wall. Her clothes fall all over the parquet floor.

"What are you *doing?*" Su cowers.

The note of dismay in her voice drives Emerald mad.

There is no point in reasoning with someone like this, Emerald tells herself. Don't engage, just get out. She proceeds to grab her clothes from the floor, shoving them into her bag. When she picks them up, she sees that Su has ironed them—even her T-shirts, even her underwear. Emerald lets out a laugh. A bitter, short bark. "There is something very wrong with you," she says as she puts on whatever's within reach—a knitted sage-green asymmetrical one-shoulder tank top, a pair of black Calvin Klein gym shorts—and goes on packing.

There are tears in Su's eyes. Emerald is galled by how Su looks so hurt by what's happening—Emerald raising her voice, tossing the basket, scattering clothes—when she *killed* her best friend.

Su blinks, opens her mouth to say something, then closes it, then opens it again. Whatever she's going to say next is going to be so bad it's good, Emerald finds herself thinking cruelly.

"I'm pregnant," Su says. "Your friend found out, and I— I didn't know how to react."

The protective layer of mocking, ironic remove that Emerald has just tried to set up for herself evaporates. Her voice is very low. "You killed Bartek because he knew you were pregnant?"

"I was trying to protect us. He knew too much." Su bends down to eye level with her. Emerald looks her dead in the eye.

"The only person I need protection from—is you."

Su actually starts to cry. Emerald has rarely seen her like this, beautiful face crumpling, slender shoulders folding in. "No fucking way, asshole," Emerald says, "you do not get to cry—"

"I did it all for you." Su is now crouching on the floor, slumped against the wall. "I do it all for you. I look out for you, I give you money, I put a roof over your head, I pick up after you, I make sure you're safe . . . Do you really think I wanted to kill Bartek, or Giovanni—"

Bells are going off in Emerald's head. Giovanni is dead, too? Who else has Su killed over the long arm of time? There is a shrinking, tightening squeeze in her chest, and she is afraid, for the first time in her four hundred years of being human, that she may be experiencing some sort of heart attack.

"We're done," Emerald says in a tiny, bloodless voice. She picks up her bag and steps past Su.

"I thought we could go home together," Su is still saying. "You, me, and the baby—"

"You know where home is for me?" Emerald spits the words. "Wherever you're not."

. . .

Emerald hops onto the first public bus that arrives at the bus stop, surreptitiously filing past the other commuters as they tap their transport cards, and takes a seat right at the back. She checks the inner pocket of her duffel bag—her passport is still there, thank god, her wallet and her phone too. She unlocks it. Several missed calls and messages from Tik. She's using her personal number.

Emerald, are you OK? the first one reads. *Whatever it is, I just want to make sure you're safe*, the next one reads. *Please call me when you see this.* And the last one just says: *I'm sorry.*

Silly, Emerald thinks, why are you sorry? She wants so badly to talk to Tik, but the best thing she can do for her isn't to call her, see her, or kiss her. She asks the driver if this bus goes into the city, toward Golden Mile Complex, and he says she'll have to change to another bus at a later stop. She boards the second bus and gets caught for trying to evade the fare this time. She only has a couple of American dollars in her wallet, but she opens it anyway. Maybe he could just accept it as a token? That's when she sees the crisp one-thousand-Singaporean-dollar bill in her billfold. She's never even seen a one-thousand-dollar bill before. Crazy Su must have gone through her stuff and slipped it in. She almost wants to throw it into the fare box so she can have nothing to do with it.

"Do you, uhh, have change?" she asks the bus driver. Gruffly, he waves her along.

Emerald alights at Golden Mile Complex. Ducks into one of the travel agencies facing the main road. Asks for a one-way ticket to New York. The cheapest is $980, Turkish Airlines, leaving the next day.

Emerald peels open her wallet, passes the travel agent the thousand-dollar bill. He raises a brow as he takes it from her, holding it up to the light to check the watermark. Satisfied, he passes her $20 in change, makes the booking on an old computer. Emerald feels better the moment it's done. She's getting away from Su. The agent prints the e-ticket for her. She notices a sign behind him. *Honeymoon Package! No Commission! Closing Down Special!*

"Are you really closing down?"

"Yah, this building, going to en bloc, you never read newspaper?"

"What's going to happen to it?"

"The usual lor. High-class condo . . ."

As she enters the building, Emerald looks around at the minimart selling dried mangoes and prawn-head crackers, the fashion kiosk with tube tops and fake nails, smells the aroma of barbecue and broth from the mookata-grill restaurants spilling out of their premises onto the thoroughfare with foldable tables and plastic stools. Pricelessness of patina and concentric circles of community, cleared out for the soulless polish of a luxury condo. She's only been to Golden Mile Complex once, and it already pains her to imagine all of this gone. What will it be like for those who live, play, and work here?

Emerald tries to recall how to get to Club Nana—Double Happiness Steamboat, JJ Hi-Fi Electronics, Ba Xian Friendship Herbal Dispensary, spiral staircase, mosaic corridor, neon sign.

An older Thai lady in a leopard-print pantsuit—P'Bee, the manager—welcomes her in. By evening, Club Nana is bustling, with a clientele of mostly middle-aged men.

"I just want to have a word with Ploy," Emerald says. "Is she around?"

P'Bee nods to the stage—Ploy is up there with a charismatic, commanding presence that she hadn't bothered to put on when it was just Emerald and Tik. Her features are accentuated with heavy makeup, and she's very pretty like this, but Emerald feels she was more attractive barefaced. She's in a sailor girl costume, long hair tied high in two ponytails, delivering a pitch-perfect delivery of Charlene's one-hit wonder "Never Been to Me."

"But I ran out of places and friendly faces because I had to be free—"

Ploy peers expertly into the crowd, emoting to the room without really looking at anyone.

"What drink you want, girl?" P'Bee asks. "Beer, vodka, chai mai?"

"Just a Coke, thanks. Keep the change."

Emerald takes her Coke, moves closer to the stage.

Ploy hits the final falsetto. Emerald is looking up at Ploy admiringly when someone bumps into her from behind. She turns to see a man in reflective polarized rainbow sunglasses, who looks to be in his fifties.

Ruddy-skinned, tanned orange like a yam. A low forehead combined with short, hard curly hair, vaguely pubic. He gives Emerald an inquisitive raise of the brows, seemingly trying to size up if she's a working hostess or an unlikely customer. He wears beige bermudas and a bright Hawaiian-printed coconut-tree-motif shirt in mismatched hues of red and green. Under his arm is a brown glazed wine jar with a red cloth stopper. He sets it down on the table as P'Bee flashes her pocket laser, tracing a heart across Ploy's shoulders, ending suggestively around her bellybutton, prompting patrons to tip her.

This man raises his hand to indicate his interest. Emerald notices that his other arm is withered away where his shirt sleeve ends. P'Bee descends on him.

"Tao rai? How much for our Princess Ploy, handsome guy?"

"Five hundred!" he declares. Emerald detects an unpleasantly briny qi. P'Bee whoops. An assistant brings a silver cloak to the stage, fastens the clasps around Ploy's slender shoulders.

Ploy accepts graciously, pressing her palms into a wai, inclining her head to the big tipper—and spots Emerald in front of him. Her eyes widen for a second, but as a consummate pro she will maintain her persona till she takes her final bow. The lights go down, and she descends in style.

"Emerald!" Ploy squeals once she gets off the platform, pulling her into a hug. Emerald hugs her back. They've only met once, but Ploy's warmth is so real.

"What you doing here?" Ploy flutters her lids. "Miss me?"

Emerald decides it's best to cut to the chase. "I came to see you because I'm going back to New York tomorrow morning, but before that, I need to ask you something, OK?"

"OK," Ploys says, wondering why she sounds so serious.

Emerald takes a breath. "Do you still have feelings for Tik?"

"Tik?" Ploy's smile wavers, then disappears. "She got new girl-friend."

"But you still like her?"

"Like?" Ploy looks at the floor, kicking her stripper heels against it. "Love na."

Yes, Emerald thinks, she's easy to love, isn't she? "OK, good." Emerald slurps the last of her Coke and crushes the can, pretending it doesn't hurt at all to bring them back together. "Listen to me. Tik told you she had a new girlfriend because she thinks that without her, you'll find a guy."

This is news to Ploy. Her big eyes widen. "A guy?" She snorts. "What guy?"

"I know, right?" Emerald is about to launch into her spiel, but P'Bee is clicking her fuchsia acrylic nails and rattling off in a stream of annoyed Thai at Ploy, who gives her an *OK, OK, I'll get to it* look. Emerald doesn't understand Thai, but she gets that she's only ordered a Coke, while the guy behind bought a $500 cloak. She hates the way the world works. She almost wishes she still had the thousand-dollar bill so she could trump this loser, but she's spent it all on her ticket back to New York.

Ploy gives Emerald an apologetic smile as she entertains the big tipper. Emerald returns a *Go do your thing* nod. Opportunistically, the man notices their exchange, and invites Emerald to join his table. "Come." He pats the empty space on the sofa beside Ploy. "Don't be shy." The man clicks his fingers to get P'Bee's attention. "Three shot glasses!"

"She don't work here, sir," Ploy tells him, but Emerald plops down beside her. She'll stay a little longer—it's her last night in Singapore.

"Promise me you'll talk to Tik?" Emerald murmurs to Ploy.

"Don't worry," Ploy whispers back. "First, I gonna scold her. Then, I gonna love her."

If it's the last thing Emerald does in Singapore, if it's the only way for her to make a real difference in Tik's life, it's this. She can hardly believe she's set herself aside to do it, but damn, she's done a good thing, and this actually feels nice. She squeezes Ploy's arm and leans on her shoulder.

When P'Bee comes to their table with the shot glasses, the big tipper uncorks his own wine jar, which emanates a sharp, vinegary scent.

"Very special whisky," he says proudly, "custom-made in China."

Emerald wrinkles her nose at the unpleasant olfactory combination of the acidic alcohol and his fishy qi. She wants to point out that *everything* is made in China these days—why would that be special?

Ploy fills the shot glasses. Just one drink, Emerald thinks.

"Chok dee." Ploy raises her glass. The big tipper holds his up eagerly. Emerald takes the last one. They clink glasses.

He makes a point of looking them in the eye, but Emerald can only see her reflection in his mirrored lenses. He grins. She tips the shot back.

And chokes the moment the drink hits her tongue.

Emerald clutches at her throat. It burns.

A vile, swirling darkness assails her stomach, throwing her to her knees. Her field of vision shrinks rapidly, and then she feels her pupils turning, flashing yellow. She squeezes her eyes shut to hide them.

"Cheers," she hears the big tipper whisper. "It's never too late to right past wrongs . . ."

"Emerald, Emerald!" She feels Ploy steadying her as she keels over and passes out.

. . .

Tik bursts into Club Nana, having sped all the way to Golden Mile after receiving Ploy's call. She told Ploy to stay away from Emerald, but Ploy made a what-the-hell sound into the phone and hung up.

Now she sees that Ploy is safe, and Emerald is unconscious. Ploy has dragged Emerald behind the bar. P'Bee doesn't look too happy about this situation. In the dim nightclub, Emerald's face looks almost the same shade of green as her hair.

"Bring her upstairs," Ploy tells Tik. "You still have key?"

Even after they broke up, Ploy told Tik to keep her set of keys. "You Singaporeans," she remarked, "how come all still stay with parents?" Ploy can't understand this mindset. Most Singaporeans remain with their families until they get married. While most first-world countries have moved or are moving toward marriage equality, the Party has instead recently made it a point to "safeguard" the definition of marriage as being strictly between a man and a woman—so someone like Tik, for whom marriage is not a possibility, is often left in limbo. As a cop who serves the state, Tik makes more money than Ploy, but she still lives in the home she grew up in. On the very same bed she slept in as a kid. "How to make love na?" Ploy teased Tik.

Tik never returned to Ploy's apartment after the breakup, but she's held on to the keys in case Ploy ever locks herself out or needs an extra set. Ploy's housemates are always changing, once every two weeks or so. Ploy has done so well at the club that P'Bee has obtained a coveted entertainer's visa for her, but the others are chancing it on temporary tourist passes. The old batch of girls just left the day before, so Ploy has the whole place to herself for the moment: a tenth-floor unit in this mixed-use Metabolist megastructure, one of few such buildings that have been physically realized in the world. A Party member has called it a "vertical slum" and an "eyesore," but Ploy loves Golden Mile Complex. The building feels like home, and because of the way it has been designed, with common spaces and joined walkways, almost all the Thais working there know each other. In Ploy's apartment, the balcony looks out over Kallang Basin and the Singapore Flyer, views now mostly reserved for the wealthy. The balcony is the only space that has not been illegally subdivided by the landlord into slices of rooms.

Tik cautiously drapes Emerald's arm over her shoulder, supporting her at the hip as they ride the elevator.

When Tik opens the door to Ploy's place, everything is just as she remembers. There's something sweet about being in an ex's home when she isn't there. Posters of Thai celebs on the walls, flimsy TV and a fish tank in the living room, basil and aloe growing in Styrofoam boxes, hand-washed lingerie on crisscrossing laundry lines on the balcony.

"Water," Emerald croaks.

Tik lowers Emerald onto the sofa and heads for the kitchen. There's a clear plastic jug of water with a sprig of basil on the kitchen counter. Tik returns to the living room with a glass, but Emerald isn't on the sofa anymore.

"Emerald?" Tik calls out.

No response. Tik hits the light in Ploy's bedroom, the first section just off the living room, a space just big enough for a single bed. Empty. She checks the next three rooms, flipping the light switches rapidly on and off—still no Emerald. Then: the sound of water in the common bathroom. Tik strides through the corridor, stopping outside the bathroom. She knocks on the door. No answer. The door isn't locked. "I'm coming in, OK?"

Tik enters the bathroom. Turns on the light. No one at the sink, but the shower curtain is drawn around the tub. Water gushes from the showerhead. Emerald's clothes are on the floor.

"Emerald?" Tik peels back the curtain.

Emerald is curled up in a fetal position, head turned inward.

Tik can't see her face, but her back is covered in scales, wetly iridescent under running water. Jewel green. Rippling like a mirage.

Tik's mind goes sweet and blank. She reaches out to touch Emerald's shoulder. The green scales are pretty to look at, but they are cold and sharp to the touch. Emerald twitches. Tik jumps, withdrawing her hand too quickly. She cuts her finger. A deep red drop of blood falls into the water.

Sssssssssssss. The hissing is so soft that at first Tik doesn't realize it's coming from Emerald. Tik is mesmerized by its melody. Gentlest breeze in her ear. A few more drops of her blood splish into the tub.

A thin, forked tongue flicks out from Emerald's mouth. Licks at the blood in the water.

13

Power's a Trip, Love's a Disease

Ploy gets back around three in the morning to find Tik sitting in the living room, staring blankly at the goldfish in the tank. A long line of ash hangs off the end of her Sampoerna. Ploy whisks it out of her fingers to take a drag. Tik's been chain-smoking, by the looks of the filled ashtray on the table.

Ploy plops down next to Tik. "Is Emerald OK? Resting?"

But Tik just stares straight ahead. Ploy looks in her room. The bed is unslept in. "Where she?" Ploy asks impatiently, waving her arms in front of Tik. "Hello-oh?"

"Shh." Tik gets up. Ploy pipes down as Tik beckons her toward the bathroom. It's dark inside. The bathroom curtain is drawn. Ploy flicks the overhead light on. Tik turns it off right away.

"What you doing?" Ploy is exasperated. "Where's Emerald?"

Before Tik can answer, Ploy hears a wet sound from the tub, like there's dank water stuck in the drainer. A pale elbow pokes out from behind the curtain. Then Emerald leans out of the tub.

Her head lolls on her neck. She reaches a hand toward Ploy.

"Emerald!" Ploy rushes forward to help her. "What happen!"

But Tik holds Ploy back—just as Emerald lunges forward.

Ploy screams when she sees the pallid green skin, forked tongue, sharp fangs.

Emerald hisses blindly, her yellow eyes blazing bright. She can't go farther than where she is, for Tik has cuffed her other wrist to the water pipe. Enraged, she hisses and twists in the tub, jangling handcuff against pipe, clawing at the curtain with her free hand till it falls right off its rod. Emerald wrestles with the fallen curtain in the tub, tearing it to shreds, revealing her lower half—

Ploy claps a hand to her mouth to stop herself from screaming.

Belly button down, Emerald's body is a snake's tail, green with dark bands of diamond patterns, as wide as her hips before it narrows inward, twisting and thrashing with a life of its own.

Outside, back on the living room couch, Tik holds a 7-Eleven plastic bag over Ploy's mouth and nose to ease her hyperventilating.

"Naga," Ploy whispers to Tik as she catches her breath. Everyone in her town back in Nong Khai province had heard about these half-human, half-serpent beings.

"You have that in Thai too?" Tik asks Ploy. Though her IC said Malay, Tik's maternal side was Balinese. When they were growing up, her grandmother had told her and her brother many tales in Bahasa Indonesia of the naga, the immortal crowned snake who could take on human form.

"Yes," Ploy says decisively, a little put off by Tik's *too*. "The village people say that two nagas, swimming, make the Mekong River. They say nagas live in the cave, near the water . . ."

Was that why they went into the Sentosa jungle? That's the last of what Tik reported to Mr. Ong. She was shaken after Marina Bay Sands, unable to make sense of it. Tik thought about calling Mrs. Ong, but Emerald had warned her to stay away. When Mr. Ong called the next day, Tik's heart couldn't stop pounding in her chest. "Have you seen her?" Mr. Ong asked. "No," she lied. It was the first time she'd lied to him; maybe even the first time she'd lied to a superior. "If you find her," Mr. Ong went on, "tell her she is no longer welcome in my home." In brief, he told Tik about how Emerald had sacked the kitchen and disappeared. "She's completely out of control."

Tik takes a breath. "I think we should hand this over to Mr. Ong."

"*Your boss?*" Ploy is appalled. "He look like he eat chili, will diarrhea!" Tik knows what she means: this is a man who can't take spice, someone who can't accept anything out of the ordinary.

Tik admits: "He told me to report to him about Emerald."

Ploy is appalled. "Why you listen to him?"

Tik wishes she could explain to Ploy how Mr. Ong exudes that power—he calls the shots and you listen, even if what he's saying is the opposite of what you want to do. She has been trained to obey. To question him is disloyalty. To contradict him feels like treason.

"This is way beyond us, Ploy. I could lose my job. You could have your visa revoked. And how do we know we can trust Emerald? What is she even doing here? I'm calling Mr. Ong . . ."

Tik picks up her phone. Before she can go to his number, Ploy takes the phone from her. "Let me tell you what she is doing here. You know why Emerald come to Nana?"

"Stop it." Tik grabs her phone back.

Ploy looks at Tik. "She come to help us."

Tik is confused. "Help us with what?"

"She come to tell me, you don't have new girlfriend. Jing mai?"

Flustered, Tik doesn't know what to say.

"You still love me?" Ploy demands. Tik is taken aback, but she manages to nod. "You," Ploy scolds Tik. "Ngoo muan kwai." She'd taught Tik that line before: stupid like a water buffalo.

Slowly, Tik puts her phone down.

"So, you want to help Emerald, or khaaaaa her?" Ploy drags out the Thai verb for *slaughter, devour, maim*.

. . .

Ploy takes Tik to the basement level and stops in front of Ba Xian Friendship Herbal Dispensary. She raps on the shutters in a specific rhythm: *tak-tak-tak-tak-tak, tak-tak*.

"It's three a.m.," Tik says.

"Uncle Lu don't sleep at night," Ploy reassures her.

The shutters roll up. A bunch of elderly Chinese uncles are smoking and playing mahjong inside. Ploy has mentioned Uncle Lu before, but it is Tik's first time inside this place.

Vintage Chinese maps and stamps are displayed in old-fashioned beveled wood frames on the walls. Curios line the shelves: intricately painted porcelain figurines of tigers and carps; triangular amulets of yellow paper with red Chinese characters; a necklace of outsize wooden prayer beads, each the size of a fist. On one side of the large room is a rosewood countertop, behind which is an ornate medicinal cabinet with assorted herbs, roots, powders, and desiccated whatnots— Tik spots what appear to be dried seahorses, a pangolin's tail, a curved deer's horn—sorted neatly into glass jars of different sizes.

Tik knows that Ploy and the other bar girls visit Uncle Lu for minor ailments and health tonics, though she can't see how drinking a soup of swiftlet-saliva nests with rock sugar could possibly improve your complexion. Ploy has also told her about how Uncle Lu does feng shui consultations for many businesses in the building, as well as the occasional Taoist exorcism. He left his hometown in Hubei, China, during the Cultural Revolution, and resettled in Singapore.

"Hu!" a jolly bald man with a long white beard and a big paunch in a gray cotton-mesh singlet declares, slamming down his tiles to display his winning hand. "Hua shang zi mo!" It looks to be a big win: the other players grumble, tossing over the chips owed to him. Uncle Lu sweeps the winnings into his drawer with panache.

"Aiseh, Ploy," he chuckles. "You are my good-luck charm."

"Uncle Lu," Ploy whispers urgently. "We got problem, upstairs."

Uncle Lu listens intently to Ploy, then asks if she herself drank the whisky as well. Ploy had not touched it, and as far as she could recall, neither did the big tipper. Emerald was the first to down it. Uncle Lu strokes his straggly white beard thoughtfully. "Is the drink still around?"

Ploy isn't sure—she was focusing on Emerald. They head back to Nana, where P'Bee is closing up. The big tipper left the earthen wine jar behind, and P'Bee dumped it in the trash. She retrieves it for Uncle Lu now. He studies the glaze of the jar. "From Guangdong province." Then he sniffs around the red fabric of the lid and asks P'Bee for a pair of tongs. "Stand back," he warns as he opens it.

There's a sour odor, and a murky glob, which appears to be a clump of aromatics. He fishes around, pulling something slippery to the surface—a perfectly preserved king cobra. "Arai wah!" P'Bee squeals in alarm, patting her chest with her hand.

But Uncle Lu isn't done yet. He swirls deeper, uncovering half of a sizable scorpion and huge-ass centipede legs. "Three-poison whisky," he tells them grimly. He explains the vicious formula. A king cobra, an emperor scorpion, and a giant centipede are sealed into an earthenware jar, where they fight to the death, concentrating their toxins into a single victor, creating a complex poison used in Southern Chinese black magic. The victor, and whatever is left of its opponents, are then drowned in wine or whisky, which masks the taste of the poison. Three-poison whisky can be used on humans for all sorts of things: to manipulate sexual partners, to cause them to behave like snakes, to create hallucinations, to fill them with madness and anxiety.

Uncle Lu says he'll make his most potent purging decoction to cleanse the poison from Emerald's system. Back in the dispensary, the mahjong players don't bat an eyelid at his late-night shenanigans.

Tik and Ploy watch as he sits on a pleather stool with wheels before his medicinal cabinet, thick brows furrowing as he consults a manual written in classical Chinese, read vertically rather than horizontally. Rolling back and forth from counter to cabinet, he gathers various herbs from several glass jars before him, measuring them out on a pair of ancient-looking brass scales. He crushes them into powder, scalds the ingredients with hot water. Stirs it with a curved deer horn. Covers up with a glass lid. Sets a timer and lets it steep.

Outside the apartment, Tik can hear clanking sounds from the bathroom even before they enter. Striding forward confidently, Uncle Lu heads in before Tik and Ploy. He is holding the brown purging decoction in a porcelain bowl in one hand, a yellow talisman with red scrawls in the other. He mutters a Taoist chant under his breath before bursting into the bathroom—but when he sees the half-woman, half-snake banging her cuffed wrist against the pipes in the bathtub, he gives a startled shout.

She looks up. Her eyes are glowing citrine with vertically elongated, slit-shaped pupils. Realizing what he is facing, Uncle Lu braces himself and brandishes the talisman at her.

She rears up—it provokes her, but that is all. Moving swiftly, Uncle Lu lights the talisman on fire, drops it into the brown liquid, and hurls the entire bowl at the bathtub like a Molotov cocktail. The bowl smashes into pieces. The creature hisses fiercely as the brown liquid hits her skin, but there is no other effect on her. The fire goes out. Uncle Lu turns as he hears a crack. The mirrored surface of the bathroom cabinet above the sink shatters. Uncle Lu lifts his arms up to shield himself from the flying glass. A shard slices his face, narrowly missing his eye.

In the safety of the living room, Uncle Lu gruffly allows Ploy to stick a Band-Aid on the side of his eyelid. He is clearly shaken. "From what you said, I thought she was a woman possessed by a snake," he tells Tik and Ploy as he wipes beads of sweat off his bald pate. "That thing inside there, that's a snake who can turn into a woman! She's a yaojing."

Neither Tik nor Ploy know the word. Uncle Lu explains that yaojing is the Chinese term for animal spirit. Three-poison whisky is used to addle and control humans, but for snake spirits, it can lead to an irrevocable reversal, detransitioning them back into their original forms. Emerald probably hasn't consumed enough of it, Uncle Lu guesses; that's why she is between skins—half-snake, half-woman.

"It's been a long time since I've seen something like this," he says, stroking his beard nervously. "I don't want to be part of this shady business, and you both better think twice about it, too." Associating with a yaojing is a double-edged sword, he tells them. These dark creatures are charismatic, and can bring wealth and influence, but their very existence openly defies the regular order of nature, and consorting with them can bring misfortune.

"I'm not young anymore," Uncle Lu says. "I can't afford to get mixed up in this!" When Ploy asks how they can help Emerald, Uncle Lu looks at her like she's daft. "You can't help her. *This* is what she is. They're not meant to be among us."

"What should we do?"

"If it were up to me, I'd give her more of the whisky, hope she turns back into a snake—shouldn't be too big—then dump her into a river or flush her down the toilet bowl."

Ploy gives him a withering look.

"Fine, be soft like tofu and figure out how to keep a demon in your bathtub." He gets up to leave. "I don't think you get it. They may look like humans, but at the end of the day, they are not like us. Yaojing can't be trusted. You'd better hold your breath around her, she may steal your qi."

"Qi?"

"Your breath, your air, your vital energy. She sucks it out of you, to look young."

So this is what Emerald was talking about when she said she wasn't feeding off her, she just wanted to know what she tasted like, it dawns on Tik. Her cheeks redden slightly.

"You mean Emerald isn't in her twenties?" Ploy looks at Uncle Lu in disbelief. He is already at the door. He turns back. "Twenties?" he scoffs. "My guess is, she's at least a hundred."

Ploy is taken aback. Uncle Lu gives her a now-you're-finally-getting-it grunt as he shows himself out. "And if anyone asks, I wasn't involved in any of this. I wasn't even here, OK?"

The door slams.

After Uncle Lu leaves, Tik and Ploy sit in the living room, at a loss. "Maybe we should call the police," Tik mumbles uncertainly.

Ploy looks at her. "You the police."

Is there protocol for something like this? Tik can't imagine what would happen to Emerald if they turned her in.

"I told you, I don't want us to get in trouble . . ." Tik interlaces her hand with Ploy's.

"But Emerald *is* in trouble. Not job, not visa. *Life* trouble."

"You heard what Uncle Lu said about her."

"I heard what he said, yes. But he don't know her. We know her."

A low moan issues from the bathroom. They go to check on Emerald. Her face is deathly pale. She is clutching her shoulders and shaking uncontrollably in the tub. The moaning is awful to listen to, wispy and guttural at the same time. Then her tail begins to writhe, and she sits up straight, like her head's been snapped back on a string by a puppet master. She thrashes her arms, wild and helpless. Her eyes roll back.

"Tik—" Ploy tugs on Tik's arm, worried.

Pushing all her misgivings away, Tik takes her phone out. "I'm going to text Mrs. Ong."

It's coming to four in the morning. *Hi Mrs. Ong*, Tik writes, unsure if there will be any response. Right away, she sees the double tick mark on the message. Mrs. Ong is awake.

This is about Emerald, Tik types quickly. *Can you come alone, without saying anything to Mr. Ong?*

The response is immediate: *Yes.*

. . .

Paul sits at the mahogany desk in his study, trying to focus. The red digits on the clock read 4:10 a.m. Parliament will be in session at noon, and he's still working on his speech. He's worried about Su, but at least she's asleep now. They would talk after Parliament.

When Paul got home from work yesterday, he was surprised to find Su scrubbing the kitchen. His wine and glassware sideboard were empty. So was the fridge. He asked what happened, and she mumbled something about a misunderstanding with Emerald, but he mustn't hold it against her. A misunderstanding? He was shocked when he peered into the colossal heap of trash—foodstuff, broken plates, glasses and bottles—Emerald had disrespected his home.

Paul was seething. "Where is she?"

"She left," Su said quietly. She looked so brittle that he didn't press for more. He told her to go and rest, that he would arrange for the helper to come in tomorrow, but Su shook her head.

"I should be the one tidying up," she said cryptically.

He put a stop to it when he saw the small cuts on her feet, by scooping her up in his arms. She was so tired she didn't refuse. He carried her to bed, gave her a Xanax and some water. She fell asleep almost immediately. She must have been exhausted. He went to the guest room—and saw that the skylight had been smashed. Now he was enraged.

The moment Emerald showed up, he'd show that ungovernable cunt the door. He could probably get her arrested for this if he wanted, but he didn't want her to remain in Singapore. Su wasn't herself around Emerald—she was abnormal. There was something black and tangled between them. He didn't like it one bit.

In the morning, Paul was relieved that Su seemed fairly normal, if quiet. She'd woken up earlier to prepare his shirt and tie, made his breakfast, and nodded vaguely when he said he would get a repairman to work on the skylight next week. He paused, expecting her to shed some light on what happened, or to apologize for her sister's delinquent behavior, but she was silent.

At work, he called Tik to ask if she'd been able to locate Emerald, but she hadn't.

When Paul got back in the evening, the whole house was dark. He found Su curled up in the guest room under the duvet. He turned the lights on. The drawers had been emptied, and Emerald's duffel bag was gone. "She came back?"

Su didn't say yes or no. "She's never said she's done before." There were tears in her eyes. Su is not a crier—one of the things Paul likes about her is her stiff upper lip. But the tears were spilling from her eyes, and she was covering her face. He put his arm around her, feeling even more threatened by Emerald. What sort of hold did she have on Su, to reduce her to this?

He told Su not to worry about dinner, he would order something soupy in. "Thanks." Su looked thoughtful. He assumed she'd say something about how understanding he was being, but what came out of her mouth shocked him: "I'm getting tired of cooking." He'd never heard her say something like that. She loved cooking for him; he loved eating her food.

Paul's guard was high by the time Su said she was going to bed, but he hid it from her. He walked her up to the room and gave her another Xanax. After she fell asleep, he went through her Birkin. Makeup compact, mints, hand cream, some business cards—and then he saw it.

An ultrasound scan with Su's name on it. Paul's heart leaped. She was pregnant? He couldn't believe it. At first he was so excited he wanted to rouse her from her sleep, but in a moment, a murky sense of foreboding came over him. Why hadn't she told him anything about it? He took a picture of the scan, sent it to one of his trusted Raffles buddies, a gynecologist in private practice.

Wilson called him immediately. "Bro, I'm so sorry . . ."

Paul took the news stoically. Then he went to the bathroom and punched the wall. After a bit of a cry, Paul tried to look for a silver lining: so this was why Su was shutting down and closing him out—it wasn't all about Emerald. He would talk to her tomorrow.

Wilson had already offered to do the abortion. Congenital deformities were heartbreaking for would-be parents. It was even rougher for them—they'd thought she was barren; this could have been their miracle baby. If it was painful for him, he could hardly imagine how hard it must be for her, the mother.

Paul placed the scan back in Su's bag and returned it to her side of the closet. He forced himself to focus on the speech he'd be giving in less than twelve hours, regarding the transgender student issue. He'd thought it over carefully, and wanted to pick the right words for this sensitive matter. He intended to clear the air in Parliament, to help safeguard those who needed protection.

Paul wakes with a start at the sound of footsteps pattering lightly down the corridor. He's fallen asleep at his desk. Still groggy, he glances at the clock. 4:25 a.m. He steps out of the study—and is startled to see Su going down the concrete cantilevered stairs in a white dress.

He runs after her. Grabs her arm. "Where're you going?"

"Paul," she says calmly, "let me pass."

He blocks her path. "Where the hell are you going?"

"My sister is in trouble. I have to get to her."

"After she desecrated our house and tore you down?"

"She needs me." The way Su says it is unequivocal.

"What sort of trouble is she in this time? Should I call the police?"

Su's eyes are the fiercest he has ever seen them. "I won't let you off if you do that."

"*You* won't let me off?" Paul mocks her. She tries to shrug him off, but he tightens his grip. "What else are you not telling me, Suzhen?" He searches her face, but it is smooth and inscrutable.

"Let go of me."

He wants her to know that she can tell him anything. "I know about the goats," he says. Her eyes widen; she is thrown off. Paul struggles to form the words. "And I know about the baby."

A vein throbs in the side of Su's forehead. She whispers: "You know about the baby?"

"Yes." His voice cracks. "My friend is a gyne, he can take care of it. We can try again."

"No," she says clearly. "I don't want to try again."

"Suzhen"—he takes off his glasses and wipes a tear away—"I understand where you are coming from, but birth defects are a statistical fluctuation. It's not your fault, OK? We must separate logic and emotion. Let me take care of this for you. For us."

"You don't understand, Paul," she says slowly.

"What don't I understand?"

"I don't think this baby is yours."

Her words ring through the still air like a death knell. He swallows hard. "There's someone else?" Paul is ready to ruin the rest of this man's life.

"No," Su says. "There's no one else. This baby . . ." Her voice softens to a hush. "It's special."

Now he loosens his grip on her. His poor, dear wife.

"Suzhen, please."

"Parthenogenesis," she is going on. "It's rare, but it happens. Especially in captivity."

"Parto-what?" He has no idea what she is talking about.

"It's more common in birds and fish, so I hadn't thought about it . . . Genetic material that's normally discarded during the egg-making process in the female animal's body acts like sperm . . ."

His heart aches. How can he tell her she is losing touch with reality, when it must feel like her reality? He takes her by the shoulders.

"You're under a lot of stress, your mind is trying to—"

He stops short. Su's irises have turned milky white. Her pupils are a thin black thread. His breath presses into his thorax. At first, he thinks it is a trick of the light. His mind races to form a cohesive thought that will make everything go back to normal, but a panicked, bucking feeling hits him in the knees. Something preternatural stares back at him—

Under his palms, Paul feels the soft skin of her shoulders turn hard and keeled. Paul lets go of her. He seems to see white scales sprouting along her clavicles—but how? Her skin is so pale, it appears luminous. He staggers back with a strangled yelp, away from her.

A bright jasmine scent pervades the air. They are indoors, but a cool breeze rustles his hair. Her voice is a silvery whisper: "*I will have this baby, whatever it takes. With or without you.*"

In the next moment, she's at the bottom of the concrete stairs. She does not look back. Knuckles blanching from gripping the banister so tight, Paul sinks to the ground.

. . .

They have been waiting for Mrs. Ong to reach Golden Mile Complex, but when she texts that she's on her way up, Tik suddenly gets nervous. "If Emerald is a naga, is Mrs. Ong also a naga?" Mrs. Ong is the epitome of a picture-perfect woman in so many ways, the thought had not even crossed Tik's mind.

Ploy takes out her phone to google "Do naga have siblings" in Thai, but there's no time for that. Tik tells Ploy to go hide in one of the rooms, just in case.

"Just in case *what*?" Ploy demands. If anything happens, she wants to be out here with Tik, fighting alongside her.

"Quick." Tik pulls her away.

Ploy only agrees because they would stand a better chance with the element of surprise. She slips into the kitchen, grabs the sharpest knife, and goes to hide in the room closest to the living room. The doorbell rings just as Ploy closes the door behind her.

Tik takes a deep breath as she opens the door. Mrs. Ong looks as prim and proper as ever in a neat white dress, her ballet flats, and the handbag that cost more than Tik's Tampines flat.

"Mrs. Ong." Tik opens the door. Her hand trembles a little as she unlocks the gate.

"Thank you for coming to me, Tik," Mrs. Ong says as she steps in. "Is this your place?"

"It's my friend's apartment, they're back in Bangkok at the moment."

Tik takes her to the bathroom. Emerald has stopped moaning. Her eyes are closed. She is still shivering, from tail to shoulders. Concern floods Mrs. Ong's face, but Tik registers the lack of surprise at Emerald's form—clearly, it's not the first time she's seen her like this.

"Sorry I locked her up," Tik blurts out, anticlimactically.

"No, no," Mrs. Ong assures her. "You did the right thing."

Tik quickly fills her in on how Emerald was planning to leave Singapore for New York the next day, how she dropped by Club Nana, how she consumed the three-poison whisky.

Mrs. Ong turns to Tik. "So you know what she is?" Her voice is quiet, her gaze impenetrable. Tik's insides turn to ice. She nods. "And you still tried to save her?" Mrs. Ong asks.

Tik isn't sure if she's imagining it—Mrs. Ong's irises seem lighter than usual, the shape of her pupils slightly thinner.

"Emerald has been nice to me," Tik says simply.

"Yes, she can be really sweet." Mrs. Ong's voice is mild, but Tik is starting to find her decorum menacing. When she asks Tik for the key to the handcuffs, Tik hesitates. "Don't worry," Mrs. Ong says. "I've been through a lot with Emerald. I know what to do."

She hands over the key. Mrs. Ong slides it into her pocket and approaches the bathtub. With a quick, graceful movement, she taps a specific pressure point in the side of Emerald's neck with her fingers. The moment she hits Emerald—with a distinct *thuck* that sounds more like wood on wood than flesh on flesh—Emerald goes limp.

Tik's eyes go wide. Mrs. Ong reaches for the key and leans forward calmly to undo the handcuffs from the pipes. She reaches into the tub, placing a hand under Emerald's arm.

"Would you mind giving me a hand, Tik?" Mrs. Ong asks politely.

Tik hurries over to help. As they drag Emerald out of the bathroom, her tail leaves a glossy, sticky pale-green trail on the floor.

They lay an unconscious Emerald on her back in the living room. Her tail twitches. Tik jumps, but Mrs. Ong's methodical, completely-in-control demeanor helps to calm her down, as if what they're doing is perfectly within the bounds of normalcy.

Then, from behind one of the closed doors in the apartment—a bright clang. Something metallic clatters to the floor, and Tik hears Ploy swearing in a muffled tone: "Chip hai!"

Mrs. Ong freezes, then turns in the direction of the noise. "You said you were alone."

Tik stands up to protect Ploy as she steps out of the room with the knife. "Don't hurt her."

"You can hold on to the knife if you like," Mrs. Ong says directly to Ploy. "I'm not going to hurt anyone, and I'm not going to let Emerald hurt anyone. Can both of you trust me on that?"

Ploy looks at Tik: *Are you sure?*

Tik nods at Ploy, who places the knife on the floor.

Together, they prop Emerald up into something like a sitting position, although her tail, flopping beneath her, makes that a challenge.

Emerald's body is slack, eyes closed, head loose on her neck—but after Mrs. Ong taps two meridian points on either side of her spine— *thuck thuck*—and two more on either side of her neck—*thuck thuck*— her upper body posture snaps upright, straight-spined. Tik and Ploy are in a half-squat, half-kneel, on either side of Emerald.

Mrs. Ong takes a lotus position behind Emerald, an arm's length away from her. She takes a deep breath, without exhaling. Shuts her eyes. There's a primordial power to her being. Her focus is so profound, it feels as if the air in the room is congealing around her. Her forehead is beaded in perspiration.

The apartment grows very still. Even the goldfish slows to a halt in the middle of the tank. The ceiling fan stops turning. The lights go out.

Mrs. Ong brings her ring and pinkie fingers to the tip of her thumb, third and index fingers held out straight together, with a snap. Eyes still closed, she extends both arms to hit Emerald in a series of meridian points along her back. Emerald groans, body jerking with each tap.

Tik and Ploy lock gazes worriedly.

"Let go and get behind me," Mrs. Ong says. "Now!"

They do as they're told. Emerald remains upright, even without their support. A second later, a viscous black secretion pours out of Emerald's mouth like projectile bile.

The bile hits the floor with a corrosive hiss, leaving a dark stain. Emerald convulses on the spot. A single black scorpion falls out of her mouth, skittering across the floor.

Without hesitating, Tik picks up the knife that Ploy laid down, twisting it deftly into the scorpion's exoskeleton. Ploy gasps as the shape of Emerald's legs—thighs, calves, ankles—becomes visible *under* her tail. The skin around her tail turns translucent, as if it is thinning out, and then it contracts. Soon all that's left of her tail is a scattering of jewel green scales. Her legs, folded under her, are milky and moist.

A dark vapor floats over Emerald, enveloping her like a shadowy wraith. Mrs. Ong makes a circling motion with her hands, and Emerald spins around to face her.

Mrs. Ong parts her lips, sending a gleaming thread of her own qi outward. Her qi is brighter than the near-invisible qi of humans. The thin stream of golden qi wavers when it meets the dark vapor, unable to break through. Mrs. Ong guides her qi forward, toward Emerald. She is very pale. Her hands tremble. Ploy pulls on Tik's arm, but Tik shakes her head. *Don't break her focus.*

A thin line of blood drips out of Mrs. Ong's nose, but she pushes more qi forward. Finally the golden qi surges through the dark vapor. Mrs. Ong pushes her qi into Emerald's mouth. As the qi enters Emerald's body, she devours it rapidly, as if she's parched, faster than Mrs. Ong is pushing it out.

The golden stream breaks. Mrs. Ong sways. Tik rushes forward to catch her.

. . .

Emerald jolts back to earth violently, her breath coming in a huge, urgent gasp. Her eyes flash open, and the first thing she sees is Su, blood on her face, leaning over Tik.

"No!" she screams, shoving Su aside. The walls spin, she is utterly disoriented, but she will not let Su do what she did to Bartek. "Stay back!" She throws herself in front of Tik and Ploy.

Su is unsteady on her feet, face pallid.

"Emerald," Tik is saying, "Mrs. Ong is trying to help—"

"She killed my best friend in New York." Emerald turns to Tik and Ploy, eyes blazing, heart pounding, head spinning. "Don't believe a word that comes out of her mouth!" Something feels very off and very raw, like a volley of electricity and amphetamines swirling in her bloodstream. The room is bright one moment, dark the next. She can't focus, their faces and voices drift in and out—

Su is coming toward them. "You need to calm down. We just exchanged qi, you could be unstable, I don't want anyone to get hurt . . ."

All Emerald hears is *qi*, *unstable*, *hurt*; all she smells is Tik's cherry cola breath; all she feels is power and panic. She lashes out at Su, blind and vicious, going ruthlessly for the soft skin of her neck, biting down in a sweep of lightning-quick stabs—

"Emerald!" Tik is yelling her name, pulling her back. "Emerald, stop it!"

Finally she lets go. Su tries to stand, but she falls to the floor. Tik runs to help Su. Emerald steadies her body against the wall. Slowly, the room swims back into view.

Tik is holding Su up. There's a score of snake bite wounds on Su's swanlike neck. Red rivulets of blood run down her collarbone in a haphazard line, staining the neckline of her dress.

"I'm OK," Su is saying in a low voice. "Don't worry, Emerald's venom isn't very strong . . ."

Tears run down Ploy's face. "How could you do that?"

Emerald sees the fear in Ploy's eyes. She was trying to protect them; why are they afraid of *her*? Bewildered, still in deep shock, she sinks down into the sofa. Limbs spent, head heavy.

Su stands up with Tik's help. Puts on her ballet flats. She looks in Emerald's direction just once. Their eyes meet briefly, and Emerald is jolted by Su's calmness, her lack of anger.

An old look passes between them. First it is tired and self-victimizing, but when neither of them looks away, it gets smelted down into: *What do I do with you? What do I do without you?* Power's a trip. Love's a disease. Every time they get back together, it's PTSD without the P. Crashing out of each other's lives, saying *never will I ever*. And yet it's only a matter of time before they begin to seek each other out again.

But this time, Emerald catches a glint of something different in Su's eyes. *You're right*, Emerald seems to hear Su say. *We're done.*

She watches as Su tells Tik she's fine, but falters when Tik lets go of her. Su gestures to Tik that she's got this, she doesn't want more help. She teeters to the table and picks up her handbag, now besmirched with a sticky lime streak. Trembling, she turns toward Ploy and Tik.

"Thank you." Her tone is benign, but her voice is shaking. She leaves, shutting the door gently behind her.

. . .

Everything seems terribly far away. Su's body is moving toward the elevator lobby, but she has no sense of being the one placing one foot before the other. When Emerald came at her, she felt herself shutting down. Colors were muted, sounds dialed down. She hardly felt any pain. All she saw was Emerald lunging at her repeatedly, but it didn't feel like it was happening to her. She was seeing it all from a distance, in disbelief. No, it was more than disbelief, it was denial.

She is watching the elevator numbers changing from one to ten when Tik appears. "Mrs. Ong," Tik says with a respectful bow. "I can send you back to Coronation Drive."

Su manages to turn around to face Tik with a dignified smile. "It's OK, I'm driving myself today." Tik holds out a damp towel for the wounds on her neck. She takes it gratefully.

"Is there anything I can do for you?" Tik asks.

"You've done more than enough." Su hesitates. "Just—if you could—don't mention any of this to Paul, OK?" Su reaches for her purse, whisks a few big bills out.

Tik refuses to take any of it. "There's no need, Mrs. Ong."

She tucks the money back into her purse. "Su," she says. "Just call me Su." The elevator arrives. Su steps in. "Can you make sure that she's all right?"

Tik nods. "Please take care, Mrs. Ong."

The elevator is mirrored. Su wipes the blood off the punctures on the left side of her neck. Each one is raised, the skin around it bruised. Her own venom neutralized Emerald's weaker venom, but it was how Emerald went at her that was the real poison. It was the way you'd go at an enemy. She hadn't held back. Mixed deep into the disorientation was the bad blood between them. Su knew she'd experienced Emerald attacking her from as far as she could to protect herself. The pain—the betrayal—was deeper than she could go in the moment. She stares at herself, wipes a tear away. She will not break down now, not until she's safe.

In the car park, Su starts up the engine. She'd almost forgotten that she could drive. It's pointless to own a Porsche in Singapore, where the maximum speed limit is a paltry ninety kilometers per hour. All for show, but soon she won't need any of this. She's leaving this place.

She's going back to Hangzhou, where she'll have her baby. That's all she has left now.

Su is going down the Marina Coastal Expressway when the road ahead starts to mist. She's in a tunnel; why's there mist? Something like motion sickness is coming over her. She takes her foot off the accelerator, slowing down. An abrupt dizziness blurs her vision, rattling her head around like a snow globe. She doesn't know if it's the qi loss, the three-poison whisky, or Emerald's venom. Leaning forward, she blinks hard, trying to keep her hands on the wheel.

The road goes askew, amber tunnel lights exploding into streaky splinters. The white Porsche careens into the road divider, narrowly missing a car in the right lane.

14

Time Heals All Wounds Is Fridge Magnet Bullshit

Sunrise on a pale beach. Gentle but dogged tide pushing out debris across the shore. Sea glass, whelk shells, coconut husks, plastic bottles. Su bathes in the shallows. So many bits of wet sand swirling in constant motion beneath her, nanoseconds trickling in an hourglass. Current pulling her down, then buffeting her up. Whiff of rubbing alcohol, faint whir of a vacuum, cold metal.

Everything is oddly bright. Su wants to get up, but she is dragged back into the shallows. Salt water swirls around her body, buoying it back and forth. Rush of sand and sludge between her legs. She is as remote from all of it as a gull or a cloud. The sun is impassively high in the sky. There is no one else on this bare stretch of beach, but Su hears a chorus of voices:

"Paul said she ran away from home, can you believe it . . ."

"How come she didn't tell us anything ah? Did any of you know?"

"Aiya, if I was pregnant with this—this thing, of course I also don't want anyone to know."

"I never imagined Su as the kind of woman who would have a breakdown . . ."

"Actually right, I can't say I'm *that* surprised. She's always been a little high-strung."

"And did you notice she doesn't like to look people in the eye?"

"She's lucky Paul dotes on her. He was so understanding . . ."

"But what was she *thinking*? Give birth to a baby without hands, without legs, with a *tail*?"

Su opens her eyes. The room is white and bright. Cloying perfume, faint disinfectant, orchid pollen. A huge spray of purple-and-white orchids, so decadent it looks fake, dressed up with bird's-nest fern and palm leaves, extends in a graceful arc from the bedside table.

She tries to sit up.

"Oh my goodness." The Spice Girls' gossipy tones are replaced by syrupy sweetness. "Thank god you've come to!" They cluster busily around Su, jostling to be closest to her. "Su-su, darling, how are you feeling?" Ping coos. "We were so worried about you!"

A wave of nausea washes over Su. She tries to shake the sick away.

"Where am I?"

The Spice Girls exchange a volley of looks.

Hanis bites her lip. "Sayang, it's for the best."

"We won't tell anyone, of course," Amrita says. "Paul asked us to come over and accompany you because he had to rush off to Parliament. The orchids are from him . . . And there's a note."

Hanis passes the envelope over. Su opens it.

Paul's cursive: "*I still love you very much.*"

"You fainted on the road, and the ambulance brought you to the hospital," Ping explains in the bright voice typically reserved for small children. "Paul transferred you to a gyne, his friend, so he could help."

A used soreness prickles between Su's legs. She forgets to breathe. She is a plastic bag ridden with holes. Leaking amniotic fluid. A choking sound in the back of her throat. She is drowning inside herself. Too little water, too much air, too late. It was a free-for-all as they knocked her out, slipped on gloves, and spread her legs. Tight gush of a suction tube. Hooked end of a curette. Scraped her clean. That little crescent growing inside her was a perfect snake. But where the soft heat of life had been, there is now a raw pit of abraded tissue.

Her baby is gone. She turns toward her pillow and starts to sob.

A strangled scream escapes her. The Spice Girls stare at one another: *Oh dear, what to do?* Ping takes a stab at it. "Sweetie—" She pats Su gingerly on the back. "It's OK, let it all out—"

"I want to be alone," Su whispers. "Please leave me alone."

The Spice Girls exchange glances: *Poor thing, she's really losing it.* "Text us if you need anything, k?" Amrita flashes Su a thumbs-up. They file out of the room, making *eeks* faces at each other, Manolo Blahniks and Jimmy Choos and Stuart Weitzmans tapping loudly against the floor as they leave.

Wilson would have left the nurses to deal with Su if she wasn't Paul's wife. He and Paul went way back—Sec 1 classmates at Raffles Institution—they'd kept in touch through the old boys' network. It was a difficult call to make to a long-time friend, to tell him that his wife's scan showed a fetus with severe abnormalities, but Paul took it in his stride. They had already agreed that Wilson would help Su with the abortion procedure; just let him know when they wanted to schedule it.

When Paul called this morning, Wilson picked up immediately.

Su had gotten into an accident, Paul said, and he was transferring her over from the public hospital. Shortly after, Paul arrived with his unconscious wife. Wilson scanned her womb.

It was one of the most unusual fetuses Wilson had seen in his years of practice. It was completely limbless, without even stunted or irregularly formed stubs. It had only one lung, and where a human had thirty-three vertebrae, this fetus had at least a hundred. He pointed all of this out to Paul. When he realized Paul was sniffling, he left the room diplomatically for a few minutes.

Paul had collected himself by the time he got back.

"Don't worry, bro," Wilson said. "We'll take care of it."

"Wilson—" Paul looked at him. "Could you do it now?"

Wilson frowned. Su was unconscious. She'd just been in an accident. Surely they needed to talk to her first? Their eyes met, and Wilson tried to intuit where Paul was going with this.

"Su is going through a lot," Paul said finally. "Between you and me"—he paused—"she's having a mental breakdown . . . She said this baby is special, she wants to keep it. Then she ran out of the house with the car, swerved into the side of the MCE tunnel." He choked up. "I could have lost her."

Informed consent is cardinal in medical practice, Wilson told Paul. It was one of the first things they'd learned in med school. All adults have the capacity to consent to or refuse treatment—

"Do I look like an idiot, Wilson?" Paul did not flinch. "Why do you think I came to you?"

He was calling in that favor, Wilson realized. Several years ago, Paul had helped to expedite Wilson's Japanese wife's immigration process, when he was at the Ministry of Home Affairs. One hand washed the other in elite sectors of society, opening doors, and greasing ladders. It wasn't true that it got lonely in high places. Wilson knew most of the men who occupied rungs of power and influence in this city from his secondary school yearbook.

"You would have done the same for Naoko." Paul's tone softened, now that they both knew Wilson was going to have to do it. "It's force majeure," he went on quietly. "A duty of care."

Wilson could see that Paul was going to go far in politics. There was already chatter among the Raffles network that Paul might be top dog once the Chief—also an old boy, of course—retired.

Though Su was unconscious, Wilson sedated her to be sure she didn't wake up midway. The procedure was easy and routine; it didn't take any longer than fifteen or twenty minutes. Paul waited outside, and when they pushed her to the recovery suite, he hovered around anxiously, kissing her forehead, nosing her hand like a puppy. He really loves her, Wilson thought. A duty of care—yes, that's what this is.

Paul told Wilson he would be back after Parliament, and asked if he could keep an eye on Su.

Damn, Wilson thought, being a politician was rough. To be rattled by a domestic emergency and still show up cool as a cucumber at Parliament House to debate matters of national importance? He admired his friend and felt sorry for him in equal measure, but there was no way he was going to be the one to break the news to Su. He didn't even know her personally. "Better to have some trusted friends around her when she wakes up," Wilson advised Paul.

Between a third-trim checkup and a fertility consultation, Wilson saw the three women who descended upon Su's recovery suite— fashionista taitai snob types—and even he had misgivings about whether they were the sort of support network that Su should wake up to. But that was above his pay grade; he'd done his part. So when one of them—a woman in cat-eye glasses who can't quite pull off cat-eye glasses—raps insistently on his office door, despite being told by the receptionist that he is busy, Wilson senses that this isn't going to end well for him.

"Ciao, Doc." She squeezes herself into his office. "I'm Ping, the editor of *Vanity Fair Asia*"—Wilson can't see how her credentials are relevant to their conversation, but never mind—"and I wanted to let you know that we broke the news to Suzhen in suite two, and she isn't doing well. As her friend, I thought I should let you know. Maybe you can personally check in on her?"

Wilson glances at the clock. It's half past twelve. Parliament started at noon. Psyching up for the task by telling himself that this will put Paul further in his pocket, Wilson goes down the corridor and knocks on the door. When he enters, Su is turned away, facing the wall. He puts on his best bedside manner.

"Mrs. Ong?" She doesn't answer, but she must be awake; he can see her body quivering. "Are you OK?"

Su turns. Her skin is terribly pale. Splotchy veins crisscross her cheeks and under her eyes. Milky white eyes, a thin black line in the middle of them. Before he can react, she reaches out and grips his chin tight, breaking his jaw between her cold hands like it's a pair of chopsticks. Pain shoots through his skull. Wilson cries out, but she clamps his broken jaw shut.

She hisses: "*Where is my baby?*"

"I didn't want to do it," he begs, barely audible through her grip. "Paul forced me to do it!"

The blanket slides back. Through the haze of pain, Wilson sees it. Where her legs should have been—twisted grace, flexing sinews—is a shimmering white tail, scales glinting under the overhead lights.

He is so shocked that no sound escapes him as it wraps powerfully around his midsection, pulling him to her. She brushes her lips over the loose gooseflesh stubble where his neck meets his throat.

Wilson whimpers. He flails his arms as she presses her forked tongue against the pulse of his carotid artery. *Chug-chug-chug*, just like her baby's heart on the Doppler machine. His frantic hand connects with something, anything—the vase of orchids—and smashes it onto the side of her head.

She doesn't flinch, even as a streak of dark blood trickles down her temple. She rears her head. Unhinges her jaw. Sinks her fangs deep into him. He moans. Before the venom can hit his heart, she dislocates his vertebrae, severing his head cleanly with her razor-sharp nails and bare hands. With an indecent squelch, it rolls onto the floor like a deflated rugby ball.

. . .

Emerald pours herself some orange juice in the passenger lounge. After checking in for her flight early and realizing she didn't have any more cash, she snuck into this priority-access-only area when the reception-ist wasn't paying attention, where she could cop some free food and drinks. She picks up a bowl of spicy laksa noodles. Spaces out at a TV screen on the wall.

A Singaporean anchor with rebonded hair is reading the news: "Five activists have been arrested under the Public Order Act for hold-ing up signs outside the Ministry of Education without a permit, pro-testing alleged transphobia and LGBTQ discrimination in the school system after a transgender student claimed that the MOE had blocked her from receiving medical care." Footage of activists with homemade signs—"Fix Schools Not Students," "Trans Students Deserve Access to Healthcare & Support," "How Can We Get 'A's When Your Care for Us Is an 'F'?"—being led into a police van. "The issue is expected to be addressed by Minister Paul Ong today in Parliament, which is currently in session."

The news moves on to a regional roundup. Emerald is eating the laksa, but she can barely taste the bold aroma of coconut milk and chili paste, ladled over thick rice noodles, fresh prawns, and curry leaves.

All she can make out is Su's qi—that clean, unadulterated jasmine. Tik and Ploy could barely look her in the eye after Su left, and even though Tik offered to send her to the airport on her Vespa, Emerald said she would take the bus. It hit Emerald, as the bus sped down the highway, that what she'd done to Su—as much as she did not want to admit it—was one of the worst things that one of them had ever done to the other, and that was saying a lot.

Some people bring out the best in each other. They brought out the worst. Time heals all wounds is fridge magnet bullshit. She wishes she could apologize to Su without the caveats she already knows she'll make. She wants to ask Su if she's really pregnant—and what was that about going home? A gummy longing lodges in her throat. Emerald swallows.

Boarding will commence soon. Emerald digs around her duffel for her sweater. When she pulls it out, she realizes that Su has tucked the Bulgari Serpenti necklace into it. She did not cry at Ploy's house; she did not cry on the bus. But now her tears are dripping into her laksa soup, and she cries even harder when she stuffs her face into the hoodie. It smells so clean, so Su.

Emerald tells herself to sober up. Wiping her tearstained face, she puts on the sweater, then the necklace. She picks up her bag and is about to leave the lounge when the regional bulletin on TV is interrupted. The news program cuts back to the Singaporean anchor.

Her face is grave. "Breaking news here in Singapore. A snake is on the loose after a brutal attack on a health-care professional at Paragon Medical. Our reporter is standing by live at Orchard Road."

On-screen, a reporter stands in front of a cordoned-off section along Orchard Road. "We're receiving alarming reports that a gynecologist has been mutilated by a venomous snake at a private clinic in Paragon Medical." Shaky phone footage of nurses and patients running and screaming as a gleaming white snake glides down a corridor.

Emerald's jaw drops. It's Su. Su, who hadn't shed in almost a decade until that afternoon at Sentosa. Su, who wouldn't be caught dead with a single scale on her face.

"It is unclear if the snake is still in the building, or how it got in.

The snake is white in color, approximately six feet in length. Police have been deployed to the area. A search party is underway. This is a developing story, we will be back with more info as we have it. Those in the Orchard Road vicinity are advised to be on high alert. If you see the snake, call 999—"

. . .

"Two teh peng, three kopi peng takeaway!" The coffee shop auntie calls out Tik's order. Tik grabs the clear packets of iced milk tea and coffee from the auntie by their orange plastic strings, and walks back from Boat Quay to Parliament House.

A few hours ago, Tik went to bed with Ploy in her arms—something she never thought she'd get to do again. She tucked her chin over Ploy's shoulder, moving with the ease of muscle memory, and the fit was just as seamless as it used to be.

After Mrs. Ong and Emerald left, Tik and Ploy looked at each other, not knowing what to say. Tik lit a Sampoerna. They shared it on the balcony. Ploy's hand trembled a little as she smoked the cigarette, and Tik put an arm around her shoulder. The sun was rising over Kallang Basin. When Ploy turned to her, Tik thought she was going to say something about the surreality of everything they'd seen. But all she said was: "I feel so heart pain for Mrs. Ong."

"Yeah," Tik said, but she couldn't help but feel bad for Emerald, too. The way she attacked Mrs. Ong was savage, but didn't she say something about protecting them? Inexplicably, Tik believed Emerald, and had a feeling that it was a misunderstanding. And if Emerald had left her with anything, it was the conviction to fight for the life she wanted, instead of simply accepting the one she'd been assigned.

Tik promised herself she would step up, for and with Ploy.

When Ploy fell asleep, Tik pulled the covers over her shoulders and pecked her forehead—she'd missed her so much.

Tik rode back to her Tampines flat, practicing her lines all the way.

Back home, Mak was peeling shallots and deseeding chili in the kitchen. "Where you go last night?"

Tik could easily have lied about a night shift, but she met Mak's eye. "I was with Ploy."

Mak's shoulders seemed to grow heavier. She looked away from Tik.

"I love her." Tik had never been able to imagine saying something like that to Mak, in Malay, but the words were not so hard, after all. "And she loves me. It's simple, she makes me happy."

Mak started pounding the shallots and chili in her granite mortar and pestle. Tik wasn't sure if Mak was tearing or if her eyes were watering from the pungent vapor of the paste.

"I hope you can accept her," Tik went on, "but even if you don't, it's not going to change anything."

Mak stopped pounding. Hesitantly, Tik reached out her hand. "She's good to me, Mak."

Mak ignored Tik's hand. She grabbed the pestle, pulverizing the spices with a vengeance.

Stoically, Tik left the kitchen, the relentless grind of pestle against mortar chafing her heart. She felt better after taking a shower and putting on her uniform, getting ready for Parliament. Her day-to-day job now mostly required her to be in plain clothes, but she donned the uniform on official occasions. The uniform was part of why Tik had wanted to join the police force. Men and women wore the same thing; she wouldn't have to worry about dressing for work. Plain T-shirt, then a soft armor vest, followed by a smart navy-blue long-sleeved shirt displaying her rank, although she did wish that the name stitched above her right breastpocket read Tik instead of

Atika. She threw on her Adidas jacket. Slicked pomade onto her hair. Spritzed some cologne.

Passing the kitchen, Tik was tempted to go without saying goodbye, but she always made it a point to salam Mak before she left the house.

"Bye," she said as she put her nose to the back of Mak's hand.

Mak nodded. Her hands smelled of shallots. Tik turned to go.

"Tonight, rendang for dinner," Mak called out. A pause. "Enough for three people."

At Parliament House, Tik passes through security checkpoints and metal detectors, heading back into the central command room. There are a bunch of commandos, from the army side, and other security officers, her colleagues from the police force, in here.

Tik joins Cheng and the rest, passing out iced coffee and tea—she'd volunteered to get drinks for her mates. "Thanks ah, Atika." They slap her on the back, then go on catching up in Chinese and Hokkien, neither of which she can understand, but she's used to it. A few guys are trying to follow the parliamentary proceedings, which they are privy to from the command room's security screen. Tik goes over to join them. Mr. Rahmat is speaking. Then one of the officers waves his phone.

"Eh, did you all see? Snake on Orchard Road!"

Snake? Tik's heart seizes. She whips her phone out and looks for news. She sees the video of the white snake gliding down the Paragon Medical corridor, which is being rapidly reshared all over social media. Tik checks the time. Emerald went to the airport early; she should be boarding her plane back to New York by now—and her scales were green. This couldn't be her. But there is something oddly familiar about this snake. Its slim, lily-white neck. The cold, calm eyes. The grace and composure with which it moves down the corridor.

Don't be crazy, Tik tells herself. Surely it isn't— It can't be—

But after last night, anything is possible. Worriedly, she types a text: *Hi Mrs. Ong, is everything OK?* Tik stares, waiting for the double tick receipt. There's none.

On-screen, Mr Rahmat has finished presenting the latest defense budget. Mr. Ong is up next. He strides over to the podium with purpose. Pauses to shuffle his papers. Adjusts the mic.

"I know this may be a divisive issue for some," he starts, then stops briefly to clear his throat. "But let me say, on my watch, that all schools in Singapore should be a safe space." He looks up. "All educators deserve a secure and well-ordered workplace to effectively impart knowledge and ethics, and in order to thrive, all students require a stable and homogeneous school environment—not one in which the foundational norms of our harmonious society have been irreparably weakened by a deviant minority." Tik tries not to flinch at Mr. Ong's words. Out of the corner of her eye, she peeks at her colleagues around the room, some listening, some nodding, some talking among themselves. No one seems to think there's anything unsound or unfounded about what he is saying. "We must ensure that our traditional values are not eroded by Western culture wars—"

A piercing, high-pitched screech of feedback drowns his voice out.

. . .

Paul twists away the microphone as the shrill squeal rebounds through the chamber. As far as he can recall, there's never been a technical fault during a parliamentary session. Paul's perspiration soaks through his shirt. He's been trying to pull himself together. He could barely focus on what he was saying—the words swam up at him from his notes.

After leaving Wilson's clinic, he went home, took a bath, popped two tabs of Su's Xanax, and lay down on the sofa in his towel. What was the protocol for when your wife revealed to you that she—but what had she revealed? He thought of calling in sick for Parliament. That wasn't leader material. He didn't want to be penalized at this stage of the race for Chief Minister. Besides, Wilson had helped to terminate the problem, and the rest of it could be talked through with Su. He forced himself to compartmentalize. Got up, shaved carefully. Gathered his speech notes. Put on the gray Armani tie Su had bought for him. *This* was her: subtle, refined, thoughtful.

Paul blows on the mic as the feedback fades. "Testing." All good. He continues where he left off. "At the same time, I wish to extend an olive branch to the student, to invite him to approach the school to clarify and discuss how we can better support his schooling—"

This time, the distortion is so grating it twists Paul's voice beyond recognition, contorting his words into a high-pitched chittering. Even the Chief Minister is covering his ears. Paul pushes the mic away, but it generates a grating scream, repeating and bouncing off the walls. Last resort—he turns off the mic altogether. The screeching stops. Nervously, Paul looks around the chamber.

The Chief nods at him to go on. Paul swallows.

He's scanning his notes when the overhead lights flicker. Paul looks up. They blink once, twice. He seems to hear a low fluorescent hum—then, all at once, a mass blowout. The entire chamber goes black. Bits of lightbulb glass scatter from the ceiling like sharp-edged confetti.

"What is going on?" The Chief Minister's voice rings out in the dark. "This is unacceptable."

Paul strains his eyes, trying to adjust to the darkness. A rumble of murmurs in the pews.

"Tech team," an aide pages for support. "Lights and mics out."

There are two security officers in the chamber, one in the front and one in the back. "Chamber to command," Paul hears one of them radio the command room. "Stand by, stand by." But all that comes back from the other side of the walkie-talkie is the pop and crackle of static.

A shiver runs down Paul's spine. At first he thinks it's his nerves—but in a moment, he realizes the temperature in the chamber has dropped. "How come so cold?" he hears a staffer saying. There are puffs of warm vapor when he exhales. Paul's shirt clings to his skin, frigid air seeping through the wet fabric.

In the dark, Paul hears the guard. "Command, do you read me?" The walkie-talkie crackles.

"Command to chamber." A solid voice comes in at last. "Backup approaching chamber—"

A discordant wail. "Chamber to command." The guard's voice is urgent. "Do you read me?"

Static streams from the walkie-talkie. What Paul hears next makes his hair stand.

Cutting in and out through the static, like a radio channel with a lousy signal, is a frantic racket of gasping and wheezing. No screams, no intelligible words. Just a group of men choking.

Abruptly, the distressed gasps cease at the same time. All that's left is grainy static. With a heavy groan, the walnut doors to the chamber swing open, but there's no one standing behind them. Then, Paul glimpses the ten or so commandos splayed farther down the corridor. No blood, but they are motionless. Someone in the chamber starts to scream, a frightened wail.

"Silence!" The Chief's magisterial voice rings out.

"Everyone, get down!" Paul hears Riz call out. "Guards to Chief!" Tumble of footsteps.

Paul sees both officers moving toward the Chief, guns drawn over flashlights. He stays behind the podium, as the others hide between the pews. Everything is happening so fast, there's no time to think.

Crouching on his haunches, his tightly wound calf muscles are quivering. Both officers train their guns on the doors. The chamber is so quiet that Paul hears every second ticking by on his watch, unbearable as a metronome cutting the air with dreadful tension—

At first, there is nothing. Then a powerful swirl of wind sweeps in, cold and bracing.

Paul's hair is blown back. His tie flutters over his shoulder.

That's when he smells it. An unmistakable powdery jasmine musk.

Su. What is she doing here? His first instinct is to call out to her.

But a growing knot of dread in Paul's stomach gnaws at him, begging him to stay silent. He bends over, clutching his knees tight as the doors slam shut, and the jasmine wind tears up and down the chamber. Skimming the pews like a wraith, searching for something, someone.

Paul starts to shake as a sibilant snarl echoes around the hall: *Sssssssss*—

Both guards whip around to locate the threat, throwing haphazard beams of light across the room. The wind gathers with a swishing susurration, like a thousand leaves crackling in a storm. Then an awful, desperate squeal breaks through the hypnotic rustling, not so different from the sound of a pig being slaughtered. Someone turns on their phone light, shines it in that direction.

Paul sees one guard being dragged by the heel of his boot across the carpet. A deafening high-pitched crack, as loud as a sledgehammer slamming into a steel wall, reverberates through the chamber as the guard opens fire—Paul feels as if his eardrums have ruptured as he crouches low to the ground, jamming his hands over his ears. Disoriented, he cowers behind the podium.

A beam of light arcs across the chamber. Something lands on the carpet with a thud. The second guard shines his flashlight on the carpet: it's the first guard's arm. His hand is still gripping the flashlight.

But from the elbow up, it is no longer attached to his body. Raw sinew and white bone stick out of the bloody stump of his severed arm.

Chaos break loose. The second guard starts to shoot in the general direction of the wind. Parliamentarians and staffers scream over the earsplitting gunfire, shoving one another in a bid to get out, but the doors are jammed shut, and they do not budge. The gunfire stops.

Paul peeks out from behind the podium. Across the room, illuminated dimly by the exit sign, Paul sees the second guard's unmoving body. Instead of hiding, the Chief staggers over, limping slightly, bending to pick up the guard's gun.

"*I will have order!*" The Chief's commandeering baritone booms through the dark chamber.

For a moment, silence. People stop scrambling.

Better able to detect the movement of the threat in this brief stillness, the Chief turns and takes aim—but before he can shoot, he is thrown back violently. The gun falls out of his hand as he struggles against something that is moving too quickly to be seen, pinning him to the wall.

The Chief kicks out as he is lifted off his feet. His hands go to his neck. He gurgles wetly.

Paul sees a diaphanous swirl of silver emerging from the Chief's mouth, collecting into a round shape, like a golf ball. The glowing sphere hovers in the air. A lean, long swathe of white scales ripple across the wall for just a second. Then it vanishes, and the Chief goes limp.

Paul hears the soft, tinkling laughter that he knows so well, blowing with the jasmine wind. Fear pulls his insides apart, but he refuses to give in. He will not be a coward any longer.

"Please." Paul grips the side of the rostrum to steady himself. "Let the rest go." His voice is not much louder than a whimper, but he knows Su will hear him. "I'm the one you want."

The chamber grows very still. The cold blast of wind comes to a stop. The doors are flung open. Panicked, crying, parliamentarians and staffers tumble out.

Paul's knees are shaking. Slowly, he forces himself to stand up from behind the podium.

15

Red Dust and Mortal Lust

Paul has come a long way in his political career. At the start, he pushed hard for a national minimum wage to ensure low-income families could get by. He opposed the Goods and Services tax hike the Party wanted to pass; weren't there alternative sources of revenue to explore, rather than passing on this burden to ordinary folks already struggling with the high cost of living? What about taking pay cuts themselves? Singaporean politicians were some of the most highly paid in the world. The Chief's salary was four times more than the US president's. Paul knew it was meant to attract and retain the brightest minds to the public sector, but did they really need a million-dollar paycheck?

Several years in, Paul was posted to the Ministry of Environment, whereas Riz had been assigned to the Ministry of Foreign Affairs—a major appointment. An old-timer, the outgoing Minister for Environment, had a word with Paul when they ran into each other in the bathroom of the Teochew restaurant booked for his retirement dinner.

"You're a good guy, Paul. Between us, Chief has earmarked you as a candidate for succession. Divya's no threat, there's no way we'll have an Indian woman as Chief Minister, but you'd better watch out for Riz. I'm only going to say this once: Chief doesn't want the best man. He's looking for someone who can be a vector of stability."

Paul argued passionately that it was precisely because he aired his contrarian views openly that the Chief Minister knew he was his guy—he had nothing to hide. If and when he was critical, it was only because he took his job seriously and loved the Party, the country, and its people.

"Dissent is the furthest thing from disloyalty." Paul was filled with emotion. "I am a patriot."

"I know, my boy." The retiring minister patted Paul on the back. He told Paul he saw a lot of his younger self in him. "I ruffled some feathers when I was your age. How do you think I ended up in Environment? Frittering Oxbridge credentials away on mosquito breeding and illegal fishing? Is that where a true patriot can do his best work? Do you want to slide, or do you want to climb?"

. . .

Paul's eyes are adjusting to the dark. It is just him in the parliamentary chamber now. The heavy walnut doors are shut and bolted. The Chief's dead body lies in the middle of the carpet with an interrupted look on his face. Paul feels the cold jasmine wind sweeping over him. "Please believe me," he calls out. "What I did, I did it for us . . ."

Her sweet voice is so soft it feels like it is in his head. "*What would you like for dinner, my dear?*"

Unsure of where the voice is coming from, he spins around—

And finds himself face-to-face with a pair of milky white eyes, shining demonically. Paul whimpers, stumbles back, falls to the ground. Something cool and smooth slides over his ankle, twisting around his calf and knee. Panicked, he tries to kick it away. He struggles, but it is stronger than he is. A muscled length pulls Paul into a standing position, clenching him in an unforgiving, viselike grip to keep him immobilized. He looks down in sheer horror. Coiled tight around the lower half of his body is a powerful and long tail, as wide as a pair of legs, row upon tessellated row of white scales.

A visceral sickness snatches Paul's stomach. Bending over helplessly, he throws up. Paul's eyes follow the tail. Dark puddle where it touches the carpet—curving into an upright position, ending in hip bones on either side, scales fusing into skin like a gradient, and that small, well-shaped belly button, a belly button he knows, a belly button he's stuck his tongue into—

Trembling, Paul raises his head to behold her face.

Su's eyes are white coals, ablaze in the dark. Her skin is so pale and glassy, it lights her up with a faint, unearthly glow. All her glossy black hair has turned pure white. Green veins run across her cheeks, debossed like vegetal spiderwebs. Where her nose should have been are two narrow slits.

"*Which dress would you like me to wear today?*" The contrast between her ghastly looks and this solicitous voice makes him shiver. The hair on the back of his neck stands as she glides to him, so close her bare breasts are touching his chest. "*I don't have to come, as long as you do.*" The jasmine wind thickens into a fog, swirling around them. For a mad moment, blood pulses into his crotch, and he wants to kiss her.

"*Don't be afraid, darling.*" Her smile is alluring. "*You can kiss me if you want.*" Can she read his thoughts, or is he hearing voices?

"Suzhen?" His voice is unsteady.

He can't afford to be afraid. This hideous thing is a decoy. He needs to get past this demon, this possession, whatever it is, back to his sweet Su. Under this miscreation is the woman who covers her mouth when she laughs, who wears a spotless apron when she bakes sourdough bread on Sundays, who copyedits his speeches in a neat cursive. She loves him, and defers to him. In turn, he takes care of everything for her. He will save her.

"Right now, you need a lot of rest—"

Su hisses. Her tongue is forked. "*Why did you take my baby?*" She fixes her unblinking, blazing white eyes on him. "*Because I made it by myself? Without you?*" Her tail inches up, constricting his chest, making it hard for him to breathe. "*How can you say you love me?*"

"The baby was making you sick." He struggles to speak up. "Your sister was making you sick. They're gone now. I'm still here, and I still love you. Come back to me. This isn't you, Suzhen."

A heinous rasp sputters out of the back of her throat. Paul realizes that she is laughing. "*This is the real me, Paulie. Can you still love her?*" She squeezes him, tighter and tighter. A series of cracks. An agonizing pain on the left side of his torso. It's the sound of his rib cage breaking.

Paul wets his pants. He is eight again, and the damp seep of urine is the only thing that can wake him from his nightmares. Dreadful domestic scenes with his mama, who he could barely recall, backed into a corner, throwing shampoo bottles, boxes of auburn hair dye, a hairdryer, at his father, who was unbuckling his silver clasp, brandishing the leather belt in his hand—

Paul snaps out of it, pulls himself together. "Nothing can change the way I feel about you!"

Su's tail loosens, and Paul is able to breathe again. Her face swims back into focus. Her eyes are less white, less empty. He sees a semblance of his beautiful wife in them.

With a shaking hand, Paul reaches out to touch her face. The bulgy green vein recedes. He'll touch and soothe every part of her that needs to be turned back, he will make it all go away. Aside from a faint glow, her eyes are almost human now. There are tears in them.

He folds her into an embrace, doesn't recoil when her scales touch his skin. "It's going to be OK." Paul kisses her cold forehead. "I'll find a way—"

"Stand back, Paul," someone calls out from between the pews in the dark chamber. Paul can't see the person, but he recognizes the voice right away. It's Riz. He has been in here the whole time.

Paul steps away from Su, turning in the direction of the voice.

"Riz, you need to get out—"

He hears the soft click of an auto pistol's safety lever being disengaged. Paul instinctively wraps himself over Su's body, pulling her back into his embrace—

Riz fires. The unsuppressed gunshots are so loud it sends a stabbing sensation through Paul's ears. Su moans, her tail whipping out violently toward the pews. There's the briefest of silences, stretched out unnaturally, in which Paul hears everything with acute clarity. The scales of Su's tail sweeping against the carpet, the pews crashing into Riz. His ears are ringing. There is an insistent pressure in his back, like a balloon has been inserted there and someone's pumping it up.

And then it hits him, hard—a red-hot iron fist punching from the back through the front. Lit dimly by Su's glow, Paul sees the gaping cavity in his belly, something raw hanging out of it.

He slumps to the ground, his red blood splattering against Su's white scales. A distraught hiss escapes Su's lips as she gathers her tail around his limp body. Her nose reshapes, her scales lose their edge as her human skin flares up. Paul lies in her luminous arms.

"Hi." He traces a shaky finger along her cheek. "There you are."

Her pure white hair sweeps over his cheeks as she bends over him. He breathes in her jasmine scent, as deep as he can. "Bai Suzhen." He brings her fingers to his lips. Ah, he smiles, she is still wearing her wedding ring. The light goes out in his eyes. Su throws her head back. Wave upon wave of unholy screams ring through Parliament House, shattering the glass in the windows.

Blinding pain radiates from the base of Riz's spine as he pulls himself forward quietly on his elbows. It feels like the sharp blade of a shovel has been wedged between his vertebrae. He hopes his back isn't broken. If he survives this—he pushes through the pain as he reaches for his gun—he will be the next Chief Minister of Singapore. There's an odd tingling in his fingers when he picks up his gun, careful not to knock into the broken wood and make any sound that would alert her.

From his position, he sees Su bending over Paul's body. An unearthly halo outlines her.

It is difficult to aim from the floor, but he's always been a good shot.

Wiping his damp palm on his shirt, Riz takes a deep breath and shuts his left eye, aligning the front with the rear sight till she comes into focus. Not her shoulder or arm. Straight in the chest—

An urgent hiss of fury. A shimmer of jewel green darts at his arm with preternatural speed, flicking the gun out of his hand. Before he can react, the long green thing twists around his neck, like a cold, smooth rope narrowing into a noose. He gasps for air, legs kicking, arms flailing. Then he sees Su hurtling toward him. Something sharp penetrates a throbbing vein in his neck.

Riz struggles—then realizes, abruptly, that there is no more pain in his spine. His entire body is relaxing as Su's venom courses rapidly through his bloodstream.

As Riz blinks his last, the green snake's shadow rises into the silhouette of a naked woman.

"Oh my god, Jie." Emerald's head swims as she looks around at the dead men in the chamber. They are both back in their human skins, naked. She grabs Riz's jacket off his body, throws it on. Runs to Paul's body, slides his eyes shut, pulls off his jacket, tosses it to Su. "Come on, let's go."

But Su doesn't get up, doesn't move. As Emerald wraps her in the jacket, she sees the bullet in Su's leg, her dark blood. "Fuck." Emerald tries to lift Su up, but they fall back down. "We need to get out of here, OK?" Any time now, backup forces will storm this place.

"*Just go*," Su whispers. Emerald hears, for the first time, their true age in Su's tone. The broken cadence of an immortal exhausted by the endlessness of existence. Emerald shakes Su. Her eyes are glassy and unfocused. An oddly peaceful expression is settling on her face.

Emerald panics. "No." She drags Su between the pews. "Don't you dare do this to me."

"*Be free. Live well, without me.*"

"You don't understand, Jie." Emerald takes her hand, lies down next to her. "I never really wanted to be human. I never really wanted to be immortal. All I ever wanted was to be with you."

They hear it at the same time. Hordes of heavy boots pounding down the marble corridor.

Emerald's heart hammers in her chest as she pulls Su close.

"*This body itself is emptiness—*"

Tik tenses up in her firing stance—feet shoulder width apart, knees slightly bent—as the doors to the parliamentary chamber are blasted open. She bursts in alongside her colleagues, all prepared for the worst—they've seen the commandos strewn dead on the marble floor outside.

Tensile force of silence and adrenaline. Then a ripple of horror— "Chief!"

"Minister Rahmat down!" another officer calls out. "Minister Ong down!"

Beside Mr. Ong's body, Tik notices a thin trail of blood, so dark it is almost black, leading away from the center of the chamber, toward the wooden pews. She files noiselessly past the pews, slowing down as the trail peters out. Steadying her grip below the trigger guard, gun pointed, Tik ducks down. Hiding under the pews in their diminutive forms, no larger than common garters, a green snake and a white snake intertwine with each other like gleaming ribbons in the shadows.

. . .

"Our nation reels as Parliament House came under a horrific attack this afternoon," a reporter says grimly as the cameraman pans to the building. "Chief Minister Edward Wee, Minister for Defense Rizwan Rahmat, and Minister for Education Paul Ong are said to be among the casualties. Acting Chief Minister Divya Anandarajah will address the nation later this evening."

The reporter has attempted to interview some of the parliamentarians and staffers evacuated from Parliament House, but the police commissioner himself intervened, ushering the witnesses away. No more specifics, he said, until the media was briefed on the official narrative, it wouldn't do for empty speculation and fake news to run rampant. Undeterred, the reporter now tries to get the attention of medics and elite security officers being dismissed from the area.

"Ma'am." She thrusts her mic in front of one of them. "Were you inside? What happened?"

Tik puts her hand up and walks away from Parliament House.

Tik's silver Vespa is parked along Carpenter Street. She mounts it, puts on her helmet, starts the engine, and rides off, moving farther and farther away from the city center.

Out on the East Coast Park highway, the cool wind feels clarifying on her face. Tik steadies herself. Takes a hand off the handlebar. Unzips the top of her Adidas jacket. Coiled around her armor vest are two snakes. White around her waist. Green against her chest.

Hesitantly, the green snake pokes a forked tongue out in the wind.

. . .

Changi Beach is the easternmost point of the island. Close to sunrise and sunset, when the tides pull back, the intertidals become exposed. Nudibranches, a purple sea star, and an orange crab are scattered across the shallows. Tik moves away from the open shore, toward the dense cover of the mangrove swamp. She wades out, apprehensively at first, growing in confidence as she gets farther in. The loud, insistent, annoyingly optimistic call of the koel bird rings through the swamp.

Ooh-woo.

When Tik is hip deep in the swamp, she removes her jacket.

The green snake emerges, then the white snake. Gleam of bright scales in the sun. Their cool, supple bodies have been warmed by close contact with her skin. Tik lowers them onto a section of raised mangrove roots. The green snake slithers behind a tree. The white snake has stopped bleeding, but its wound is still fresh.

"Tik." She turns when she hears Emerald's voice. Emerald steps out from the mangroves, naked. Tik reaches out to drape her jacket around Emerald's shoulders to protect her modesty.

Emerald picks up the white snake. It curls around her arm, then drapes with ease over her neck. Emerald nuzzles the white snake's head. "It's a long way out." Emerald squints beyond the sea.

"Where will you go?" Tik asks.

"I promised I would take her home," Emerald says.

Tik looks worried. "How will you make it to New York?"

"We're not going to New York," Emerald tells her.

Then she places something shiny in Tik's hand.

"Take this," Emerald says. It's the Bulgari Serpenti necklace. All the diamonds glitter in the sun. If Tik sold it, maybe she could take a leap, quit her job, or write off the down payment for a flat of her own, a place that she could share with Ploy.

"No." Tik passes it back to Emerald. "It's too valuable . . ."

"Take it," Emerald threatens, "or I'll drop it into the ocean like the old lady in *Titanic*." When Tik still doesn't accept it, she takes a step closer, tucking it safely into Tik's pants pocket. "Tik?" Emerald looks into her eyes. "I just wanted you to know that you taste like cherry cola and cloves."

A gentle wave pushes them together. Tik reaches out to touch Emerald's shoulders, the nape of her neck where her green buzz cut ends. Pulls her into a tight hug. Emerald's skin tingles.

"Will I see you again?" Tik asks. They pull apart.

She kisses Emerald chastely on the cheek.

"Maybe"—Emerald smiles a little sadly—"in another lifetime."

Fiery golden beams cast a pink and coral wash over the horizon. The sun is going down, and the water is still warm. With the white snake wrapped around her naked body, Emerald steps into the sea, farther and farther. When her feet can touch the ground no longer, she strokes gracefully through the current. Intermittently, she turns back to see if Tik is still watching, still there.

Tik waves. Smaller, fainter, as the sun goes down.

When Emerald turns around again, she can't see Tik anymore, but she waves anyway, in case she's still there. *Bye, Tik. I never got to tell you that my favorite thing about Singapore is you.*

A silent, genial reptilian head bobs up in the water. Leathery skin, long snout. A saltwater crocodile. And then three more. The flotilla of crocodiles guides Emerald and the white snake out of Singapore's waters, toward the South China Sea.

"Come on, Jie," she whispers. "Time to go home."

A thousand years ago, the Chinese emperor postulated that the world was carried on a giant turtle's back, and sent armadas out to map the seven seas. Now American billionaires jizzed up the sky with rockets, jostling for the first space colony. In the end, it is all red dust and mortal lust. There and then, here and now, Bai Suzhen and Xiaoqing have each other.

I love you in metric. I love you in imperial. I love you through the Copernican revolution, the rise of communism, the fall of capitalism, the final hour of the Anthropocene. Love you enough to swallow an ocean, to shoot down the sun. Love you in any and every form, be it corporeal or even immaterial, love you in every direction of space and time. A snake can shed its skin a hundred times, but it will always remain a snake. To be sisters with you in one lifetime is not enough.

After

All the snow has melted away from the scenic bridges. West Lake in spring is akin to heaven on earth, surrounded on three sides by cloud-capped hills, riverbanks blanketed by newly budding peach and azalea trees. Red-tipped herons are returning to fish in the lake.

This winter just past was harsher than before.

But in a terrain as ample and abundant as this, no matter. There were boundless features such as tree stumps and underground holes for creatures seeking shelter from the elements. It was a rush and a push for the best hides, and yet the green snake did not oust a family of squirrels from the moss-lined hollow of an oak tree, though it would have been easy enough for her to intimidate these small mammals.

Picking up a scented invitation off some dead bark, the green snake cautiously poked her tongue into a communal pit. It had been dug out by other snakes below the frost line and secured with heavy logs, but the pheromones circulating in the hibernaculum were off-putting. The green snake had no intention of bedding down with a huddle of garter males through the bitter cold. She could take better care of herself—and her sister.

The white snake's wounds were long healed, but she remained torpid in her movements. She had to be coaxed to eat at all. Despite the green snake's best efforts, the white snake grew thin. Her excess skin hung loose like a shadow. Her once-iridescent white scales had lost their luster.

The green snake found a cave secreted away in the forested foothills of Nanping Hill, not far from Jingci Temple. The cave's entrance was narrow, but once you wriggled through, it opened into a roomy grotto. She insulated the walls with bird fluff and dried peat. Covered their scent by scattering dried nightshade around the mouth of the cave.

The white snake spent most of her time curled up in a corner, head tucked inward. The green snake told herself it was all right—winter was upon them. Soon the white snake would lower her metabolic and heart rate, drift into deep sleep. With her sister in a weakened state, the green snake was determined, however, to protect them both, and refused to let her own body slide into brumation. As she strived to keep awake through the cold, she found herself turning back, for the first time in her long life, to self-cultivation.

This body itself is emptiness. Emptiness itself is this body.

She'd never comprehended it, but this time, existing alone—the white snake was here, but she wasn't present—in the dark, the green snake felt the words unfurling in her mind like tea leaves scalded in hot water.

Their proximity to Jingci Temple was helpful in this regard.

In the mornings and evenings, an apprentice monk pulled back a suspended log to strike an enormous copper bell. The green snake let the profound sounding of the bell ripple through her.

Since her return to Hangzhou, it was one of the only human things she allowed herself to hold on to: a marker of time. All through the frigid winter, the green snake saw no one else, ate nothing, indulged only in a few drops of melted snow, and started to see how impetuous they were back then, taking on their human skin transitions before they had even known themselves as snakes.

She shared her findings with the white snake, signing with her tongue like they used to, but they no longer seemed to share that primordial language. Glassy-eyed and unresponsive, on some days the white snake even turned her head away from her.

Winter is ending, Jie. Can you hear me? I miss you.

It has been a rejuvenating retreat for the green snake. Silent fast through a season of snow. Mastering mind over matter in pure darkness. Emerging from the other end to realize that the light at the end of the tunnel was a glimpse of her own radiance.

Emerald was more well rested, more at ease, more powerful, than she's ever been, and self-cultivation was no longer a means to an end, but an end in and of itself. She was beginning to surpass mere *understanding*, moving toward pure *being*.

Yet enlightenment is far from unidirectional. Virtue sleeps next to idleness, rubbing shoulders with envy, giving lust a boner. And sometimes, all it takes is waking up to a whiff of sugar. Nothing more, nothing less. And so it is that on the first day of spring, before sunrise, the green snake pokes her head out of the grotto and catches the moreish scent of candied haws on a breeze.

At first she resists. Sugar is merely a chemical equation, a mortal invention, the most childish of temptations. But then she looks at her sister: her dour mouth, the sag of her washed-out skin, quiet and incurious in the corner, almost as if she's punishing her.

Fuck it, it's spring. Just one bite.

And so the green snake slithers out of the cave, following the irresistible smell of rock sugar and fresh hawthorn like a butterfly in avid pursuit of nectar. She stumbles over damp moss and flat rocks, going faster as the smell grows stronger.

Amid the evergreen conifers of Sunset Hill, in a small clearing close to Leifeng Pagoda, is a tanghulu seller under a bare, stocky ginkgo tree.

The sight of those bright red haws, thickly coated in rock sugar syrup like a sweet stalactite, makes her mouth water. A low fire heats the sugar in a wok. Fresh fruits await dipping.

Dressed in a fusty old khaki Mao-collared jacket and a matching beret, a crinkly-eyed, tan-skinned vendor is busy arranging skewers of candied hawthorn, tangerine, and cherry onto a straw display.

His jaw drops when he sees her. That's when Emerald realizes she's in her human skin—and stark naked. She'd meditated in the quiet of her mind to an unprecedented peak. It now required no effort to slip between skins. The thought of the taste of sugar was enough to alter her body. Emerald notices the glossy locks flowing over her shoulders—her hair has grown out now, long and dark.

"Young lady," he stutters in northern-accented Mandarin, "are you OK?"

"Yes." Her tongue slips on the word. She can make words again. "I'm OK."

Averting his eyes humbly from her nakedness, he removes his faded jacket. Grateful, she takes it from him and slips into it. The rough-hewn khaki material is itchy against her soft skin. "Thank you." She is still reeling from the newness of sounds in her mouth.

"You're not from around here, are you?" He smiles broadly. His qi smells like anchovies.

"Actually, I was born in Hangzhou," she tells him. "But I've been away for a long time."

"Ah." He holds a stick of candied haws out to her, fresh off the wok. "Welcome back."

"I don't have money on me right now," she confesses.

"Don't worry about it," he insists. "This one's on me."

She swallows, longing to taste it. "Are you sure?"

"It's the first day of spring," he declares pleasantly.

She takes the candied haws from him. Red as roses.

Bites into the hard candy, the soft hawthorn within.

To throw it all away for sugar, baby. The sugar coating breaks on her lips, drips down her chin as she licks the hawthorn, tasting all the sweet artifice and sticky shambles of this mortal realm.

A thousand years of prayers would never be able to wash away the red of her desires—

Spring is here, and she is sick of being a snake. Exhausted from taking care of someone who won't even look at her, who refuses to eat, who maybe doesn't even want to live anymore. Emerald is different: no matter what happens, she'll always have a lust for life.

Beyond their cramped cave are all the wonders of the world.

Mountains upon mountains, cities upon cities, people upon people. She wants: *words words words*. The glorious imprecision of language, that impossible endeavor of saying what you mean to another. She sees, with benevolent distance, how hopeless and winsome it is to be in this skin. How *human* it is to attempt a futile expression of your innermost secrets to another by vibrating strings in your throat to make an avalanche of sentences. To laugh, to sing, to cry out loud. How we all wish so badly to be heard.

Dawn is breaking. Emerald wanders away from the tanghulu seller and the old ginkgo, sighing at the diffused glow of the lavender-streaked sky. She touches the gnarly trunks of trees and the tender buds of leaves with the tips of her fingers, relishing their hardness, their softness. As she traipses through a cluster of poplars, starry-eyed and sure-footed, seeing and sensing the world anew, in love with every last bit of it, the giant copper bell at the temple is struck.

She stops in her tracks and closes her eyes, focusing solely on its inviolable timbre.

Deep and delicate, the bell releases its sacred resonance all over West Lake. It is a singular, spectacular sound. Time is dilating. Seconds are suspended in the deep echo of the bell's vibrations.

The great bell's tolling ripples the surface of the water. A magnificent cormorant screeches as it swoops over West Lake, folding back its wings to scoop up a black carp that flaps fiercely for its life in its hunter's merciless beak. A lustrous fox slinks under Yang Causeway, three fatty pieces of Dongpo pork in its mouth, stolen from the dumpster behind the new-fangled restaurant nestled into Winery Yard's folds. A golden monkey scales a tall sequoia overlooking the rebuilt octagonal facade of Leif-eng Pagoda, where a gleaming gunmetal escalator cuts directly into the steep hill.

Under the ginkgo tree, the tanghulu vendor chews on a candied tangerine, crooning Teresa Teng's sentimental ballad "What Do You Say to That?" "*I recall you so clearly, but you've already forgotten me . . .*"

Biting the stick between his teeth, he lifts his grubby beret to scratch his short, curly hair. Digs into his pockets for a small bottle of hard liquor. Holds that up to his teeth, uses his crooked dentition to twist off the cap—hidden by his rumpled long-sleeved shirt, he has only one arm. Swishes sorghum liquor through his mouth. Finishes the candied tangerine. Blows out the fire.

One moment he is extinguishing the fire under the sugar wok. The next, he is no longer there.

All is quiet but for the hypnotic murmurs of the temple bell.

Very slowly, a beady eye on the end of a hoary tendril the length of an index finger pokes through a shirt sleeve. Upright, shrewd.

An orange horn-eyed crab, large as a melon, with just one pincer, emerges from the pile of fallen clothes, scuttling sideways on its eight legs through the broad-leaved evergreen glade.

Emerald wipes the sugar from her mouth on the back of her hand as she moves toward the rich toll of the bell. It sounded so far away when she was in her snake skin in the grotto, but now, as she is walking on her two feet with her head held high, the source of that exquisite sound is well within reach.

Dragon gargoyles adorn the majestic roof. Red silk lanterns hang from the eaves, swaying gently in the morning breeze. A saffron-robed monk is sweeping the spotless stone steps leading to the temple's main hall. Its chrysanthemum-yellow walls, landscaped gardens, and serene gazebos are well kept.

Emerald takes a reverential breath outside Jingci Temple.

Unnatural creatures are not welcome in holy places. All those years ago, she and Su beheld the temple from afar in their snake skins, balancing on rocks, craning to see what lay within. Emerald was merely curious, but Su yearned to be let in, to kneel in the hall where she could offer up her prayers. If they'd tried to enter these sanctified grounds, they would be shooed with sticks, if not shot by arrows.

Now she slips in noiselessly, avoiding the main hall where monks are chanting morning prayers. Glides past the sutra repository, pausing momentarily at a lotus pond. It is too early in spring for flowers, but she sees a few buds in the muddy water. Behind the pond is a corridor of red wooden plaques hung up on a bamboo fence.

Each plaque has handwritten words on it.

At first, Emerald thinks it's ancestor worship. But as she gets closer, she realizes that these are the wishes of temple visitors.

In big, blocky Chinese characters, the plaque nearest to her reads: *STRIKE LOTTERY!*

I pray for my mama's good health and happiness, says the one next to it. *May she live to a ripe old age.*

She glances through the others on the same row.

Help me get into my top choice for college.

Curse my boss to hell! Crash his Maserati!

I'm in love with someone who doesn't know I exist how long to wait before I move on?

Most of the wishes are in Mandarin, but she spots a few in different languages. Japanese, German, Arabic, and then there's this messy scrawl in English: *Yo Buddha please send an ethereal goth girl who will let me suck her toes and unironically get off on Muse with me to Austin TX kthxbye!!!*

Emerald laughs out loud. The sound of her own laughter, soft and silvery, a tiny bell of her own making, is thrilling to hear. She laughs again, but it's not the same as the first time. She picks up an empty red plaque and a black pen. Right away, the muscle memory of writing returns. Without overthinking, she starts to scribble. Blows on it to dry the ink—and for luck. Reads it over. Wipes the cool tears springing unexpectedly to the corners of her eyes. Hangs it up on one of the bamboo hooks. Not on a new row. Somewhere between all these earthly banes and fiery desires, hidden in plain sight. She runs an idle hand along the secrets of strangers. Red plaque after red plaque, the wooden edges tap against each other. A wind chime of mortal dreams. The unbroken clinking brings a simple pleasure to her ears. Emerald looks up in wonder at the big, rapidly brightening sky. The rising sun is more brilliant than she ever recalled it to be. She sticks her forked tongue out.

Loamy roots. Melting snow. Faint hint of bus diesel. Lake algae.

And then, from afar: the unmistakable, elegant musk of jasmine.

She marvels at how intoxicating such a familiar smell can still be.

Inhaling so deeply it hurts, filling her lungs to the brim, she follows.

A novel by
Amanda Lee Koe

Agent	Jacqueline Ko
Senior Editor	Sara Birmingham
Senior Editor	Gabriella Doob
Publisher	Helen Atsma
Associate Publisher	Miriam Parker
VP Publicity	Sonya Cheuse
Publicity Director	Cordelia Calvert
Senior Marketing Director	Meghan Deans
Foreign Rights Director	Catherine Barbosa-Ross
Senior Art Director	Allison Saltzman
Senior Designer	Jennifer Chung
Cover Image Illustrator	Maya Lin
Production Manager	Michael Siebert
Senior Production Editor	Lydia Weaver
Copyeditor	Miranda Ottewell
Proofreader	Nora Reichard
Proofreader	Carla Jablonski
Editorial Assistant	TJ Calhoun
Publicity Assistant	Nina Leopold
Director, International Sales	Dan Vidra
Senior Manager, International Sales	Shannon McCain
Manager, International Sales	Stacey Lai
Marketing Coordinator	Erin Gilroy
Creative Director, Audio	Suzanne Mitchell
Agent, United Kingdom	Jessica Bullock
Agent, Foreign Rights	Sarah Watling
Assistant Agent	Thomas Wee
Co-Agent, Film & TV	Michelle Kroes
Co-Agent, Film & TV	Will Watkins
Author Photographer	Lenne Chai

Acknowledgments

I had so much fun writing *Sister Snake* it might be criminal. Let my colluders, patrons, kindreds, compatriots, and loves be known:

My visionary agent, Jackie Ko, whose razor-sharp clarity and acuity paves the way forward for whatever direction I want to go in.

My wonderful editors, Sara Birmingham and Gabriella Doob, for their far-reaching perspicacity, care, and enthusiasm.

The New York Foundation of the Arts, the National Arts Council of Singapore, and the DAAD Artists-in-Berlin program (in particular, meine Lieblinge Silvia Fehrmann, Mathias Zeiske, and Laura Muñoz-Alonso).

Additionally from the Wylie Agency, the intrepid Jessica Bullock and Sarah Watling, my UK and foreign rights agents. My exuberant film/TV co-agents, Will Watkins and Michelle Kroes from Creative Artists Agency. The entire Ecco team across departments from publicity to production, as honored in the credits roll.

Angel booksellers and librarians everywhere, for putting this book into the hands of readers. Sweet baristas from Cafe Grumpy in Greenpoint (where I started this story) to Little Rogue in Katong (where I scrutinized the second pass), who provided this Americano-guzzling tropical cyborg a semblance of safe harbor.

My bio fam, for always having my back. K.J. Lee and Nancy Koe, for your unconditional love and boundless support; Darrell and Adeline, for being my first playmates—I honed the seeds of my storytelling on the expanded canvases of our shared imagination.

Kirsten Tan, dream believer and feedback whisperer, for having walked through so many cyclones of waking and writing life with me, 何不潇洒走一回?

Carol Hong, my dearest sister from another mother, for the steadfast heartbeat of unswerving friendship, honesty and loyalty.

Police ops officer C and ob-gyn Dr. W.K. Tan for fact-checks. Beta and sensitivity readers Thomas Wee (also from the Wylie Agency), Ad Maulod and Darrell Lee (my long-standing, long-suffering pro-bono legal adviser—appreciate all the billable hours, Pet). Prabda Yoon for reviewing my Thai slang. Lenne Chai for zhuzhing up my author portrait.

That unforgettable night with the raucous Purnrao KTV crew at the now-defunct Golden Mile Complex and the late architect William Lim—sabai sabai.

Film legends Maggie Cheung and Joey Wong for playing the archetypal animal spirits that set my childhood imagination on fire. As with most folklore about shape-shifting women across cultures, Legend of the White Snake, one of China's Four Great Folktales, was passed down in an oral tradition since the Tang Dynasty (AD 618–907) as a cautionary morality tale, but these actresses were so entrancing in *Green Snake*, Tsui Hark's madcap 1993 adaptation, that all I wanted was to be a hot snake queen with an existential crisis.

Scholars, I feel your ennui. Submit, subvert, or sublimate?

Singaporean politicians, I know you're reading this with the cover wrapped in brown paper. You won't admit it to your aides, but secretly, you can't say you didn't enjoy the read. Breathe, daddy, it's fiction ;)

Beautiful queer folx everywhere, especially in places that do not recognize our full humanity and equality—the ways in which we've had to learn to reach for our own freedom mean that we are organic trailblazers of self-determination by necessity. Autonomy and ardor will always be the polestars in our night sky.

And to you, reading this, we're still on the same page for a moment more. Because I want to feel free, in life as in art, I never think about an audience while writing. But right now, outside the frame of the story, I am imagining you, on the other end, wondering if you're more of a Su, or more of an Emerald.

Reading is a conspiratorial act that completes. By spending time with my words and worlds, you make them real for—and with—me.

ALK